# Burn the Rabbit

# Rabbit in Red

# Volume Two

### By Joe Chianakas

Four Phoenixes Publishing

United States    Canada    United Kingdom

Printed in the United States of America

First Printing, 2016

ISBN 978-0-9976205-3-5

www.joechianakas.com

www.facebook.com/chianakas

# Cover Art & Design by Camron Johnson

**www.camronjohnson.com**

Whether it's for a personal collection or a professional illustration, go to www.camronjohnson.com for fantastic, original work.

Also check out Johnson's own comic, *Thy Neighbor*, coming Fall 2016.

# Dedication

This one's for Brandy. Here's to twenty years of friendship, and for being willing to read my stories even if they have scary clowns and spiders in them. That's true friendship. I'm also hoping Mark Wahlberg gets cast as one of my characters in the movie version and that you're forced to watch that, too.

I know. "Why do I put up with you?"

Because best friends are family. Thanks for always being there and believing in me.

# Part One: Cruel Summer

"I think of horror films as art, as films of confrontation. Films that make you confront aspects of your own life that are difficult to face."
– Wes Craven

# Chapter One

His forehead glistened with sweat from a feverish nightmare plagued by a single image: the rabbit soaked in blood, a constant reminder of his warped past and a harbinger of a crumbling future. Each day he looked in the mirror and the reflection that stared back at him twisted in agony. Only wicked thoughts could make him smile now, so he'd contemplate sweet revenge and grin at the possibilities.

He had a simple morning routine. Pouring a scalding cup of coffee, hot enough to burn off any normal person's taste buds, he enjoyed the bitter taste that accompanied the pain. Pain was good. It would harden him, make him tougher, make him invincible to Rabbit in Red. Carefully holding a newspaper article about JB's Rabbit in Red Fright Fest from last year, he read it over and over again. If asked, he could recite the words JB had said, the twisted, manipulative language used to paint a picture of imagination and heroics.

"Bullshit," the man said. JB wasn't imaginative and those kids weren't heroes. JB was a villain and those kids were his prodigies, little slices of his madness, clay being shaped in the image of a mastermind host. He drank more coffee, burning his mouth a little each time. He had as many blisters as he had yellow stains on his teeth. After the events of last year, he'd let himself go.

After his coffee, he moved to the living room and turned on the TV. He had saved a number of televised news stories and interviews on his DVR. He picked one each day to watch and recited the words along with the interviewee. Today he watched an interview of Jaime, and like all of the contestants, the now soon-to-be first year students at JB's so called Horror College, he studied their body language and non-verbal behavior, too. He was determined to learn everything about them.

Because he planned on destroying all of them.

"What has JB told you about this Horror College?" a reporter asked Jaime.

"You can imagine JB likes mystery," Jaime said, laughing her carefree laugh, "so he's been ambiguous. But we know we'll be leaders. We'll be creating horror, designing sets, simulations, and stories much like JB did for us last Halloween for the initial contest. We will be inviting new participants, too. We're all flying out to Rabbit in Red Studios early this summer to prepare. During the first couple of months, we've been told that we'll help design a new contest for this Halloween, and then we'll begin more formal studies in the fall. As formal as JB can get, that is."

She brushed the hair out of her eyes. Her leafy-brown hair danced just below her shoulders now. It had grown out since last fall. The man smiled and watched closely. What did her hair smell like. Innocence? Did innocence have a smell? It wouldn't smell like that for long.

"So JB will be having a contest like last year every Halloween?" the reporter asked.

"That's my understanding," Jaime said. "It will be completely different each year, but still some kind of challenge. We need fresh blood every year."

She laughed again, and so did the man watching. *If fresh blood is what you want, I'll give it to you.*

"What happens after the next contest?"

"We'll study and create. I'm hoping we'll get to make our own movie."

"Why do you want to return to Rabbit in Red? Quite a few people, and I'm one of them, consider what JB did last year to be unethical. To be, well, almost evil."

Jaime smiled. "We thought the same at first. There's always a little madness in any genius. But I'm returning, not because of the madness, but because of that genius. We'll learn things no traditional college or textbook could teach. It's all hands-on creation."

She put both hands on her hips and held eye contact with the reporter. She looked strong and confident, especially when she took a deep breath, the man thought. He enjoyed watching her chest move.

The interview continued, as they all had a tendency to do, by reviewing the most exciting and scariest parts of last year's contest. Footage previously broadcast on frightfest4d.com, JB's website, showed images of Jaime Stein in a game chamber as Ash from *Evil Dead*, cutting off her own arm in a virtual simulation, then jumping to a live action battle where she smashed a bottle over a stunt actress who played Annie from *Misery*.

But the man had seen enough of that. He watched Jaime's smile, the focus in her brown eyes, the way she blinked and took a short breath before answering questions. She was smart. Maybe the smartest of the four who had been selected as first-year leaders. That was why he studied her as much as he could.

But he'd be lying if he said there wasn't another reason. Sure, Jaime was attractive, and maybe he'd feel just a little guilt after he hurt her. Maybe he'd give her a chance to like him first. Maybe he could tell her that the way she brushed her hair out of her face aroused him. She'd be the last one he'd destroy. He pictured what could happen. He'd pin her down on the floor and wrap his arms around her neck. Then he'd offer her a chance of redemption, if only she could feel for him what he felt for her.

Thinking about her this way, he decided he would spruce himself up. In the bathroom, he took out a toothbrush and scrubbed vigorously. He wouldn't lose the blisters or stop drinking scalding hot coffee. The pain was necessary, but he could cover up the pain like makeup hides a pale face. He could be one person on the outside and someone entirely different on the inside. Wasn't that the way most people were anyway?

Jumping in the shower, he washed hair that had been unclean for days. It was a hot spring, an early summer really. The schools had recently closed, and he spent most of these past few days inside without air conditioning, bathing only in his own sweat and stink.

He continued with his normal routine, the shower a temporary distraction, and proceeded to the kitchen. Turning on two burners on the stove, he placed a pot of water on one and ran his hands over the other. The flames felt good. Like the blisters in his mouth, he wanted to deaden his skin, to stifle all feelings, to immunize himself to pain. When the water started to boil, he'd drop his hands in deep, keeping them there as long as he could. Each day, he was able to hold them in the boiling water longer and longer. He'd grimace and even scream on occasion, but it felt good, like pain from hot sex, or so he imagined.

Then he'd return to his bedroom and take out a black, leather-bound notebook. On the first page, he glued a picture that had been taken from Rabbit in Red. It featured all original nineteen contestants with JB in the middle. Jaime, Bill, Rose, and Wes were of course directly in front of JB. Clenching his fists, he simply pondered all that he would do to them and then wrote those ideas in his notebook.

JB had sent a packet home with everyone last year that included the theme, and the media had already begun discussing the possibilities as to what this year had in store for first-year students and new contestants.

"Burn the rabbit," the man whispered. "If that's what you want, JB, that's what you'll get." He grinned at himself in the mirror. He could clean up nice when he had to, and he had more than one costume in his closet. He could become anyone he wanted to be.

*Then why do you stay you?*

*Shut up!*

His thoughts yelled back and forth at one another. He turned on the water in the shower again. He couldn't get enough hot water. Not the hot that relaxes you at the end of a long day. He needed to feel pain. He needed to feel what they were going to feel. Taking his clothes off, he looked in the mirror.

*Would Jaime like this sight?*

He rubbed his chest, feeling the muscles that could pin Jaime to the ground—no, that *would* pin her to the ground! His hand glided over his belly. *She'd like that pressed against her*, I'm sure. Then his hand dropped lower. *Oh, yes. This was the treasure he'd give her, and she was going to love it.*

He stepped into the scalding-hot shower again, and let the water pour over his head. He inhaled the steam, and just stood there. Minutes later, he heard a voice.

"Honey, I'm home," a female voice called from the living room. "Where are you?"

He heard the voice over the water pouring on his head in the shower, but he didn't respond. Now that she was home, he closed his eyes and imagined he was someone else.

"Honey?" The voice was closer, and soon a creak from the bathroom door alerted him that she was entering the bathroom. "Oh, you're showering. Good. How is your cold?"

"I feel better," he said.

"It's this wicked weather," she told him. "These temperature changes. Didn't we just have the heat on last week? And now we need air conditioning, but the damn thing isn't cooling. It's no wonder you've been in bed sick for so long. Well, I'm glad you feel better. And I'm glad you're showering. I didn't want to tell you, but you were beginning to smell." She giggled.

He tried to laugh back, albeit a fake laugh. Having her by his side was necessary. He was never really sick, but when the madness overpowered him, it became a convenient excuse. She'd give him space, and he could wallow in his ideas. But the summer program at Rabbit in Red would begin soon, and the first years, as JB called them, would be returning. He needed to be strong. He would eat her cooking, go out with her in public, smile, and pretend the world was normal, when on the inside all he could picture was the beautiful destruction of fire.

"Do you feel like eating?" she asked. "I picked up some groceries. I have your favorites. I'll make some if you feel like eating."

"Yes, I can eat." Trying to remember his manners—he had to get accustomed to this façade—he added, "Thank you."

"Great! I'll get started in the kitchen." But she hadn't left the bathroom. Instead she paused for a moment, and he wondered if she might peek in the shower to check on him. After all, this shower was the first time she had seen him out of bed in days. He wandered around the house when she was gone, but otherwise, he wanted to be alone. He wanted the time to think and plan.

"I love you," she said finally, and he heard her turn around, getting ready to leave.

He looked down at his naked body as he scrubbed the dirt from his skin. Although he had been getting used to it and had actually liked it—it was like a shell, like armor—he knew he needed to keep up appearances and clean himself up. He saw something else when he looked down, something he typically only felt when he imagined himself on top of Jaime, his arms wrapped around her neck. He was aroused.

"I love you, too, Mother," he called back.

When he heard the door close, he shut his eyes, leaned his head against the wall, and let the stream of water pour down his back. He pictured Jaime. Would she want him the way he wanted her?

Or would he have to . . . could he even . . .?

The thought rose slowly, but when it entered his mind, it was like thunder. *Do I have what it takes to kill her?*

He smiled. The thought excited him. Reaching down with a calloused and hardened hand, with an image of Jaime in his mind, he pleasured himself in the shower.

# Chapter Two

"I know an old lady who swallowed a fly. I don't know why she swallowed that fly. Perhaps she'll die."

Tara giggled as she sang and laughed even harder when her big sister rolled her eyes.

"You know I hate that song," Jaime said and pushed her.

"And of course that's why I'm singing it to you, stupid! It's my graduation present to you."

She stuck her tongue out at Jaime, but everything about Tara was one big smile. Jaime shook her head, but then she laughed.

The big graduation day was finally here, and looking at Tara, Jaime nearly started to tear up. Excited as she was about the future, leaving her little sister behind would be the hardest thing she'd ever done.

She shook the thoughts out of her mind. "How do I look?" Jaime asked, adjusting the cap and gown in front of a mirror in her bedroom.

"Weird. Why do they make you dress like that?"

"Oh, they say because of tradition, but more than likely it's all about another company making money off these damn rental fees they make us pay."

A ringing came from Jaime's computer. It was a Skype call. Jaime ran over to the computer. "Oh my God."

"What is it?" Tara asked. "Bill?"

"No, it's—it's Dad."

"What? Answer it!"

Jaime nodded and answered the call before she could change her mind. She hadn't talked to her father in—how many years now? Not since her eighth grade graduation, actually. She got a birthday card and a Christmas card, but that was it. Her mom had e-mailed him about her graduation. Jaime, as usual, had tried not to get her hopes up.

"Hello?"

"Jaime? Sweetheart? Is that you?" It was beyond strange to hear a voice that should have been familiar.

"Um, yeah. Tara, too. Where are you?" The webcam was fuzzy, and they could barely see him. But they heard his voice perfectly. It was a beautiful voice.

"Honey, I'm in Brazil of all places. It's a work thing. I just wanted to say happy graduation. Listen, tell your mom I'm okay. I love you both. The connection here is very weak, so I'm afraid I don't have much time. But I love you both and I miss you both. One day I'll get home again to see you. Congratul—"

"Dad!" Jaime and Tara shouted in unison.

"Damn! We lost him," Jaime said. "I can't believe he called."

"Me, neither," Tara said. She looked up at her sister. "I don't know whether to be excited or mad. Is that weird?"

"No. I feel the same way." *It's only been a decade since I've actually talked to my father. He's been gone forever. Then suddenly a happy graduation call?*

"Hello?" a voice called from downstairs.

"Aunt Megan!" Tara called. "We're up here!"

"Hey, Jennifer," Jaime greeted, after her cousin and aunt had walked up to the bedroom. "Thanks for coming."

"You know we wouldn't miss it," Aunt Megan said. "Where's your mother? And are you really going to this Horror College and not a real college? That's crazier than ice skating naked."

"I'm right here," Jaime's mother called from downstairs, "and I've told her the same damn thing a dozen times."

They all walked down from the bedroom together, and Jaime watched Mom and Aunt Megan hug briefly. Seeing them together always made Jaime a bit sad. They both had experienced such great pain. Aunt Megan had lost a husband to suicide. Jaime's own dad was never around. Uncle Tim and Dad, brothers that should have spent more time together, she thought. Today, watching Aunt Megan and Mom hug like strangers too close to one another on an airplane, Jaime laughed.

"That's a gorgeous dress, Janet," Aunt Megan told her. "Wherever did you get that? I love that blue!"

"By the way, mom, it's not crazy," Jaime said. "I've told *you* that *a dozen times*."

"Would you laugh if I told you this is from TJ Maxx?" Jaime's mom said, ignoring Jaime's attempt to argue. "They have some great sales."

"Typical," Jennifer said. She walked to Jaime, while their moms talked sales and shopping. "Mom will criticize me and jump into another conversation without even listening." Jennifer rolled her eyes but smiled. Jennifer and Jaime walked back toward the kitchen.

"I heard that," Megan hollered.

"At least your daughter's not into this horror shit," Jaime's mom complained. "I still don't understand it."

"You guys, we're gonna be late to the ceremony," Tara called as she ran down the stairs. "Jaime, did you tell Mom?"

"Tell Mom what?" Janet Stein asked.

"About Dad," Tara said.

"What about your father?"

"He called on Skype," Jaime said. "Just before Aunt Megan arrived. He said to tell you he's okay. He wanted to say congrats on graduation."

"Of course that son-of-a-bitch couldn't be bothered to actually show up." Janet walked up to Jaime and hugged her. "Oh, Jaime. I'm sorry. I really tried to convince him to come see you."

"It's okay, Mom. Really." Jaime shrugged and her mother hugged her again. "I wasn't expecting anything, so the quick Skype call was a nice surprise."

"Well, we've got a ceremony to get to," her mom said, and they walked outside and squeezed into Aunt Megan's SUV.

In the backseat of the SUV, Jaime put her arm around Tara, and Jennifer smiled at them. "You two make me actually wish I had a sister."

"When I leave, you can have her," Jaime joked, and Tara elbowed her ribs. "Ouch, brat!"

But she smiled at Tara. It was already turning out to be quite a day. Jaime tried not to talk about their father too much. He had left when Tara was born, and Jaime didn't even remember him. She must have been about three years old when he left. Her mom had gotten so mad that she even threw out all the pictures, and in a pre-digital age, those weren't the kind of things you could get back.

Today, for the first time in ages, she was able to see his face, even if it was fuzzy, and hear his voice. Maybe it was just her imagination, but Jaime thought she looked like him.

*****

Across the country, on the exact same day, Bill Wise put on his cap and gown and got in the car with his mother.

"It's a big day, Bill. I can't believe how quickly time has passed." Sally sighed. "When do you head back to California?"

"Next Thursday. You know that because you've made me a promise, Mom." He eyed her closely, looking for signs of hesitation. Or even an outright lie. *She better go,* he thought. She had promised.

"Yes, yeah, I know. Are you sure you want to go back there? Some of these news stories are scary. I can't believe he did all of that to you kids."

The way she changed subjects so quickly made him worry, but then she looked at him. He saw something in her eyes he hadn't seen before. It was a fire. A burning, a desire, something that wasn't there before. The fires burned for different reasons, but for one of the first times since he was a child, he thought he could see a bit of himself in his mother's eyes.

"We're not kids. Not then, and definitely not anymore. And I told you. I'm going back not because I completely trust JB but because I completely trust my friends. I want to see them again. Plus, I told you what he did for us."

"The news never said that, Bill. Only you said that."

"He found Dad's killer," Bill insisted. "Using *his* resources. That's why you don't have to worry. It was a gift to me. I really think it was his way of saying that I could trust him and should come back."

He stared out the window as they drove by another farm, the corn just beginning to grow. Soon it would be as tall as him, and that was always remarkable. Then by fall, there'd even be corn mazes. That was his favorite.

His mother sighed, and Bill looked back over at her. At a stop sign, she paused long enough to look into the driver's side mirror and put on some lipstick. Her hair had grown, and what once was fully blond now had plenty of gray. Bill felt his mother staring, and he turned to the side, his head nearly touching the roof of the car, and his long legs stretched as far out as her little Kia would allow. She smiled at him and patted him on the leg.

"It's such an incredible story, that's for sure. Almost hard to believe."

"It's the truth. Besides, you're changing the subject," Bill said. "You promised me, and I'm dropping you off myself before I leave. Oh-right?"

She looked at him with worry in her eyes, but Bill also saw that fire. He hoped that meant that she'd keep her promise, that something was changing inside of her. Over the last several months, they had discussed her drinking multiple times. Many such times ended in fights or just more drinking. But Bill, remembering his promise to himself at Rabbit in Red, never gave up. He had managed to get his mother to agree to enter a rehab program while he was away for the summer. They had timed it perfectly and arranged Sally Wise's first day of inpatient rehab to be the day Bill would return to Rabbit in Red.

"Okay," she said finally. "Let's just enjoy the day. I only get to see you graduate high school once. And with your strange choice in 'college'," here she made air quotes, "I don't know if I'll ever get to see you at a formal graduation ceremony ever again."

"I wouldn't worry about that, mom. I bet JB's got something much, much bigger planned than a cap and gown ceremony. I can only imagine what his would be like."

Bill laughed, and his mom gave him another nervous look, that same look she gave him years ago when he wanted to watch *Gremlins* over and over again. It was a nice look—he knew it meant that she cared—and an even nicer feeling.

*****

Jaime walked across the stage as her name was called and shook the hand of her high school principal. The moment took only a second, but she looked out at her classmates and all of those who attended the ceremony. When she walked off this stage, she would be a different person, and she had something no classmate of hers did. She wasn't leaving one school of standardized tests and textbooks to go to a college with even more tests and textbooks. In a few days, she'd be on a plane to a brand new adventure, to create art, to live in a spectacular world of horror with her best friends.

Scanning the crowd, she saw Susannah Price, the homecoming queen, the prom queen, the kind of person Jaime never was. Susannah and her followers—one couldn't exactly call them friends—had teased Jaime before Rabbit in Red. When Jaime returned, she'd hoped she would have earned some kind of respect. But no, she should have known better.

*When you find success, those at the top work even harder to keep you down*, she thought, recalling Uncle Tim's words of wisdom. She wished he were here. Uncle Tim had been the father figure in Jaime's life, and she missed him every day. She could talk to him about anything, from high school to horror movies. She wished he had been around now so she could talk to him about Bill, too.

She wanted to talk to someone about her feelings for Bill, she realized. But not today.

Today, Jaime smiled at Susannah, realizing that these four years of high school were simply a coming-of-age necessity, an assembly line of education from day one until now that all must complete. Graduation represented the freedom to make one's own choices. Her mother might disapprove, and Jaime knew she'd miss her sister more than words could express, but it was her time now.

Tara enthusiastically waved her hand at Jaime, and Jaime returned the gesture. She continued scanning the crowd as she exited the stage and stopped suddenly at the sight of a figure in the very back.

It would be impossible to miss his Frankenstein's monster-like body, almost a beast of a man, really. At first, it appeared that he tried to be discreet, but if his large body wasn't a giveaway, his hat was. He wore a black baseball cap with a Rabbit in Red logo: a white rabbit in a bloody red box. It looked a little odd considering he was wearing a suit jacket and dress pants as well.

As small as it was from Jaime's point of view, she'd recognize that Rabbit in Red symbol anywhere. She fantasized about its possibilities during the day and was haunted by some of the more dreadful memories at night. Maybe she was crazy to return. Maybe they all were. But there he was, a man in all black. He tipped his hat at her, and Jaime smiled at JB.

She returned to her seat, anxiously awaiting the end of the ceremony so she could say thanks to JB and introduce him to her family, but by the end of the ceremony, he had disappeared.

"I'm sorry, baby, that your father didn't come," her mom said, perhaps seeing a look of disappointment on Jaime's face. "I looked all over for him. I had hoped for a moment that maybe he'd show up."

Jaime flinched; she'd actually forgotten about her dad. "Oh, yeah. No, it's okay, Mom. I saw someone else. I just wish you could have met him."

"Who are you talking about?"

"JB himself. He was in the back."

"You're kidding? Wow. Well, it's a good thing he didn't stick around." Her mom tightened her lips. Jaime knew that look. That was her mom's famous *you're about to get it* look. "I have a few words I'd like to say to him in person, you know. That gives me an idea. I'm going to write him a nasty e-mail and your father one, too."

She faced Aunt Megan and a wicked smiled flashed across her face. "What do you say, Megan? Want to join me for some wine and hate mailing tonight?"

*And that's why JB didn't stick around,* Jaime realized. *Still too bad, though.*

"Sounds delightful." Aunt Megan laughed.

"Say what you want to my father, but please, Mom, don't embarrass me with JB," Jaime begged. "He's not that bad."

"That's the thing about youth," her mother said. "You can be blinded too easily. You can see villains as heroes and heroes as villains."

"He's not a villain, Mom." Jaime clenched her teeth, trying her best not to snap at her mother. "I wouldn't go back if I thought that."

Janet shook her head. "I pray that you're right."

Jaime had told her mother about almost all of the simulations, all except one. She never had told her mother about the fear simulation with Uncle Tim. Her had mom freaked out at all of the others. Generally, her mom was pretty easy-going and Jaime, always a good student, was allowed to do almost whatever she wanted. She usually had made good choices. But it took a lot of fighting and persuading to get her mom off her back about returning to Rabbit in Red.

Of course, her mother couldn't control her actions now, but Jaime didn't want to leave on a bad note either. So she never said anything about the simulation with Uncle Tim, and she planned on keeping it that way. She couldn't imagine if her Aunt Megan or her cousin Jennifer ever found out either. True to his word, too, JB never let that footage be revealed to the public, but of course if that had been revealed, he'd also be under a lot more scrutiny than he already was.

Jaime walked with her chin a little higher that afternoon. Out of all of the contestants who were graduating this weekend, it was she JB had chosen to see walk that stage.

*But why me?*

She shrugged off her own question. Seeing JB made her feel even more important, and she couldn't wait for the next few days to pass by to continue the adventures at Rabbit in Red.

*****

At the end of Bill's graduation ceremony, he hugged his mom and his grandparents. He watched his classmates throw their hats in the air and joke with one another. They got into cars, played loud music, and drove off like a *Fast and Furious* movie, gearing up no doubt for a plethora of parties. Bill's party consisted of a small cake with his grandparents. There were no friends to invite. The rest of his senior year after last Halloween's Rabbit in Red adventure didn't result in ridicule like Jaime's. In fact, several people wanted to hang out. Bill gave everyone a chance, but after a night or two of hanging, everyone pretty much asked the same question.

"Do you think you could get us a part in one of JB's movies?"

"Are you gonna meet anyone famous?"

"Don't forget us here when you make it big, Bill! You won't, will you? We're best friends!"

After such questions, Bill had realized that he didn't really have friends. There were people amused with his new connection, but they didn't want to get to know who Bill really was. They wanted to know what Bill would be able to do for them.

He looked at his phone on the drive back home. He wanted to call Jaime, but he knew she'd be celebrating with her family. He thought of Rose and Wes and wondered how they were. At the end of today, all four would now have graduated. Wes had graduated last week, and Rose the week before, but now that all could finally say they were done with high school, they had planned a Skype call at midnight to congratulate one another. That was the party Bill was looking forward to.

"What exactly is this college again, Bill?" his grandmother asked when they were home. "I don't think I've ever really understood."

It was a question he had been asked a lot by several different people. He smiled and did his best to answer when a text alert came on his phone.

*I want to go with you guys! Take me please!* It was Tara, Jaime's sister.

*You'll be able to visit. I promise!*

*I'm so jealous.*

Bill rolled his eyes. *I think you're the only one. Everyone else thinks we're crazy.*

*You are crazy. But I'm still jealous.*

*LOL.*

Bill was having more fun texting Tara than hanging out with his family, but as they were just about to have cake he reluctantly signed off. He'd just turned toward the table when he heard a loud thud from outside. It sounded like someone had smashed against the front door. He dropped his phone and ran out front, his mother and grandparents behind him. They were immediately blinded by flames, and Bill's mom screamed.

"I'm calling the police," his grandfather stated.

Bill stared, speechless. Someone had slammed an axe into their front door and lit it on fire. Through the flames, he could see a message that had been written on the axe, a message certainly intended for him. He swallowed hard as he read it.

*Prepare to burn.*

# Chapter Three

"You are NOT going," Sally Wise told him. "Someone threatens us, threatens you about this stupid horror shit, and you *still* want to go?"

Bill closed his eyes and rubbed his temples. This wasn't the first time they had had this argument since the "incident."

"I'm not going to be controlled by fear! I learned more about myself in one weekend last year than I learned in all four years of high school. I love you, Mom, but you're not stopping me." He opened his eyes slowly, expecting her to attack him once again. She glared but remained silent.

Then she marched out of his bedroom and walked down into the kitchen. Every footstep sounded like the beating of a drum, but then Bill heard a noise that made him shoot straight up in bed. It was the clinking of ice cubes in glass.

"Mom, what are you doing?" Bill leapt out of bed and down the stairs to the kitchen.

It was exactly what he was afraid of. There she stood pouring a glass of vodka. They hadn't even eaten breakfast yet.

"Relaxing," she snapped. "Do what you want, I guess, but don't tell me what to do." She took a long swallow.

Bill fidgeted and broke eye contact with his mom. She better not do this to him. *To us.* "I leave tomorrow. You're still letting me drop you off at the rehab hospital, right?"

Several deep swallows of her favorite drink replaced any kind of verbal answer. Then she sat the glass down and walked over to him. He could smell the alcohol on her breath. For a moment, he thought she might slap him.

"What is wrong with you?" Sally asked.

"You don't . . . you don't understand. If I don't go, whoever did this to us wins. That's what they want, don't you see?" He sighed and looked at his mom to see if she was getting it. Or was the liquor already going to her brain? "The safest place for me is with JB at Rabbit in Red. I'm old enough to make my own decisions, and that's what I'm doing."

She shook her head and walked away. He marched back upstairs to his bedroom and did what best distracted him. He watched a movie. This one was called *The Final Girls*. It was completely ridiculous and satirical, but it had some heart, too. There was a scene between the main character and her mother that nearly made him tear up. He spent the rest of the day glued to the TV, streaming one horror flick after another, or online browsing Fitz of Horror, his favorite horror entertainment page. He didn't need or want reality.

And the next morning, bags packed for both of them, Bill drove her straight to rehab on his way to the airport.

He thought his mother would cry or at least tear up, but her eyes only twitched with anger. "I wish you wouldn't leave me alone. What if whoever slammed that axe in our door comes back and I'm all by myself?"

"I thought we talked about that. You'll stay with Grandma and Grandpa for a while, at least until the police make any connections. And I told you. I'll tell JB about it. He can probably find out more in a day than the police will all summer."

He hoped she'd believe this. Hell, Bill wasn't completely sure he believed it. But he had to get back. It was about more than horror or making movies.

It was about her. Jaime.

He had to see her. He had to hold her. He had to tell her how he felt and how terrible it was to be away from her for so many months. Sure, they talked, and FaceTimed, and Skyped, and texted, and did every kind of technology they could. But it wasn't enough, not anymore. He knew what it was like to have her by his side, to have her head on his shoulder, to hear a sweet snore as she slept. He wanted that again. He hadn't been able to tell Jaime that over the phone. Ever since they had said their good-byes last Halloween, he had promised himself it would be the first thing he'd do when he got to see Jaime in person again. He'd grab her and kiss her and tell her he might die if she didn't become his girlfriend.

Bill noticed his mom was fishing through her purse while he was day dreaming. He wanted to tell his mom that maybe the real reason he needed to go was because of Jaime, but he worried his mom would only use that against him. *See, you know you shouldn't go, and all you're doing is risking your life for a girl!* He shook her voice from his head.

"Oh, Bill. I think you're putting too much hope in one person." His mom sighed and kept digging through her purse. Bill gasped when she pulled out a pack of cigarettes and lit one up.

"Mom! When did you start smoking?"

"The day I quit drinking."

Bill wanted to say something about replacing one addiction with another, but he chose to keep his mouth shut. They were outside of the drug and alcohol rehabilitation clinic now. It was time to see what this kind of place could really do. Bill parked and walked his mom inside.

"JB is sending a car to pick me up here. I'll leave the car in the back of the parking lot for when you're ready, but I hope you'll complete the program and stay for as long as they recommend. Then go to Grandma and Grandpa's."

She inhaled the cigarette deeply, threw the butt to the ground, and crushed it out with her heel before stepping inside. "I appreciate what you're doing for me, Billy. I do." She hugged him then, her head barely reaching his chest. He wrapped his long arms around her.

"I love you, Mom."

"I love you, too. Please be safe. Please. I have a bad feeling about all of this. About you, I mean."

"I'll be fine. I promise. You'll see. After our summer program, you'll come visit. You'll see how cool everything is. And how safe." He tried to smile, but it was forced. Was he fooling himself, too?

"If you say so," she replied.

"Bye, Mom. I'll call you."

He watched her check in at the front desk and hoped that she would be safe, that she'd find some kind of recovery here, and that it would work. He turned around and walked back to the car. It was time to return to Rabbit in Red.

*****

"Bill! Over here!"

Wes and Rose ran toward him, and Rose gave him a surprisingly hard hug. Her red hair seemed brighter somehow, and even though she was a pretty short girl, she looked taller and stronger. Maybe it was confidence, or maybe she'd been working out since last Halloween. Bill thought for a moment that if she wanted to, she could snap his back in two.

"Rose," he said. "It's so good to see you! But you're crushing me, girl. Damn."

"I'm sorry!" She giggled, and that shy, innocent expression he'd seen when he first met her returned to her face. "I've just been really looking forward to seeing you guys."

"Me too, man," Wes said and extended a fist. Bill laughed, picturing the first time they all saw Daniel and his group of idiot followers last year, fist bumping like stupid jocks. Bill reminded himself some of those idiots would be back, and that maybe he should give them a decent chance, since they all might have to work together this summer. Bill then closed his fist and tapped knuckles with Wes.

"You look good!" he told Wes. Wes was still overweight, but he looked stronger, too. He had grown an inch or so, probably one last final teenage growth spurt.

"Rose sent me this cool app. You walk and jog, but then it tells you that zombies are chasing you. It makes you outrun the zombies. I've been doing that for a few months. Nothing crazy, but I'm trying."

"That's awesome. You seen Jaime yet?" He looked around. It was nice seeing Wes and Rose, sure, but the one he needed to see wasn't here. The only thing he had thought during the plane trip from Chicago to L.A. was what he'd say to Jaime when he saw her. He had a little speech planned. It would start and end with a kiss. Where the hell was she?

"No, you beat her here. Come on in, man. We wanted to hang outside for a bit. JB has all new themes inside!" Bill wanted to share in Wes's enthusiasm, but the smile he returned was fake. He wanted to experience this with Jaime.

"Of course he does," Bill said.

"Come inside!" Rose grabbed his hand, pulled him forward, and once again Bill was surprised at her strength.

"What are you guys doing outside anyway?" Bill asked. Rose and Wes looked at one another and giggled. "Ha, never mind," Bill added. He knew that look. They were outside making out or holding hands or being all happy.

The entrance that had previously split into two main halls based on *The Shining* and *Halloween II* had been redecorated. On their right resembled Freddy's nightmare world. It was a boiler room. Along the walls, metal bars enclosed what would have been Freddy's workplace. It was dark and dingy, but the best part of the hall was at the end. It would appear that in JB's remodeling he had installed an actual boiler.

"Listen closely," Wes whispered. They stood outside of the boiler, and it hissed at them. Following the hiss, the unmistakable cackle of Freddy Krueger bounced off the walls around them.

"Some kind of surround sound effect?" Bill asked.

Rose shushed him. "Just listen. And watch."

The boiler rumbled and came to life. A real fire formed inside, and flames spit out at them. Bill jumped back several feet and yelled, "Damn!" Rose and Wes laughed, and Bill found himself smiling too, even with flames dancing inside the boiler. Then Freddy's laugh changed. It became a piercing scream, and they had to cover their ears.

"That's sick," Bill said. "I love it."

"Isn't it awesome?" Rose had a twisted grin on her face. "I just love fire. This is gonna be a great summer." "What's down the other hall?"

"Come and see." Wes led the way, and as they entered the hall to the left of the entrance, they were in a school setting. The previous *Halloween* themed decorations and hospital rooms had now become classrooms. Lockers lined the hall.

"Is this also *A Nightmare on Elm Street*?" Bill asked.

"We're not sure," Wes said. "I couldn't find any specific enough details to place it. It could be any number of settings."

"I'm sure JB has something up his sleeve for this part of the studio," Rose told him. "But c'mon. The best parts are next."

As they moved forward down what used to be the *It* hallway, they entered hell, or what was designed to look like hell, that is. Digital flames flickered all along the sides. The walls looked like the inside of a volcano, and although these flames weren't real, JB obviously had used his 4D technology to enhance the setting. Vents spit intense heat at the three as they walked forward.

"This kind of heat in a California summer?" Bill asked. "Crazy."

"Yeah." Rose wiped a hand across her forehead. "We're not sure if this is meant to just be hell in general, or a specific hell from a story. *Hellraiser*, maybe?"

"Maybe," Bill said. "There are a lot of hells."

"This is the best part!" Wes pointed at the end of the hall where they would enter the commons. The flames fizzled out near the end, but they were greeted by the giant face of Candyman.

"Oh, that is creepy as hell," Bill muttered with a smile. "Wow."

It was a giant black face with sharp white teeth. Candyman's eyes looked up toward the ceiling, and they had to crawl into his mouth to enter the next room. In the Clive Barker inspired movie, this image of the haunting Candyman appeared in a run-down ghetto building, the monster's secret lair. Inside the lair was art and graffiti that represented Candyman.

As they walked through his mouth, they looked around at the re-designed commons. It wasn't exactly Candyman's lair, but it was inspired by it for sure. They were surrounded by horror art, fantastically detailed drawings, paintings, and sculptures of all of horror's greats. Bill recognized the artist. He had hung several works of art by Camron Johnson Illustrations on his bedroom walls at home. Jason, Freddy, Michael, Pinhead, Ghostface, Leatherface, Jack from *The Shining*, Pennywise the clown, and many more, including art depicting the assistants from last Halloween: Captain Spaulding, Samara, Pumpkinhead, Sam.

The commons itself resembled a cave, and where the stage once stood was now a giant, curved screen. It was like a movie theater, but instead of posters there was a variety of the most unique horror art they had ever seen. Instead of rows of seats, there were a variety of wooden benches.

"It's so dark," Bill said. "Amazing." Bill walked up to each work of art, taking his time to soak it all in like he was in a museum. *In a way,* he thought, *that's exactly what Rabbit in Red is.* He took his time in front of Jack from *The Shining.* Jaime should be looking at this with him. It would be the perfect time to bring up the old argument as to what's better: King's book or Kubrick's movie?

*Dammit, Jaime, where are you?*

"Isn't it?" Wes said. "Like I hope JB lets us have movie nights here. This is the coolest theater ever."

They looked around, and several of the contestants from last fall were here, mingling. No one had come to speak with them yet, but several were sure staring.

"You know, guys," Bill said, "we're supposed to be the first-year leaders. We should mingle. Make sure no one feels like we're better than them or something, you know?"

He tried to focus on the moment. *Just keep busy. She'll be here before you know it.*

Wes and Rose both nodded, and they stepped toward the other first years who had returned.

"Should we wait for Jaime?" Wes asked.

"We can talk to them again when she's here," Bill said. "You can tell just by the way they're looking at us that they all seem unsure. Let's at least say hi."

They walked closer to all of the returning students, who quickly quieted.

"Has anyone seen JB yet?" Bill started.

They all shook their heads and stared at Bill intently. Bill looked at his two friends, who nodded at him, giving him the okay to speak for them.

"We just wanted to say hi. We're excited to be here. There was a lot of . . . of competition last year," Bill said, trying to find the right words. "We want everyone to be friends, to work together. It's been a while, so why don't we re-introduce ourselves? I'm Bill Wise. This is Rose Dawn and Wes Pike."

They all started shaking hands. There were a dozen names for them to remember. They smiled at Annie Walker and Leroy Birch, the two "missing" contestants from the games last year. There were eleven others though, and as they shook hands and said hello, Bill felt the tension in the room dissipate. Everyone was talking, laughing, and smiling, but Bill kept looking over his shoulder.

*Where the hell is Jaime?* It was starting to make him angry.

As they were talking, a man walked out in front of the giant screen. He had long sideburns and a gray, receding hairline. He swung his arms in a way Bill found familiar. Not quite as big as JB, he was still pretty thick and muscular.

"Hello, everyone." He smiled, and that smile Bill recognized.

"My name is Chester Malcolm. You might remember me better dressed as Captain Spaulding."

The students exhaled a long "Ohhh."

"This summer," he continued, "is about learning. No games yet. You'll see us in our true colors. I'm JB's right hand man, so to speak. If JB is the president of our Horror College, I'll be like your dean, working directly with you while he takes care of . . . all sorts of behind the scenes stuff. Let me introduce all of JB's top staff, all of your deans, so to say. First, here is Donnie Chase."

A young woman approached, short like Rose, but with hair as black as a raven. "Donnie, you'll remember, played Samara last year."

Two more men followed Donnie Chase, and Chester Malcolm, aka Captain Spaulding, continued. "Let me also introduce Michael Quinn, who played *Trick R Treat's* Sam, and Thomas Lance, our Pumpkinhead. Try not to confuse the two," he laughed.

"I also want you to welcome Bonnie Villa and Marcus Everett," he said, and two more lined up by his side.

They'd recognize Bonnie anywhere. She looked just like Kathy Bates from *Misery*, and Bill shuddered at the flashback, the first "real" fight they had last Halloween. Marcus was a tall, thin man, and if he only he had worn all leather, they'd have recognized him right away, too. He'd played the man shooting and chasing them in *The People Under the Stairs* room last year.

"Our faces are new but familiar. It will take time to learn everyone's name, but you may call us by our first names." Chester opened up his arms and made an exaggerated gesture. "We're a team here. JB has organized us to help get you settled. We'll take you to your rooms, and we'll break into small groups, and one or two of us will also participate in your groups." He made a deliberate effort to look each of them in the eye. "Our first task is a competition of sorts. We'll determine this year's Rabbit in Red contest for new recruits. Each team will brainstorm ideas, and then we will vote on the best. Then everyone will work to design and prepare that challenge." He smiled so wide that his lips looked like they could have touched his ears. "This is hands-on horror, and now you are the creators! It's going to be a spectacular summer!"

Murmurs from the crowd of students echoed throughout the commons, but Bill spoke up. "Where's JB? Will we see him? And do you know where Jaime is?"

"JB has a surprise for you, as he always does." Chester chuckled and clasped his hands together in excitement. "He wanted us to get you started. There's much to do. And we expect your friend to arrive shortly."

Rose put her hand up, and Chester called on her. "No need for such formalities, young lady. Speak your mind."

"Last Halloween," she started, "we were told we'd have to make a decision as to whether . . . whether Daniel would be returning. Is that something we still need to do?"

"Oh yes," Chester replied. "Once everyone is in a group, we'll discuss that. But for now, let's show you to your new rooms. Behold!"

Chester pointed behind them. Unlike last year, where the halls behind the stage in the commons led to different sleeping quarters, a new section of the studio appeared. Directly behind them, the wall vibrated and slid open, revealing an unexplored area of Rabbit in Red.

As the movable wall glided open, they saw what resembled some kind of space ship. Long, cylindrical metal pipes lined the walls, and the floor consisted of metal grating. A variety of pipes and retro-looking gadgets were placed all throughout, and it led to the one thing that popped out in the middle of the hall: a ladder.

"Go ahead," Chester said. "Explore. Up the ladder and down the hall, you'll find your rooms. Guys to the left. Ladies to the right."

Bill looked around one more time, hoping to see Jaime. He was excited to see the new rooms, but disappointed she had yet to show up. Where was she?

"Let's check it out," Wes said, leading them forward.

"Oh, I know what this is all about," Rose stated, sliding her hand along the metal pipes.

"Nostromo." Wes nodded. "Excellent!"

"Ladies first," Bill told Rose. She slung her purse, the same black purse with the purple lettering, over her shoulder, and climbed the ladder. They waited for everyone to climb before turning their separate directions.

"Meet you back here in a few minutes?" Rose asked.

"Yeah." Wes grinned. "We'll check out our rooms. You lead the rest of the girls. See you in a few."

Bill and Wes led the guys to the left, and as he had expected, they found a room full of pods. Long, white sleeping pods, almost shaped like coffins, but curved like bananas, were spread out in a circular fashion around the room.

Leroy had jumped up to Bill and Wes's side. "*Alien*?" he asked.

"Most definitely," Bill said. "This is awesome."

Each of the guys claimed a pod for the bed. It was larger than those that appeared in the movies, at least the length of a full size bed. Inside the pods, they discovered the master host spared no expense. Each pod had its own smart screen with a variety of features. It was basically like their very own computer within each pod. The screen had all the apps they would need, from Netflix to Facebook, iMovie to Pandora.

"Amazing!" Wes cheered.

"Think of the porn you could watch on these things!" Leroy said.

Bill rolled his eyes. "Um, not when we're sleeping in the same room, please."

As they amused themselves with all of the technology in the pods, the lights went out. Darkness filled the room, and a pulsating, electric beat of music blasted from all the pods at once. It was a terrifyingly creepy sound, and all the guys covered their ears.

"What's happening?" one of them tried to shout over the music.

Bill and Wes could only shake their heads. The music was deafening. Then a single image appeared before them, a 3D hologram projected from somewhere in the dark. It was the rabbit, spinning and dancing. The rabbit snarled at them, and then burst into flames.

"Follow the rabbit," a voice projected over the music.

The rabbit screamed in what seemed to be a combination of pleasure and pain. It hopped away, and the guys followed. It took them deeper into this unfamiliar section of the studio. The rooms continued to look like that of a spaceship, but in this new room, the rabbit hopped toward a giant metal slide.

"Follow the rabbit," the voice repeated, and the burning rabbit jumped on the slide.

Unable to speak over the loud music, Bill and Wes looked at one another, trying to figure out what was happening. Bill turned to the rest of the guys, and nodded his head toward the slide.

He hopped on first, Wes right behind him, followed by all of the others. They flew down the slide fast, like sledding down a steep wintery hill. The slide curved, the music pulsated, the rabbit shrieked in front of them, and they all screamed as they flew down.

The slide dumped them into another new room, one that reminded Bill of JB's monitoring station where he observed all of the games last year. There were multiple monitors, each showing a different section of Rabbit in Red. They fell onto a soft surface, some kind of foam padding. In the middle of the room stood the two people Bill was most curious to find: JB and Jaime.

From across the room, he saw all of the girls slide and spill onto the floor. The music slowly softened, and JB, tall and strong as ever, stood in the center and spoke.

"Welcome back, my friends! Welcome to your summer of horror!" He laughed over the music until the electronic pulses were completely silenced.

"We have much to do and much to discuss," he continued. "You must be wondering about this room, and why my rabbit led you here in such dramatic fashion."

That smile lingered on JB's face, and Bill's flesh erupted in goosebumps. JB might be a genius, but there was also most definitely a good percentage of madman in that brain.

"These sections, including your rooms, are all new modifications made since Halloween. We will embark on the biggest horror ambitions you can imagine, but my friends, we have enemies. Rabbit in Red has had many threats, as have some of you. In the case of an emergency, the music will play, the rabbit will appear, and you are to follow the rabbit to safety. In this room, we will be able to watch any section of Rabbit in Red. Behind me, a tunnel will lead us out of the studios to the outside. I'm afraid an escape plan is absolutely necessary, and while I don't want to scare you, I do need to prepare you. For *anything*."

The way JB looked as he said it sent a chill all through Bill's body. This didn't sound like JB's facetiously sadistic nature from last year. This sounded . . . well, *real*, Bill thought.

While the other students looked around at one another, Bill stared at Jaime. He tried to ask *how are you* and *what's happening* with his eyes. He thought she understood, but she bit her lip and looked back at him with a fierce sadness. The only time he had seen this look on her face was during the fear simulations last Halloween, when she watched her uncle nearly hang himself again. He put a hand over his chest. Something hurt inside of him, seeing her like that. Bill widened his eyes, but she looked away. Then JB continued.

"You may be wondering why our young Jaime is with me here and was not with you earlier," JB said. "I'm afraid to say we already have a missing person, and it's not part of a game this time. Jaime's sister Tara has been kidnapped. Jaime's mother and sister drove her to the airport. When Jaime's plane took off, her mother and sister drove home, but a car crashed into their vehicle. Her mother is okay, but the driver of the vehicle took Tara. I received a message immediately. It read, 'Burn down Rabbit in Red. Or I burn Tara.' I assure you we are doing whatever it takes to get Tara back. In the meantime, we are on high alert at the studio, and are working closely with authorities. We'll find the psycho who did this. I promise you."

When he had finished, Bill ran to Jaime.

"Oh my God. Are you okay?" Bill's body shook and the words came out like a stutter.

Jaime looked at the ground, and Bill could see a lump in her throat as if she were swallowing back tears. Then she looked up at him. "I don't know what to think or do, Bill. I should go home to my mom, I suppose. But then I'd just be sitting and waiting. I know JB cares." Bill reached for her hand, and she took it. "He picked me up at LAX personally. As soon as I saw him, I knew it was bad news. But if JB could find your dad's killer, then surely he can find whoever took Tara, right?"

Bill hugged her then, and Jaime put her head against his chest. He didn't say anything. He just let her cry. He thought about whoever had slammed an axe in his door. He thought about what his mother had said, that she had felt something bad about all of this.

Maybe she was right after all.

## Chapter Four

Jaime stared at JB as Bill hugged her. In this panic room deep within the Rabbit in Red studios, she watched their master host take charge. He walked with a heavier step this year, she noticed. But something bothered her. When he welcomed everyone down here, why did he even try to be humorous and inviting? *Welcome to your summer of horror*, he had said.

No shit.

But what he had already done and what he had told her he was going to do sure made it seem like he cared. *Let's see what he can really do,* she thought. *But why all the drama? Just call a goddamn meeting and let's get started.*

Bill held her close, and it was Jaime who had to pull away. She had missed his smell. Old Spice. Wasn't that what his father had used, too? She thought he had told her that once.

She and Bill had talked every day after leaving Rabbit in Red last Halloween. Every single day. And not once did he ever actually ask her out. Sure, they lived a thousand miles away from one another, but wouldn't you think he'd eventually say in his cute awkwardness, "Hey J, so you and me . . . are we official?" But no. Never happened. She prided herself though on knowing Bill better than anyone else, and in the back of her mind, this was supposed to be their moment. He'd wait to ask her in person. All those months apart would make the attraction stronger.

But none of that even mattered any more. Tara was gone. *Why? And who? And just what the fuck?* Thoughts bounced through her mind like hail slamming against a roof. If someone wanted to get her or do something to hurt Rabbit in Red, why go after her sister? She had no idea, but JB had better prove he had the resources to find Tara, and find her quickly.

"Oww," Bill said. She looked down and realized she had grabbed his hands and squeezed.

"Sorry," she mumbled. She looked back up at the handsome, tall boy who hugged her so tightly. It should have been a hug of a different kind of passion though, she thought.

JB had given them a few moments to say hello, but now he wanted everyone's attention again. "Team, I know this is difficult. Finding Tara is of the utmost importance. When something happens to one of our own, we fight together as a family."

Jaime felt Bill's grip on her hand tighten, and he stepped closer to her. Everyone had turned to face JB in this strange panic room.

"You know the whole 'too many cooks in the kitchen' idea?" JB continued. "It applies here. I will spearhead a search for Tara myself, and Jaime of course will accompany me. The rest of you—we need your thoughts and prayers. But the best way for you all to move forward is to keep busy. The busy bee has no time for sorrow, as they say."

Jaime saw JB nod at Bill and lock eye contact with him. Bill's grip tightened on her hand more. "Yes, I know you want to help," JB continued. He spoke to the group, but his eyes never left Bill's. "Trust me. There is work for you to do here." He paused, as if waiting for Bill's understanding.

Bill looked at Jaime, and she leaned in close, whispering in his ear, "I trust him."

"My team will lead you on your first project," JB said. "There's nothing you all can do at the moment. I assure you I'm putting all of my energy into finding out who is behind this kidnapping. We have a choice to make." He looked at each of them in the eye, lifted his chin, and spoke even louder. "We give in to fear, and we let Rabbit in Red die because of this person's horrible actions. Or we continue. We make it stronger than ever."

The other first year students were obviously concerned, but they all nodded reluctantly. JB was right. Sitting around would only drive everyone crazy. It was better to keep busy.

"Let me stay with you." Bill addressed Jaime but looked over at JB.

"No, Bill," JB said firmly. "I know Jaime appreciates it, but there really is nothing you can do. You have to trust me here. I'll get to the bottom of this. I promise."

Jaime bit her lip. She would have liked Bill by her side, but truth be told, she didn't know what JB had in mind. And she felt like she could explode any second. A ticking time bomb just waiting for a trigger. Did she really want Bill to see her like that?

After a moment of silence, she mumbled, "It's okay. Believe me, as soon as Tara is okay, I want to get back to work, too. It's what we're here for, after all."

Bill studied her. She wasn't entirely sure he believed her. That would make two of them. He hugged her again and looked up at JB. "I don't know if I'm going to be able to concentrate on anything here, JB. Whatever you have planned for us, it's just going to drive me crazy until Jaime is back. Please let me come."

"Son, I'm not even sure I want Jaime to come. This is all very serious. Between just the three of us," JB said, softening his voice and looking around so the rest of the first years wouldn't hear, "we're in real danger. That's why I wanted all of you to see this panic room right away. If something happens while I'm gone, this is where you'll be directed to go. As for what's out there and for who took Tara . . ."

JB sighed and looked up. His face tightened. It was an expression Jaime hadn't seen on him before. "Look, the fewer who are in danger, the better. You're safe here, inside. This is my final decision. Jaime can come, but no one else. It's a risk even with her."

"But, sir, please!" Bill wrapped an arm around Jaime. She looked up at him, and a feeling of warmth blanketed the cold she had been feeling.

"That's the end of the discussion, Bill." JB walked back to the center of the panic room, coughed, and got everyone's attention. "I do have one nice surprise for everyone. This was going to be a gift anyway, but I hope now it will help distract all of you until we get back. This is for all of you, but Bill, you may like one of the surprises more than most. You'll see."

JB's face twitched, something like a smile. *It would have been his classic grin if some psycho didn't have my sister,* she thought. Jaime looked over at Bill. There was no smile on his face.

"Chester will give it to you back in the commons. I hope you all like them." JB motioned for Jaime to follow him. It was time to go.

"Jaime," Bill started. He grabbed her hands, and she wished more than anything in that moment that she could read his mind. He leaned in, and for a moment she thought he'd kiss her. He wrapped his arms around her and pulled her close. He hugged her so hard his arms shook. "Please be careful," he whispered in her ear. "I don't like this at all. Text me every second you get. Please." He pulled away slowly.

In that moment, she wanted to say how much she loved him. She blinked and felt her eyes moisten. She nodded.

She turned around and followed JB. In the back of the room, there was an elevator. Jaime and JB got in, and they faced Bill, who looked as if he was losing his best friend.

Jaime held eye contact with him until the elevator doors closed. Then she and JB went up and out of Rabbit in Red to find the evil that had taken Tara.

*I hope the next time I see you, Bill, Tara is by my side. Oh, God, please don't let anything happen to my baby sister. I'll do anything, anything at all. If this psycho hurts even a single hair on her body, I'll kill him. I swear to it. I'll fucking kill him.*

*****

The other first years had gathered near the slide that had dropped them into this sanctuary of sorts.

"Do we climb back up the slide?" Wes asked nervously.

"No, look." Bill pointed to the corner of the room, where the 3D rabbit hologram waited. There was a staircase that led them back upstairs. It was narrow and winding, but they climbed up it. The staircase led up to the new sleeping quarters, near the ladder. From there, they scaled down the ladder and walked back out into the commons, where Chester was waiting for them.

Bill didn't know how he would be able to get through the next hours or days or weeks or however long this could take. He loved Tara. He had always wanted his own little sister or brother, someone he could scare in the middle of the night with a classic horror movie but also someone he could try to inspire. And why couldn't he go with JB? This wasn't fair.

*Screw this contest or whatever the hell we are supposed to do,* he thought. *I should be by Jaime's side.*

Chester greeted them once everyone had gathered back in the commons. "I'm sorry for the bad news, everyone. But trust me. If there's anyone you want on your side in a time like this, it's JB. We need to get to work, but first, JB has a gift for all of you. Something that I hope will lift your spirits."

Donnie Chase, who had previously played Samara, walked out into the cave-like commons area with two little surprises. "JB thought some animals would bring some smiles to your faces. First, meet Falcor."

An almost all white cocker spaniel leaped forward and ran into the crowd of students. He wagged his tail furiously and licked the faces of virtually everyone. Bill understood why JB said he'd appreciate this gift perhaps more than others. The little cocker spaniel reminded him of his old family dog, Sparky, whose last night alive was the same as Arnie Wise's last night, the dreadful night of the home intruder.

"Falcor?" one of the students asked.

"Falcor is the name of one of JB's all-time favorite movie animals," Donnie said. "And now, your second mascot. We thought it was time to host an actual rabbit. Meet Lester!"

Bonnie Villa, who played that terrible Annie from *Misery*, walked out then with a white rabbit in her arms. "This little girl will need some extra special care. She's not as independent as Falcor. So we'll rotate, among those who are interested, who will take care of her. Who would like to take care of her first?"

Rose shot up her hand quicker than anyone else. "Very well, Rose. Meet little Lester." Bonnie handed her the rabbit.

"Adorable!"

Falcor had made his way over to Bill, who sat on the floor and gave the pup some love. The pup rolled on his back and let Bill give him a big tummy rub. *Damn you, JB*, he thought as he smiled. He didn't think he should be happy or distracted or doing anything but thinking about Jaime, but JB knew what he was doing. *He just better know what he's doing out there, too.*

"It's time to make our teams," Chester announced. "Bill, Rose, and Wes, as previously arranged, you will each be a group leader. We will divide everyone else into these groups of three, and we'll be working with you. Your first task is as follows. You must develop a new challenge, like the Fright Fest you experienced, for new recruits. Jaime asked last year if we'd do the same test each year. The short answer is no. The long answer is that it's up to you to determine the kind of test new recruits who want to be students at Rabbit in Red must experience." Chester moved among them, patting some of them on the back even, trying to rally the team. "Bounce your ideas off of us. We'll help you determine what is practical and what we can actually make happen. Spread out. Use Rabbit in Red as your inspiration. You can get started now. You also have another item on your agenda. Take some time to discuss that too, and we'll hear your initial thoughts when you come back for dinner, which will be served at six."

The assistants divided everyone up. Surely, they would have preferred to work together, Bill thought, and more importantly, they would have preferred that Jaime were by their side and that everything was okay. But Bill knew they all had new responsibilities this year. They were the student leaders, and they needed to act like it.

*****

Across the country, a man stared at a scared little girl in a hotel room. Tara wore a wet blindfold, soaked from all of the tears. The man wore an oversized hooded sweatshirt, the hood covering most of his face, in case Tara's blindfold slipped off somehow.

"Why are you doing this to me?" Tara asked.

The man stomped around the room, repeatedly checking his phone. He breathed aggressively through his nose and turned to look at her.

"I have to get their attention."

"Whose attention?"

The man ignored her and refreshed the news feed on his phone. He wanted to know what the authorities knew. Social media made crime all too easy today. The authorities thought that by posting a news article with information about what they were seeking they would get others to help find the criminal. But really, it helped the criminal hide. If they had a description of him, he'd change his appearance. If they had an area in which they suspected he was residing, he'd move somewhere else. Playing it very smart and safe, he'd stay a step ahead of everyone else. The only one who worried him was JB. He knew what JB was capable of. So the man had bought a burner phone, never used a credit card, and stayed away from any camera.

"Whose attention?" Tara asked again.

"Your sister's. And JB's."

"Why do you want their attention?"

"Shut up," he mumbled.

"But why?"

"Shut up!" he shouted. "I'm concentrating." He needed to send another message to JB and Rabbit in Red. His initial warning, he knew, would only prompt a search team. They wouldn't take him seriously, not yet, not until he found a way to make them take him seriously.

He looked at Tara, crying and struggling in the chair on which he'd tied her arms and legs. Then he reached into his pocket and pulled out a book of matches. He looked at the matches and then over at Tara. A smile stretched from cheek to cheek as he thought of what he needed to do. Approaching Tara, he lit a match.

*****

Rose sat down with her team, and they spread out across the floor. Her arms shook like they used to before giving a speech in school. She'd never liked public speaking, that was for sure. But now she was a leader.

She liked the idea that a leader didn't have to be loud or talk all the time. A leader, she hoped, could also be quiet and lead by example, not words.

*What would Jaime do?* A picture of Rose's little brother floated through her memory. She had lost her little brother tragically, and not a day went by that she didn't wish he were by her side. She understood the agony that Jaime was going through.

Rose focused on her thoughts on the people in front of her. Her team consisted of Annie Walker and four others she was trying to learn more about. A few of the other returning students from last year that were in her group consisted of Dennis Kasper, Brandon Rice, Caitlin Delores, and Venus Bowers. The first agenda item was to discuss whether or not to invite Daniel back to Rabbit in Red.

"You hung out with him last year," she said to Dennis and Brandon. "What do you think?"

"It's totally uncool that he got violent," Dennis said. "But I don't think he's a bad guy. He just . . . got wrapped up in the games."

"He's a total ass and super competitive," Brandon added. "But sometimes you need a guy like that. If Rabbit in Red is really under a threat, I kinda want a guy like Daniel on our side."

"What if Daniel is responsible for what's happening somehow?" Venus asked. Rose wanted to know the meaning behind the name Venus, but she didn't interrupt. Venus wore flip flops and a cut off shirt that revealed her stomach with a belly button piercing. Looking at her, Rose really didn't need to ask the obvious.

"I agree," Caitlin said. Caitlin was a tall girl with light brown hair. She wasn't as tall as Bill but was definitely the tallest girl here. "How do we know if we can trust him?"

Rose had considered this. Could Daniel be the one who had kidnapped Tara? Could he be the one who had threatened them? Who else could it be? There was Dexter. Rose reminded herself. There was most definitely something scary about him. Even JB had seen that, as Dexter's return wasn't even up for discussion. And then there was Chester's brother, Sid Malcom. Sid had been locked up under the funhouse last year during Halloween weekend. Could Sid be out for some kind of revenge?

"If he is an enemy," Rose jumped in, "then maybe it would be even better to have him here. Keep your enemies closer, as they say. If he's up to no good, we'd know for sure if we were able to watch him here."

Caitlin and Venus looked at one another and shrugged. "Okay," Venus said. "I can understand that. If the other two groups want him back, then we'll support that."

Rose doubted the decision but, given everything that had happened, it would actually be good to have Daniel here. Brandon was right. Sometimes you needed an asshole on your side. *And if he's guilty of the threats to Rabbit in Red and has anything to do with Tara's kidnapping, then why would he even return? They'd know for sure if he were the villain then, right?*

"Okay, that's settled," Rose said. She liked leading this group. She liked that she could ask questions and get them to think and discuss without telling them what they should think. "Now, what are your ideas for the new recruits?"

"I have an amazing idea. Picture this." Venus explained her concept, and it was a great start. Each of them added something to the idea, and by the end of the night, they had come up with something new, workable, unique, and terrifying. In other words, it was perfect for Rabbit in Red.

*****

Back in the monitoring station, the same one past the game chambers he used last year, JB talked with local authorities in Jaime's hometown. She sat by his side, talking to her mother on the phone. JB had turned off the cell phone blockers he had installed for last year's Fright Fest.

"You should come home," Janet Stein told her daughter.

"JB is seriously doing everything he can for us, Mom. I think it's better if I'm here to help him and you're there to be a direct contact for the local cops."

"Oh, Jaime, why did this happen?"

"I don't know, Mom." She had been wondering that same question. Why Tara? Why not go after someone actually at Rabbit in Red? It felt almost without purpose, a random act of violence maybe, and that scared her even more.

"If they hurt my little girl, I'll strangle them!"

"Have you told Dad?" Wherever her father was, he'd want to know about this, right? How could someone not care? She shook her head.

"I've tried all of my contacts and the bastard still won't get back to me."

"I can't believe that." *Or at least I don't want to believe that.*

"It's true," her mom said. "I'm going crazy over here. I wish you'd come home. Wouldn't you be safer here?" Standing near her, JB nodded. She and JB had talked about this before she called her mother.

"This place is like a war bunker, Mom. You'd be safer *here*, actually. JB has invited you to stay with us here."

"Well, I certainly can't go anywhere until we find Tara."

Jaime watched all of the monitors. JB had a local news channel from Jaime's hometown streaming on one. His personal e-mail was open on another, and news feeds from social media popped up on another.

"Um, let me call you back," Jaime said when she saw a new e-mail arrive for JB. He noticed it too, disconnected his phone call, and opened up the message.

The subject of the e-mail read *Tara burns.*

Jaime gasped and grabbed JB's arm. She squeezed it tight. "Oh, please, no. Please, no!"

"Let me open it, Jaime. You might want to look away."

But she couldn't. She wanted to, but her body wouldn't move. Inside the message was a video. Jaime held her breath as JB pressed play.

The video showed Tara tied up to a chair wearing a blindfold. Then her hair went up in flames. The fire appeared to engulf her entire face, and her screams made Jaime burst into tears.

A single message appeared at the end of the six second video.

*Your choice is simple. Either I see all of Rabbit in Red burned to ashes, or you'll see all of her burned to ashes.*

# Chapter Five

Chester Malcolm walked once again to the center of Candyman's den back in the commons. Bill saw Rose smile at Wes and wished that he could smile like that. In their own ways, Bill thought, everyone had become some kind of leader. That was more and more obvious with each passing minute of the summer. Those who followed the rabbit were no longer simply followers.

"We're excited to hear your proposals," Chester began. "But our first line of business deals with Daniel Lloyd. What have your groups decided?" He looked over at Wes, who stood up to address the crowd.

"Our group voted yes," Wes told them. "We should invite Daniel back."

"And what is your rationale, may I ask?"

"Everyone deserves a second chance. We're willing to give him that chance," he told Chester.

Bill tried to study Wes as he spoke. Bill didn't think Wes looked like he believed this. Maybe he was just reporting what the majority of his group had decided?

"Very well." Chester nodded and turned to Rose's group. "And what about you all?"

"We agree. We've decided to let him back." Unlike Wes, Rose looked certain. She may have been short, especially in comparison to Bill, but standing there, she looked tall and confident. Yeah, everyone really was starting to look like leaders, Bill thought.

"And your rationale?"

Rose held Lester the rabbit who started to squirm in her arms. "Um, well, forgive my choice of words here, but if Rabbit in Red is under threat, we decided it helps sometimes to have an asshole on your side."

Chester laughed. "Very well, Rose. Very well. And you, young Bill?"

Bill stood up and Falcor the dog barked by his side. "Our group," Bill started, looking carefully at Rose and Wes, "has voted no."

"And your group's rationale, Bill?"

"If Rabbit in Red is already unstable, we don't want to risk it by throwing a stick of potential dynamite in our home base."

He sat down. He felt the stares from Rose and Wes, but he didn't look them in the eye. His group's decision was made, not that it would matter much.

"All very interesting responses," Chester continued. "JB has given me the authority to make the final decision based on your group responses. As it is two groups against one who vote for Daniel's return, I shall invite him to join us. Of course, you never know if he'll actually accept. He could be off doing any number of different things."

Bill felt his stomach tighten. *What were the other groups thinking? Daniel is an asshole, plain and simple.* He was someone who had demonstrated that he could not and should not be trusted, and there was no way in hell Bill would support bringing him back.

He thought of his mother then and wondered how she was doing. *We'll become a fool for those closest to us, always believing and hoping for the best. But why become the fool for anyone else? How does that saying go? Fool me once, shame on you. Fool me twice, shame on me.*

Bill worried they had all just become fools.

"On to our second order of business," Chester stated. "Let's hear your initial ideas for our new recruits."

"What about Jaime and Tara?" Bill interrupted. "Do you have any updates for us?" He hadn't received any texts from Jaime in a while, and all of this work wasn't distracting him from the situation. It was just making him crazy.

Chester sighed empathetically. "Unfortunately, I do not have any updates for you yet. I assure you Jaime is by JB's side, and he is working tirelessly to help Tara. When we know something more, I'll tell you."

Bill frowned, and Chester continued, "I know that it's difficult to focus on the moment. It's difficult perhaps to make this fun again when you're worried for the safety of others and yourselves. I cannot emphasize enough though that you should have full confidence in your master host. JB . . . he has . . ." Chester scratched the top of his head. "He had more resources and experience than you can possibly imagine and understand. In time, you'll learn more about that. What we have here is terrible, don't get me wrong. But it would be as if a tiny 3$^{rd}$ world country tried to declare war with the United States. No one is a match for JB, and this madman is surely a fool. You'll see in time."

Bill wanted to trust these words, but it was difficult not to have Jaime by his side. He took out his phone and texted her quickly. *Please tell me you're okay.* He stared at the phone as Chester continued, and several moments later, he heard from Jaime.

*It's really not, Bill. It's not okay at all.*

*What does that mean?* His stomach tightened, and for a moment, Bill thought he'd throw up. His hands became fists, and he wanted to throw the phone across the room and punch someone.

He tried to relax. He could barely text, and if it weren't for autocorrect, nothing he typed would have made sense. *Where are you? What's going on?*

He waited impatiently, constantly refreshing his phone to keep it lit up.

*Actually getting ready to fly back home. With JB. On his private jet. It's all so crazy, I don't even know where to begin. I'll text when I land. Promise.*

Bill looked up at Wes and then over at Rose, wanting nothing more than to get them alone. He needed his friends now more than ever.

*****

Thousands of feet overhead, Jaime sat next to JB in his private jet. They were flying to Boston, where Jaime's mother and sister had driven her not all that long ago. JB had told her the kidnapper would likely still be in the Boston vicinity.

"I know this is hard," JB said, looking at Jaime. He stood up then, his thick chest taking deep, slow, deliberate breaths. Jaime's eyes were puffy from crying, and she shook her head.

"I don't understand," she whispered. "Why do this? What's the motive? To destroy a horror studio?"

"Our world is as big as we make it, and everyone's world is as important to them as yours is to you. Your mother's world is you and Tara, yes? Your world is your family, your future, your friends. My world is Rabbit in Red. Our worlds are about the people and interests in our lives, no matter how many. A truly psychotic person isn't all that different. His—or her—world is whatever they make of it. This madman can only see Rabbit in Red, nothing more. Its success or its failure is the only thing that matters."

He sat back down, not able to get comfortable it seemed. He looked ahead, never quite looking at her. His hands were interlocked and resting on his lap. He had a look of determined, focused patience, but it didn't comfort Jaime.

"But why?" She shifted in her seat and fidgeted. She saw Bill's texts on her phone, but her hands were too wet from wiping her eyes to text back.

"Just as some take great pleasure from creating, others feel the same from destroying. That's the difference between a hero and a villain. A hero creates. A villain destroys."

Jaime clasped her hands together and squeezed them tightly. "Does it make me a villain then that I want to destroy whoever did this to my sister?"

At that, JB turned and looked at her. He leaned back in his seat, and when he faced her, she could feel his breath. He looked at her for a moment before responding. "In reality, there are very few people who are fully a hero or fully a villain. In reality, that line blurs, and we wear whatever mask is appropriate for the occasion." He exhaled deeply. "Do you think that to destroy a villain you must become one?"

"I think a lot about your tests from last Halloween. You made us become the villain in part of the games to see the world through the eyes of evil. I know you did that for the sake of movies and art, so that we'd better understand the bad guys we are to create. But now it makes me wonder . . ."

She paused and looked out of the window of the plane. They were flying through the clouds, and a steady stream of grey engulfed the airplane. *I wonder what I am capable of.* Somewhere deeper, another voice echoed in her head: *You know what you can do, and you know what you will do if you have to.*

She looked back at JB, who was still staring at her. "It makes me think that sometimes in life you do have to become the villain for the sake of others."

JB nodded softly, as if reading her mind. "We will do whatever we need to do."

*****

Bill heard different people speaking, but he wasn't listening. He checked his phone obsessively.

"Again, I understand how difficult it is to focus, but focus we must," Chester Malcolm repeated. "It's time for you to present your project proposals. What are your ideas for recruiting fresh meat? Wes? What did your group come up with?"

Bill tried to listen to Wes's proposal. "We start with a two-part test that anyone can do on an app. We think new recruits should understand what we've already experienced. Not the same thing necessarily, but something similar. So we have a proposal for a two-part game. The first part would be trivia relating to horror and fire, like the riddles we solved but focused on movies with fire as a theme. The second part would be a video game where they re-enact the scenes we had to do in person."

Bill sighed and looked at his phone again.

Wes paused for a moment after Bill's sigh, but then continued. "They play as Jason or Freddy, then Ash, then there's a round to save the victims, then there's a round to become the villain, but it's all done on their phones or tablets. The highest scores would be those who understand what we've already experienced. That's who gets invited to Rabbit in Red this year."

"Very interesting idea," Chester said, turning to Bill next. "Bill? Bill? What is your idea?"

Still staring at his phone, Bill said, "I'm just worried for Jaime."

"I understand, Bill. Are you able to discuss your project idea?"

"Yeah, I can." He sighed again. "Um, we thought we'd have a different kind of test. Since the goal is to be a part of a horror college, let's see what each applicant can actually do. They submit a piece of original work based on what they want to do in the horror industry. If they want to direct, they create a short film. If they want to write, they submit a screenplay. And so on. Then we judge the quality of their work and decide who we want to work with."

"Okay," Chester said. "Another interesting proposal. And Rose? What did your group determine?"

"Well, it started as Venus's idea," Rose said. "We all added to it, but she's got a pretty fantastic concept. Venus, why don't you explain it?"

Venus smiled and stood up. "Let's take Rabbit in Red to the world and show them what we can really do."

Venus explained her idea, and Bill finally forgot about his phone. He looked at everyone as Venus talked, and their expressions, even those of Chester and the assistants, clearly revealed that this was the idea they would adopt. Bill had known that his group's idea was mediocre at best. He didn't have the energy to really think about it. But for the first time since Jaime and JB had left, with the exception of the brief smile when meeting Falcor, Bill's thoughts drifted away from the real horror Jaime had to face to this idea that Venus was proposing. He felt chills as she described it.

*Yes,* he thought, goosebumps forming on his arms, *that is what we have to do. This is what Rabbit in Red was built for!* For a second, he felt guilty about his enthusiasm for Venus's idea. *Dammit, JB, you get Jaime and Tara back here. Jaime would love this idea.* It would be a massive undertaking, would require extra staffing and finances, but Bill knew that JB would love it, too. It was exactly the kind of horror that would make him smile because it was exactly the kind of horror that would terrify the world.

"This kind of contest gives us the chance to discover those who love fear," Rose added when Venus finished her explanation.

"It's twisted," Chester laughed. "But we want this to be a consensus. Let's put all three projects to a vote."

Every single hand in the room shot up with excitement, a unanimous vote for this final project idea. This was the perfect kind of project for them to build. This was why they had returned to Rabbit in Red. This was what would make horror fun, original, and powerful, not just to the first-year students sitting in the commons, but to all the fans across the world.

*Oh, Jaime, you're gonna love this. Just get back here in one piece.*

"It's a perfect idea!" Chester cheered. Bill looked around. Everyone's eyes were glowing. It was like . . . like they all had discovered chocolate for the first time. It was going to be that epic. "Now, let's get to work making it happen."

*****

"They're coming for you," a man said to his reflection in a hotel room mirror.

"And they will be so surprised at what they find!" The man giggled, a squeaky, maniacal laugh. He picked up a small can of air freshener and turned around. "It stinks in here!" He sprayed the air freshener all throughout the room. "Ugh! What a terrible smell!"

Then he turned and faced the mirror.

"Are you ready?" he asked the reflection.

The face in the mirror smiled back at him. He looked down at a folder he had on the desk and took out a sheet of paper he had printed earlier. Looking closely at the paper, he scanned the words written on it. It was a one way air ticket from Boston to L.A. It would depart at the same time he suspected JB would arrive. But that was okay. JB and Jaime would find a present waiting for them, a very special present indeed.

He turned then to look at the girl who sat motionless in a chair in the center of the room.

"Good-bye," he said, grabbing a bag as he walked out the door. "Tell your sister I said hi and that I'll see her soon,"

But her eyes were closed, her head limp and fallen against her chest, and she said nothing.

# Chapter Six

"How will you find her?" Jaime asked as the plane landed at Logan International Airport.

"I'm fortunate to have the best technology available," JB said. "When we created the 4D game chambers last year, we worked with terrific engineers and innovators around the world. I have access to an app that will pinpoint Tara's location."

Jaime's eyes widened. "What? How does it work?"

"It finds . . . how should I say it? You can search for things out of the ordinary, and it will tell you locations. For example, some police stations are using a new system that notifies them when a gun is shot and the location of the shot. It's an extremely effective tool to find and stop crime quicker. The particular system I'm using can find more than gunshots."

The plane slowed, and JB faced her. Jaime felt a chill for a moment. JB had such a habit of looking straight ahead when he was speaking. Whenever he looked her in the eyes, she saw something she couldn't quite explain. His dark eyes hid a mystery, decades of life of which Jaime knew only the very tip of the iceberg.

"You can search for sudden changes in temperature," JB continued. "You can find fire. Just like finding gunshots, this system could help fire departments locate fires more quickly. Imagine a local fire station with an app that synced to the nearest cellular tower that could instantly alert the station of any sudden, rapid increases in temperature. Firefighters could be on the road the exact moment a smoke detector would go off. It's amazing technology. I'm using the technology to search for locations that had a sudden increase in temperature during the time before we received the video of Tara."

JB faced the front of the plane again, just as it came to a complete stop.

"That's incredible." She took out her cell phone, thinking maybe she'd text Bill. She hoped this technology was capable of finding Tara quickly, and that Tara would be okay. Then she felt a pressure in her chest and didn't have the energy to text Bill. She put the phone away, and JB stood up. They walked to the plane's exit.

"Yes. The only limitation in the program's beta stages is that you can only access the area in which a tower is connected, so we have to be here in person. However, I can tap into the airport's central communication feed and access all surrounding towers from right here. We also know from the video that the Tara was in a hotel room. It shouldn't take long to find possible locations."

They exited the private jet, completely avoiding the main part of the airport. Outside, a black Lexus awaited them. "Mr. Bell," a driver greeted and bowed. "Where may I take you, sir?"

"Hop in," he told Jaime, as the driver opened the back seat car door. "Just a moment, driver."

JB searched the listings that the app had discovered, and Jaime looked over his shoulder. She watched JB scroll through several locations, focusing on cheap motels that would be ideal for privacy. He swiped left and right, looking at data she didn't understand. It was like a strange Tinder app that revealed locations and temperature changes over a certain amount of time.

"Here! This has to be it," JB stated. "Driver, enter this address into your GPS, and get us there, fast. Jaime, call your mother. I'll alert the authorities. We'll be there in no time at all."

Jaime's chest hurt again, and her heart jumped into her throat. She hoped he was right, and Tara better be okay. Or someone was really going to pay.

*****

Bill barely heard the other first years discussing the project. He was too busy staring at his phone, constantly refreshing feeds and hoping Jaime would send a message any second.

"Are we sticking with the number nineteen?" Venus asked Chester. "How many will be invited this year?"

"JB has instructed that the magic number this year is eleven," he told them.

"Why eleven?" Rose asked.

Chester nodded to Bonnie Villa, last year's Annie, who answered for him. "So the place was called Taberah because fire from the Lord had burned among them."

"What does that mean?" Wes asked.

Bonnie and Chester shrugged. "More riddles," Rose said. "Wonderful." She looked over at Bill. "Are you okay?"

"Waiting to hear from Jamie. Something is very wrong."

"I'm sorry." Rose reached up to put an arm around his shoulders, but had to settle for his waist. "It's going to be okay."

Bill looked down at her, and she smiled. She still had her black purse with its purple lettering strapped over one shoulder. She never went anywhere without it, it seemed. Bill thought of what was inside Rose's purse. The picture that she kept close. They had all experienced so much. They had all lost so much.

"I hope so." He looked at his phone again. *Why isn't Jaime texting? C'mon!*

"JB's the man, remember?" Wes said. "It will be okay, Bill."

Bill nodded but didn't speak. *I can't lose anyone else. None of us can. C'mon, Jaime, please text with some good news.*

"Each of you will be responsible for designing a section, but you are to collaborate with your groups on each part. So if you have a group of five, we need five sections from you."

Chester's instructions pulled Bill ever so slightly from his thoughts. Their creation, this new Rabbit in Red design, would be the best horror creation ever. The fact that it was so awesome sucked too though. He couldn't get completely excited about it or fully invest his energy in it. Not until he knew Jaime and Tara were all right.

"My section will have clowns," Wes said.

"Mine will have lots of insects. But mostly bees," Rose grinned. "What about yours, Bill?"

He looked up at the ceiling in the commons, which resembled that of a cave more than a room anymore. He observed the entrance to the commons, the wide hole through Candyman's mouth, wondering how far away Jaime was and how long it would be before she'd return. Would everything be okay? Did any of this shit here even matter?

"Nothing," he finally responded. "My section will be about . . . about darkness. We'll scare the shit out of them by completely isolating them from everyone and everything else."

After a moment, Wes said, "Well that'll do it. This will be scariest haunt ever created."

Wes tried to smile, but Bill couldn't smile back. He was glued to his phone. The scariest things in the world weren't clowns or spiders or bees or monsters in your closet. The scariest thing was darkness and the possibility that life may never be bright again.

*****

Daniel Lloyd hung up the phone and sprawled out in bed. He wore green athletic shorts and a gray muscle shirt. He was just about to return to the gym for a second visit when he received the phone call. It had been Michael Quinn, who introduced himself as the assistant who dressed as Sam from last year.

"I've been instructed to invite you to return to Rabbit in Red, if you wish. The majority of your classmates have decided that you should be welcome here, if you'd like."

"Why isn't JB calling me?" Daniel scoffed. "It should be him. Not you."

"JB is away on urgent business," Michael said.

"Of course he is. Why should I return?"

"I do not care if you return or not," Michael said coolly. You must make the simple decision whether a traditional college education or the unique experiences at Rabbit in Red would best serve your current and future interests."

Daniel was silent for a moment. "They really want me back? Everyone?"

"I cannot tell you the specifics except that it was put to a vote, and the majority voted that you should be invited to return."

"I'll be damned," he said, looking into his bedroom mirror and flexing his arm. "When should I return?"

"First year students are already busy completing the first project. The sooner the better."

"Will someone pick me up like last time?"

"That can be arranged. When will you be ready?"

He looked in the mirror again and smiled. "I'm ready now. Send a car."

"Very well. We'll see you soon. Good-bye."

He stared at the ceiling. He knew he was smarter than all of them at Rabbit in Red, including Bill. Especially Bill. JB had tricked him last year. That was all it was. Bill and Jaime and the fatso and the redhead: they were all out for themselves. They didn't really care about him. They used him for information to help find the missing contestants and gave him no credit at the end.

After last Halloween, Daniel spent his time working out and studying. When he wasn't in the gym, he read up on the history of horror. From history, he studied psychology. After that, he watched every movie he could, but he focused primarily on one theme: revenge. He had waited for a moment to return, invited or not, and now was his time.

He knew he'd get back there sooner or later, but the fact that the returning students voted to give him a second chance was surprising. *Your kindness is what will kill you,* he thought.

He looked in the mirror and smiled. He had quite a few ideas, and yeah, he wanted Rabbit in Red. He wanted horror. But most of all, he wanted to see the looks on all of their faces when his ideas fully blossomed.

That would be a moment worth remembering.

*****

Still looking at his phone, Bill listened to more instructions while waiting for Jaime's text. Perhaps only minutes had passed, but it felt like hours.

"By the end of this creation," Donnie told everyone back at the commons, "we want eighteen sections. The final two will be determined by Jaime and Daniel, with the help of all of you of course. One section in honor of each of you, as you described, Venus. We'll have to wait on their return before we can finalize, but start working on the specifics for your section."

A section for everyone but Dexter. Dexter would have made for nineteen, Bill thought. Where was Dexter? Was he involved in this?

The mention of Jaime grabbed Bill's attention. He watched the other first years discuss and plan their sections. Donnie Chase approached Chester and whispered something in his ear. Bill glanced at his classmates. They were enthusiastically sharing ideas. He walked closer to Donnie and Chester.

"JB will love this," Bill heard Donnie say.

"Absolutely," Chester replied. They didn't even notice that he was a few feet away. Like his classmates, they seemed too excited by this new idea.

"It will be the *American Idol* of horror." Donnie laughed.

"A Rabbit in Red inspired custom haunted house at eleven locations throughout the country," Chester said and nodded. "I particularly enjoyed the method in which they've determined who will be selected from each location."

"They are definitely a unique group." Michael Quinn said, jumping in from behind them both. Quinn smiled at Bill, who took his phone out quickly and pretended to be messaging someone. Quinn lowered his voice, but Bill could still hear. "I've contacted Daniel and sent a car to pick him up. He'll be here before the night is over."

"Good," Chester said. "I know they don't all trust him, and they probably shouldn't, but he'll add a certain something special to this creation."

"Any more updates from JB?" Donnie asked.

"He's in pursuit as we speak," Chester said, checking his phone. Bill froze. *In pursuit of what? Or who?*

"And if the girl is dead?" Donnie asked. Bill tasted vomit in his mouth instantly at the thought. *Are they talking about Tara? What do they know?*

"The show must go on," Chester said. "You know that."

"I don't like this." Donnie shook her head and looked around the room. "If JB doesn't find who did this to Jaime's sister, they're all in trouble. And so are we."

"Death is a part of horror. A part of life. If anyone wants to leave, we can't stop them," Chester whispered. "But I have a feeling something else might."

Bill wanted to approach them, but clearly he had heard everything they knew. JB was in pursuit. So was Jaime still by his side? Jesus. He could barely type, but he managed to send one message.

*Please tell me you're okay!*

No response, and Bill couldn't hold in what he had been feeling any longer. He sprinted to the closest bathroom.

*****

JB's car pulled up outside of a shady looking motel. It reminded Jaime of the motel in the original *Psycho*, and she wasn't at all surprised by that fact. An intense and rapid change of temperature had been detected from this exact place only minutes before they received the video back at Rabbit in Red earlier in the day. Jaime followed as JB marched ahead. He hadn't told her which room number they were going to. But she had a feeling that—just like Marion Crane—this psycho had used room number one.

No authorities had arrived yet, and Jaime was shocked to see how quickly JB could move. He glided out of the car and flew over to the rooms. Once again she thought of Frankenstein's monster, and then she gasped as JB lifted his foot and kicked down the door—it was door number one, Jaime noticed briefly—without hesitation. She ran right behind him. A pungent smell knocked at their senses. It was a smell Jaime would never forget. She remembered burning some hair playing with her mom's curling iron in the past, but that was such a small amount, a few strands, and yet the odor even then was overpowering. Here, though, the smell was all-consuming, a dreadfully overwhelming scent of hair on fire.

And there was Tara, tied up and limp in a chair. All of her hair was gone. JB turned on the lights and ran to the girl.

"Tara!" Jaime pushed JB aside and shook her sister hard. "Tara! Please, no! Wake up!"

*This can't be happening! This CANNOT be happening!* "Oh, God, no! What did they do to you?" Jaime yelled and hugged her sister's body close to her own. *I'll kill them, I'll kill them, I'll fucking kill them! Oh, Tara!*

JB reached between them and placed his fingers on Tara's neck.

"Jaime!" JB said. "Jaime, she's alive. Her pulse sounds strong. She must just be unconscious." JB pulled at the rope and untied her.

"What? Really?" She pulled back a bit and looked at Tara closely. *Oh, thank God! Tara, I don't know what I'd do if I lost you.* She let tears spill out from her eyes and hugged her sister again. All she could smell was the powerful odor of burnt hair, but she breathed it in deeply and willingly.

"Tara," JB said. "Tara, can you wake up?"

It took a few more shakes but her head finally lifted from her chest. Tara's eyes opened and she saw her sister.

"Jaime! Oh, thank God you're here!"

Jaime lunged in and hugged her sister.

"I'm so glad you're okay! Who was it, Tara? Who did this to you?"

Tara looked down again, and Jaime saw dark red scars and blisters on her scalp. "I never saw his face. He covered up his face. And he burned all my hair! I thought he was going to kill me." She sobbed. Tara and Jaime hugged again while JB explored the motel room.

"It doesn't look like he intended to kill you," he said. "It looks like he wanted to scare us into thinking he would kill you. Look." He pointed at a bottle and sniffed it. "Chloroform. He knocked her out with this. Judging by the blisters on her scalp, he put the fire out very quickly. Not quickly enough to avoid any pain or scarring, I'm afraid," he said and put an arm around Tara's shoulders. "But you're going to be okay."

Tara sobbed and Jaime held her.

"Whoever did this wanted us to find you," JB added. "I don't know how, but he must have known about the technology to which I had access. He filled up the bathtub with lighter fluid and set it on fire. He also removed all smoke alarms." He looked straight at Jaime. "The fire from her hair may not have been hot enough or long enough to get a reading from my app. But the fire he lit in the bathtub sure was. Whoever did this set this all up perfectly."

Jaime's mind jumped all over the place. *Who in the hell would do this? Thank God she's okay! Who else would know about the technology JB used? I'm going to fucking kill whoever hurt my sister!* Tara cried for several minutes. Jaime simply held her, and JB stood next to them and remained quiet.

After a few minutes, Tara asked, "What do we do now?"

"Your mom and the police will be here any minute," JB answered and put an arm around her shoulder. "You'll have to help them fill out a report so they can look for who did this to you. I'm going to need to talk with you too, okay? I know you're exhausted and hurt, but I'm going to find who did this. I promise you that. I'll just need your help, all right?" His voice was calm, sensitive, not the powerful voice Jaime had grown to know.

Tara made a half-smile but grimaced in pain. "Okay," she said. Finally, police sirens rang from outside.

"I'm going to need you to do some convincing, Jaime." He stared into her eyes, and Jaime saw something between anger and determination. "Your mother may not like this, but the safest place for Tara will be right by our side. I know you won't want to leave her alone, and I can't offer the best protection from across the country."

He started pacing again, and he looked like he wanted to hug her and sprint after whoever did this. "The police will need to interview Tara, and they'll take her to the hospital. The moment she's released, I need the two of you by my side. We'll get your mom to come as well." Worry flashed across his face. Perhaps he wasn't so certain about convincing Mom, Jaime thought. "I imagine the hospital will keep Tara overnight, so I'll have my jet available for you first thing in the morning. All right?"

"It's not going to be easy to convince my mother," Jaime said loudly, since the sirens were increasing in volume.

"You'll just have to make her come."

"Okay." Jaime wasn't sure that would be possible, but she'd sure as hell try. It would be nice to have everyone together. JB turned to leave. "Where are you going now?"

"I'm not resting until I know who did this. I'll have my driver take me to get a new car, and I'll send him right back so he's with you all night until you're ready to return to us." He paused for a moment and looked more closely at her. "Will you be ready to return to us?"

Jaime looked at Tara, her beautiful sister who was now bald with a blistery scalp, then back at JB. "Yes. We will most definitely be ready."

JB smiled. "Good. I need to go now, or I'll get held up by the police. I'm going to start searching now. Tell the police everything, Jaime. I'll be in constant contact. I just want to start looking now. Is that okay with both of you?"

Jaime and Tara nodded, and they held one another closely. Seconds before the police pulled up, JB and his driver sped away in a different direction.

"He's like Batman," Tara said.

"Yeah. Something like that, I guess. So what do you think? Would you rather we stay here? Or do you want to stay at Rabbit in Red? I will stay with you, no matter where."

Tara smiled a little and didn't wince as much at the pain as she had previously. "I'd rather stay with Batman. At least until they catch who did this to me."

The cops ran out of their cars, and the noise at the motel intensified quickly. "Just hold my hand and let's get through this night," Jaime said. "Then I'll take you to see the bat cave."

# Chapter Seven

In the *Alien* pod dormitories, Rose Dawn sat on Wes Pike's lap in his bed. Wes wrapped his arms around Rose, and they were watching a horror film on the personal sized screens that accompanied each bed. She held Lester in her lap and petted the soft bunny's head.

"The baba . . . baba . . . baba . . . DOOOOK!" Rose cheered. "This is great!"

Wes laughed and looked over at his best friend. Bill sat alone across the room, playing a video game in his bed. Wes had watched Bill grow more and more distant since they had found out what had happened to Tara. JB had returned to Rabbit in Red, and he was supposed to address them all today during lunch, but Jaime had not yet returned. Wes worried Bill wouldn't snap out of his daze without her, although Jaime texted all of them that both she and Tara were coming back. Wes and Rose tried to comfort Bill, tried to include him whenever they did something, like watch a movie. Sometimes people need to be alone, and so they gave him space but were always close by at the same time.

Still, it was awkward. Wes had never felt closer to another person in his entire life than he did with Rose. He watched her watching the movie. He couldn't help but smile. How did a guy like him get a girl like her? Then he looked over at Bill. Sometimes he'd catch Bill giving them almost a dirty look. Wes understood though. He spent four years in high school just like every other teenager, but unlike nearly every other teenager, Wes Pike never went to school dances or kissed a girl under the bleachers at a football game. He understood the pain of looking at someone else who was ridiculously happy when all you really felt was total loneliness.

In short, it sucked. So Wes did his best to understand and be a good friend.

"Have you seen this one, Bill?" Bill looked up briefly from his phone. All he did anymore was stare at that thing. Wes had no idea how it even had any battery power left. Bill nodded but didn't smile. Falcor looked up, too. The little pup shadowed Bill's emotions. The more distant Bill got, the closer Falcor appeared to snuggle.

Wes thought of asking if Bill wanted to squeeze in on the small bed and watch with them, but then he thought that idea would probably only make Bill groan. *One day it will get better. Bill and Jaime, me and Rose. That will be nice.*

An alert popped up on everyone's screens and interrupted Wes's thoughts. The message said that it was time to come downstairs to the commons. Wes sighed, but Bill moved quicker than Wes had seen all summer.

They climbed down the ladder and took their seats in the cave-like commons, and their fearless leader, Jay Bell, stood in the back center of the room, almost exactly in the spot he had first appeared as Freddy Krueger last Halloween. He wore black dress pants and a bright blue button up shirt, a formality that juxtaposed their current setting.

"Good afternoon," JB greeted. "Please have a seat. We have a few things to discuss, and then lunch will be served." He smiled gently at all of them, and Wes hoped it would be good news.

"Let's discuss the rabbit in the room, pardon the bad pun." He tried to smile bigger to comfort everyone, but no one laughed. "Here's what we know. A madman did kidnap Jaime Stein's sister, Tara. He threatened to hurt her if we do not 'burn the rabbit' or shut down what we are doing here. Unfortunately, he did hurt her. He burned her hair, which resulted in some minor scalp burns."

Tara was *burned*? Jesus, Bill would go ape-shit. Wes looked at Rose, whose face had paled at the news. Tara may not have been "one of them," but she was Jaime's sister, and that made her family to them all.

JB held up his hands. "The good news is that Tara is perfectly fine. Bald, but fine. For her safety, I've invited her to stay with us. Home alone with a single mother may not the safest place right now. In our fortress here, we have the ultimate security and strength in numbers. I'm also bringing in a team of counselors who will work with her as well as any of you who would like to talk to a professional. We don't want to bury our nightmares. We want to confront them and manage them. Jaime, Tara, and their mother are on their way here now via my private jet. I've set up a separate sleeping area for Tara and her mother with even stronger security."

"Who did this?" Bill asked. Wes saw tears form in Bill's eyes, and Bill didn't bother to wipe them. They rolled down his cheeks, and he stood up, his face flushed with anger. Rose squeezed Wes's hand.

"I'm working on that, but we have our suspicions."

Wes had talked about his suspicions with Rose. What about Chester's own brother, Sid, the one he had locked up last Halloween? And what about Dexter? And, of course, JB must have known thousands of people in the industry. Wes could easily imagine a few people being jealous or simply crazy after working with JB.

"What happens next?" Wes asked.

"You all have a choice. You always have a choice," JB said. "I hope you will choose to keep working on your projects. We have quite an exciting year ahead of us, and I haven't even introduced your studies yet. This summer is for designing our new Rabbit in Red challenge. In the fall, you will begin your course studies. Is there an extra element of danger? Yes. I won't lie to you. We've been threatened. We've been attacked. But don't you see? Whoever is behind this wants us to stop. I never stop pursuing my dreams because of the jealousy, anger, or fear of another. In fact, it makes me work even harder."

There was no smile on his face this time. Wes saw something else. It was a fierce honesty, a look that said, *go ahead, test me. We will endure, no matter what happens.* Wes felt a chill. If something happened to one of them, JB would just keep going, wouldn't he? They could be murdered one by one, but as long as someone was there to work on his damn projects, he'd never stop.

Wes looked around at everyone else. He sensed a renewed energy in the room. JB had that effect. Yeah, a nuclear bomb could be approaching and somehow JB would motivate them to keep working. Everyone was mad or upset or confused, but somehow JB could twist that into motivation to keep moving forward.

Even Bill. Last year, Wes would have argued that Bill was the smartest of them all. But Wes saw something frightening in Bill—a blind trust in JB. Too much trust.

"So the question is, are you still with me?" JB asked. "Stand if you are with me."

The murmurs around the room continued, and everyone looked over at Bill. Wes wanted to tell Bill that maybe it was time to say no. But he knew Bill would keep following that damn rabbit.

Bill stood up and faced JB. "I'm with you," he said. Wes stood next, briefly releasing his grip on Rose's hand.

He looked down at her, and then she stood up. Wes couldn't say no. He didn't have the trust that Bill did, but he'd never leave his friends. They would protect one another, no matter what. Wes smiled at Rose, and she reached out for his hand again and held it tight. Everyone else in the room stood up, too.

"Excellent," JB said. "I knew we had chosen the right crew for the job. Now, we're short a couple people. Jaime will be here tonight, but we have one more to add to our group right now." JB turned to his right, and they all looked over at the Candyman's mouth entrance. Standing right inside, waiting to be called, was Daniel Lloyd.

"Come forward, son," JB called.

Daniel walked in cautiously but confidently. He kept his chin high and looked only at JB. He wore a muscle tank and khaki shorts. As he approached JB, Daniel put out his hand, and JB shook it.

"Your peers, Daniel, have voted for you to get a second chance. I welcome you back. You certainly have talent and a deep, unique knowledge." He turned to face the rest of the first years. "Let's use that talent to come together, to create and influence our world of horror. That's what we are here for. This is no longer a competition among any of you. It's time to work together."

Wes remembered the first time they had decided to trust Daniel and give him a shot. They teamed up once before, back when they were searching for Annie and Leroy, contestants who had gone missing during the games last year. But then Daniel dumped them and paired up with Dexter, a truly disturbed individual. What were JB's final words to Dexter? Wes tried to remember, and he thought that JB had told Dexter that they'd speak privately. But Dexter wasn't here. Daniel was, and Daniel would do anything it took to win, and maybe that was why JB had said what he did. It was no longer a competition. Daniel looked around the room and took a seat next to Leroy.

"I am very excited about the project you have envisioned," JB continued. "We will build a test model here in the studio. Not only will each of you get a chance to walk through your haunt, but at the end of the summer, when it is complete, I am inviting all of your families to join us for a week. I know that they must be worried about you, so we will invite them here and show them nothing is wrong."

Here, JB smiled. It was the grin of a kid allowed back in the candy store. "Well, nothing but our twisted, passionate, and creative minds, that is! The haunt will consist of eighteen sections, one section inspired by each of you. After we test it and work out all of the kinks, I will hire a team of builders to construct these houses in eleven locations across the country. We will invite others such as yourselves to walk through our haunted challenge. Based upon the unique way you've developed to evaluate each contestant as they walk through, we will invite one person from each location to join us again this Halloween to experience the next round of your creations. You will study horror in the most unique way imaginable! At our family week, I will introduce your professors. You will be working with the most genius minds in our field, and with their guidance, you will create new rounds of horror for our fresh recruits. I cannot wait to see what you come up with!"

Wes looked over at Rose whose smile matched JB's. *Man, we are all messed up,* he thought, but then he leaned in and kissed Rose hard, right in front of everyone.

*****

That evening Bill sat in his bed with his eyes glued to his phone. He had texted Jaime a few times and was eagerly waiting to hear from her, hoping that she'd return to the studios any minute. He thought of how far they'd come in their friendship over the last couple of years. What had started solely online—debates in horror forums, serious discussions about death and losing loved ones—had turned into an adventure. He smiled at the memories of them solving the Rabbit in Red riddles on their phones over the course of a sleepless weekend. But what they thought would be mostly an amusement park adventure turned into something darker.

He recalled watching her save her Uncle Tim during the fear simulations, seeing her cry, and then feeling such anger for JB. They had come out of those challenges stronger, but he had to remind

77

himself of what JB had done to them. Their master host argued he did it *for* them. He stared at the ceiling above the bed and bounced his legs nervously. Did he believe that? That JB did this for them?

Now, the shit was getting real. They were designing terrifying things that capitalized on people's fears. On one hand, it was very exciting, but on the other, he had a voice telling him to be careful. *You're doing to others what JB has done to you.*

And then of course there was the terror outside of Rabbit in Red. Was the person who attacked Tara the same one who threw an axe at the front door of his house after graduation? It had to be, right? Bill had every confidence that JB would discover this madman. After all, JB had uncovered the identity of his father's murderer, something authorities had never been able to do. JB never even took the credit for it. In fact, on all of the news stories and articles Bill had read since the beginning of the contest, Bill realized he had never even seen a single picture of JB.

There was nothing he could do but wait and he tried to shake the thoughts from his mind. He put in his ear buds and listened to his favorite band, hoping the music would drown out the thoughts. Selecting "Slightly Dead" by Terribly Happy, he let the music take him away. He wanted nothing more than to shut up his mind, and the music perfectly matched his mood.

He closed his eyes, his thoughts dissipating with the music, and moments later he felt a familiar touch on his arm. When he opened his eyes, he jumped up so quickly the room started to spin.

"Jaime!" He sprung up at her, arms wrapping tightly around her body. "Are you okay?"

She didn't look like herself at all. Her eyes were puffy from lack of sleep and no doubt shedding too many tears.

"I'm better now," she said and put her head against his chest. "This is all just so unbelievable. Seeing Tara like that . . . her hair burned, her scalp scarred . . . Bill, I could kill someone. I could kill whoever did this to her, and that thought frightens the shit out of me."

He held her close and his heart beat quickened. He buried his face into her hair. He felt those damn tears return to his eyes. He wanted to hurt whoever did this, too. This lunatic who had taken her away from him, who had ruined everything this summer. Bill wanted to hold Jaime forever. *Don't leave me again.*

"It's okay," he said. He paused for a moment and then spoke softly. "I'd be more worried if you didn't feel that way. This psycho deserves everything he gets. And I promise that I will be right by your side to help make sure he gets it."

He held her for a few minutes, and like the best of friends, there was no need to speak. Just being together was enough. Enough for now, anyway. *One day, ONE DAY, this shit will be over, right? One day, maybe I can have what Rose and Wes have. Will things ever be normal?*

"How's Tara?"

"She's here, and so is Mom. Mom didn't want to be alone either. She's taking a leave of absence from work, and I think she plans on staying here until they catch whoever did this. Plus I don't think she'll ever let Tara out of her sight again." She attempted a smile. "What's going on here? What are you guys working on? I need a distraction."

Just the fact that she tried to smile and that she looked up at him made his heart skip a beat. Maybe JB was crazy for making them work, for continuing these projects. Or maybe he was a genius in more ways than one. If Jaime needed a distraction, then Bill would be happy to help with that. They needed to feel that excitement that had brought them to Rabbit in Red in the first place.

"It's gonna be sweet. Rose's group came up with the concept. We're basically designing a nation-wide haunted house challenge. And we design the haunts."

Her eyes widened and somehow appeared to darken as well, and Bill felt a chill at the look on her face. "Wow. Well, let's be sure to add fire. Make them think they're gonna get burned. Really make them feel it."

There was no humor in Jaime's voice, and Bill studied her face. She sounded completely serious, and he'd be lying if he didn't say that she scared him in this moment.

"Burn them," she said and rested her head against Bill's chest again.

# Chapter Eight

As the summer continued, the first years designed and assisted in building the Rabbit in Red haunted house, which for its public event now possessed a formal name: Rabbit in Red: Hellfire House. Since the theme of the year, in more than one way, had been "burn the rabbit," they wanted a few sections devoted to fire. Besides, including fire in the haunted house was a giant middle finger to the psycho who threatened them. Although the psycho had yet to be discovered, all had been quiet enough to allow everyone to return to a normal pace of work, or as normal as it got at Rabbit in Red.

The test model for Hellfire had neared completion and would be unveiled during family week, when the parents of the first year students would visit and see the inner workings of the studio.

Bill hadn't seen his mother in nearly two months, but after a couple of nagging phone calls and the promise of a free plane ticket provided by JB, she agreed to visit along with all of the other parents.

Bill waited outside of Rabbit in Red for his mother to arrive. When she did, he ran to her. He couldn't wait to show her everything, but there was one question he had to ask first.

"How are you, Mom? How's . . . um . . . everything been?"

"You can say rehab, Bill," she said wryly. "They teach us not to be ashamed and not to hide from our disease. Hiding and shaming can cause relapse. I've been sober since the day you left."

He hugged her. "I'm so proud of you! Come inside. You've got to see this place!"

Bill led his mother through the various hallways, the *A Nightmare on Elm Street* hall, the school house, *Hellraiser*, *Candyman*, and of course the *Alien* bedrooms.

"How in the hell does anyone sleep at night?" she asked, but Bill only laughed.

"Isn't it fantastic?"

"Uh, as fantastic as a funeral I'd say." She rolled her eyes but gave Bill a half-smile.

"Oh, give it a chance. It's all in good fun."

"Meth addicts would say the same thing."

"Mom!" He laughed and put an arm around her shoulders.

"I'm just sayin', Billy," she said, but at least she was laughing a little.

"Look, there's Jaime and her mom. I want to introduce you."

"Oh, is this *the* girl?"

"Don't embarrass me," Bill said. "Hey, J!" Tara was by their side too. Her hair had started to grow in, but it looked like a military buzz cut. In an attempt to make her feel welcome, they shaved the shape of a rabbit into her hair one night. She liked it, and they kept it trimmed so that on the right side of her head, the silhouette of a rabbit became a symbol for what she had endured. It had become a popular style, and the first years each buzzed the outline of a rabbit in their hair, too. Her humor and good spirits had gradually returned as well, largely thanks to the dozen plus students who did everything they could to get her smiling and keep her smiling.

"And hey, T!" Bill ran a finger through the outline of the rabbit on her head. "Hi, Ms. Stein. This is my mom, Sally Wise."

"Nice to meet you," Sally said.

"You as well," Janet Stein replied. "It will be good to have another mother here, as well as finally someone who isn't a horror junkie like all these kids."

Sally Wise laughed. "I have never and will never understand why they like this shit."

"Agreed! How can you willingly like to be scared? And after all they've experienced?"

"Okay, well at least they're bonding," Bill whispered to Jaime, leaning in close. Then he turned back to him mom. "C'mon, you have to meet JB!"

"What's he like?" Sally asked Janet.

"Well, he's nice enough to give me a private section so I don't have to live in all of this horror. But I've actually not seen him. He always sends an assistant."

"Bill talks about him all the time, like he's a freakin' hero or something." Sally stuck out her tongue and rolled her eyes.

"Jaime is the same way. I don't know why they look up to such a weirdo." Janet pursed her lips and shook her head.

"Mom!" Jaime and Bill said together, then laughed.

"C'mon, you guys," Tara said. "Everyone is in the commons, and I think JB is going to welcome everyone."

They led their mothers into the commons, where Chester Malcolm stood in the center of the room.

"Welcome, parents, to our first annual family week at Rabbit in Red," Chester greeted them loudly. "Mr. Bell has been called away on urgent business, so I will be your master host this week."

Bill frowned and Jaime raised her shoulders as if to say, *typical JB*.

"I promise to do my best to fill his shoes," Chester continued. "Please, help yourself to some appetizers and take a seat. We will preview for you the special events we have in place this week."

After everyone grabbed something to eat, Chester lowered the screen that had previewed last year's games. "We have a lot of fun in store for you this week. We will begin by letting you experience some of the fun your sons and daughters had last year with a special parent battle. We're re-opening the game chambers and creating a special parent tournament." On the screen, the familiar images of Freddy vs. Jason and Ash vs. his hand appeared.

"You will be asked to re-enact these horror fights. We'll be watching you out here on the big screen, which I'm sure will be plenty of fun!"

"Oh my God, I can't even," Rose said from behind them. "My parents haven't even seen these movies. It's going to be great."

"Right?" Jaime said. "My mom and Bill's hate them, so yeah. This will be fantastic."

"Then tomorrow night," Chester continued, "they'll get to play the villain. Like all of you did, we'll have them become Michael Myers and see who can kill Laurie Strode first!"

"Thank God they're not putting them through the fear simulations," Wes said next to Rose.

"What's the fear simulation?" Sally asked Bill.

"Um, nothing, Mom, nothing you have to do." He shrugged and looked at Jaime, who looked similarly relieved. There would always be some things they just weren't going to tell their parents.

"On Wednesday, you all will be the first to see the most recent feature film our master producer has made. And then on Thursday . . . Thursday will be the best day. Each of you gets to be the first to walk through and experience Hellfire. We assure you that it will be a most memorable experience."

Chester laughed. "But now, let's eat. Spend some time with your families and explore wherever you wish. The first round of our family games begins tonight!"

Bill turned to his mother. "Okay, Mom, I don't know what the prize is if you win, but let me tell you what you need to do."

Jaime, Rose, and Wes turned away and began discussing the games with their own families.

Afterwards, Sally Wise said loudly enough for everyone to hear, "I have to do *what*?"

*****

They suited up all the parents in the game chambers. For those who had two parents present, each would play one of the scenes. For Bill, his mom would have to re-enact both Freddy vs. Jason and Ash vs. his hand. In took some persuading from Bill to get Sally in the game chamber. But he succeeded. Jaime didn't have such luck. Her mom wanted nothing to do with it.

The large screen showed the parents trying to figure out all of the equipment. Sally Wise screamed when the floor below her moved, and once more everyone laughed. Chester and the other assistants monitored from the station beyond the game chambers, and they rotated in and out among the parents so everyone had some time on the big screen.

Bill's mom chose Jason, and when Freddy attacked her, she screamed, "What the fuck is this?" Her screams were almost as loud as all of the laughter from the commons.

"I don't think my mom is going to win," Bill said.

"Oh my God, there's my dad," Rose said. Mr. Dawn chose Freddy, and he stabbed Jason over and over with his clawed hand, but with each stab, he grunted, "Argh, argh, argh!"

Rose put her face in her hands and giggled. "I can't even watch!"

"Why is my hand moving on its own?" Sally yelled when the games moved on to Ash vs. his hand. They remembered the special technology in the gloves that moved their hand to make it feel like it was really attacking them.

"Jesus Christ!" Sally shouted again as her hand swatted at her face. "What am I supposed to do?" She looked around the room for the chainsaw, grabbed it, and shouted, "Oh, Bill, this is ridiculous!"

The players rotated burn and out, and Wes cheered as his dad started the chainsaw and cut off the possessed hand. "DIE HAND!" Mr. Pike yelled, and Wes cheered, "Go, Dad!"

Bill's mom watched her hand move on its own and throw things at her. She shook her head, did absolutely nothing, and said, "This is fucking ridiculous. I'm done." Then she walked out of the game chambers.

Bill and Jaime laughed so hard they fell on the floor holding their sides.

When the games were over, Chester walked the parents back out to the commons and everyone gave them a standing ovation. The parents couldn't help but laugh, too. Some of them even bowed.

"Our winner," Chester started, "for being the most correct in re-enacting the films at a whopping 9% accuracy is . . . Mr. Pike!"

"Yeah!" Wes cheered.

"And your prize for this evening is . . . this!" Chester handed Mr. Pike a small box, and Wes recognized it instantly as what he always thought of as Pandora's box, the mystery puzzle box from *Hellraiser*.

"What am I supposed to do with this?" Mr. Pike asked.

"Hold on to it. It contains a secret that your son will no doubt need when the time is right." Chester smiled at Wes. Of course there would be more secrets to unravel. "Ladies and gentleman, you were fantastic. Your children will show you to your sleeping quarters. You'll get to sleep where they did last year. We hope you enjoy the scenery!" Chester chuckled just like JB would have, and Bill wondered again what JB's urgent business was.

He looked around the room, suddenly feeling that something was off. He counted the number of first years. There were only seventeen, which meant one was missing. It occurred to him immediately who it was, but it was no mystery as to why. Daniel was absent from tonight's event. Although Bill didn't know anything about Daniel's mother, he knew enough about his father to know that Daniel was most likely alone right now. It would appear that he didn't have anyone from his family come to visit.

*****

"Parents," Chester said, "are you ready to *kill*?" He cackled as the screen on stage revealed their next fun challenge, another smaller version of what the first years had to complete last year. Michael Myers chased Laurie Strode, then the screen changed, and Hannibal Lecter enjoyed a delicious meal of human brain.

"They're kidding, right?" Sally Wise asked Janet Stein. "I mean, virtual or not, there's no way I'm eating that shit."

Janet nodded and sighed. "How did you kids do this? I'm only watching, and I'm completely grossed out. There must be something wrong with all of you."

Jaime and Bill had been giggling so much that they were out of breath. No sounds came out of their mouths. It was the dry-heaving of laughter. It had been a remarkably fun week at the studios, something everyone desperately needed. Wes and Rose joked with their parents as well, who were making similarly disgusted faces at the images on screen.

"Boy, I won you one prize," Mr. Pike told Wes. "I'm gonna get you another here."

"Not if I have anything to say about it," Mr. Dawn jumped up. Rose's dad shared her red hair and freckles. He had a chunky body, but it suited his laugh. He looked like a more grown-up, red-headed, pale version of Wes.

"Mom, do you think you can try at least?" Bill managed to ask in between laughs.

"I guess." Sally groaned. "I run after that girl and stab her? Then I kill the other girl and eat her brain? Jesus, who would have thought that's what I'd be doing this week."

"You can do it," Bill encouraged. "You too, Ms. Stein."

"When this is over, I'm taking your mother out for the strongest margarita they make in Hollywood," Janet promised.

"I like the sound of that!" Sally said.

"Mom!"

"Yes, I know. Kidding, son. Oh, Janet, they don't let me drink anymore. But maybe I deserve one if I win, *oh-right*?" Her tone may have been sarcastic, but Bill wondered if there was some truth or hope in what she said.

The assistants escorted the parents back to the chambers for a final re-enactment of last year's 4D Fright Fest games. The screen projected multiple people at once this time, and when the chase began for Laurie Strode, Mr. Dawn fell hard on the floor. He had tried to get a running start, but he apparently tried too hard for his own good.

"I'm okay!" he shouted and stood up.

Mr. Pike was the first to catch Laurie out of all of the parents, however, and Wes cheered as his father stabbed her.

"This is really quite sadistic if you think about it," Rose told Wes.

"You're just saying that because my dad was faster," he said and poked her gently in the side. "Besides, I try not to think too much."

For those with two parents, like Rose and Wes, they had to switch players for the second game. Among the four of them, it was all of their mothers competing against one another.

As Clarice Starling approached Hannibal's cell from *Silence of the Lambs*, they all simply stared at her.

"Bill! What do I do?" Sally called.

Not that she could hear him. "Kill her!" he called anyway.

JB—or whoever had programmed these simulations for the parents—made it a little easier on them. Suddenly, a gun appeared in their hands.

"I guess I'm supposed to shoot," Janet said from her chamber. Multiple bangs went off from the guns, and as must have been so conveniently programmed, the gun shot splattered open Clarice's head and brain oozed out of her skull. Now in the simulations, a fork replaced the gun.

"Nope, fuck no. Not ever," Sally said and walked out. Bill winced. Maybe this was a bad idea. Shooting someone in the head was probably not the best game for his mother to play.

"Nasty!" Another parent yelled, but her fork went into the brain. However, Rose and Wes's moms had beaten them all to it. It seemed the friendly rivalry between their dads rubbed off on the moms.

"I'm eating it! Look!" Mrs. Dawn called out. She stuck her hand right in the brain. She squeezed the virtual tissue and juices squirted her in the face. She opened her mouth wide, laughing and playing along. She took a giant piece of the brain, lifted her hand above her head, and squeezed again. This time she let the virtual juices drip into her mouth, and then she swallowed it whole. She grinned wide and shouted, "I hope this makes you proud, Rose!"

"Oh, my God," Rose choked out in between laughs.

"Congratulations!" Chester called over a microphone that echoed throughout the commons and the game chambers. "We have a winner. Head back to the commons, and you'll get a prize!"

Once everyone returned, Chester announced the winner. "In tonight's game, we applaud Mr. and Mrs. Dawn! You have earned a prize for Rose, one of Rabbit in Red's many secrets. Rose, come here and help claim your prize."

"What's this?" Mrs. Dawn asked, as Rose joined them to claim the prize.

"It's a femur," Chester said.

"A femur bone?" Mr. Dawn examined the so-called prize. "Is this human? Is this real or a prop?"

"Rabbit in Red is full of secrets, sir." Chester grinned. "Your daughter will figure it out when the time comes, I'm sure."

"Well, isn't this lovely, honey?" Mrs. Dawn joked. "A femur bone. Just what you've always wanted, I'm sure." They sat back down at their table.

"You all have been fantastic sports," Chester said. "We wanted to give you a taste of what your sons and daughters experienced. Many of our games helped us determine not only their knowledge of horror, but many other qualities such as creativity, spontaneity, and their ability to deal with fear and evil. They are embarking on quite the journey here, and we are only getting started. So many more exciting things in their studies and experiences here are yet to come." Chester grinned, but it felt odd to not have JB speaking to them.

"And with that in mind, it's time to preview your next challenge, parents. Tomorrow, you will be the first ever to walk through Hellfire." The smiles fell from their faces. "Over the summer, your children created a special Rabbit in Red haunted house. You'll walk through on your own, experiencing eighteen chambers of horror."

Bill looked at his mother, who rolled her eyes.

"You'll each be evaluated in a unique way that our first years conceived. We'll tell you exactly what that is when you've finished. First though, you must survive and walk through all eighteen sections. Can you handle it?"

Chester laughed again, and Bill still missed JB. Chester did a great job filling his shoes and previewing each section, but there was something about the way JB spoke that made the games even more frightening and fun. Where was JB? What exactly was he doing? It certainly wasn't like him to miss anything related to Rabbit in Red, and so Bill could only imagine that he was going after the kidnapper. As resourceful as JB was, Bill also couldn't help but be worried.

"Let me ask you this now," Chester continued. "Are you ready to experience our new creation? This is the scariest, largest, and most technologically advanced design ever fashioned by Rabbit in Red. Ladies and gentleman, welcome to Hellfire!"

# Chapter Nine

Tara visited Jaime upstairs in the *Alien* pod bedrooms. "I wish I could have seen Mom play. That would have been hilarious." She sighed and Jaime put an arm around her shoulder.

"I know, but JB wants to make sure you're fully healed before exposing you to any of our games. And not just here," Jaime rubbed Tara's head, "if you know what I mean."

"So Rose and Wes's families won prizes?"

"Yeah. Well, they're for us. Rose and Wes, that is. There's always a game here at Rabbit in Red."

"I like Rose and Wes," Tara said.

"Me, too. They're good people." Jaime paused for a moment, examining the small patches of hair that had formed on Tara's head, running a finger through the rabbit outline they had cut for her. "Unofficially, you know, this means you're a Rabbiteer. How are you doing?"

"I like the idea of being a Rabbiteer. I'm fine." Sitting on Jaime's bed, Tara looked down and frowned in a way that didn't exactly boost Jaime's confidence.

"But really," Jaime pressed, "I mean like deep inside that head of yours, how are you?"

Tara looked up at her big sister and shrugged. "Okay, I guess. I've been talking a lot to the counselors JB arranged. It helps."

"What are they telling you?"

"Basically that emotional scars can last a lot longer than physical scars, and that it's okay to be angry or sad, and the best way to manage those feelings is to talk openly about them."

"That's good advice," Jaime said. "Do you feel angry or sad?"

"I was sad for a while, but not once I got here. Being with you and Bill, getting to know everyone else, that's been really cool." She smiled a little.

"What about angry?"

Tara shrugged again, and Jaime saw the little girl inside her sister. She may only have been a few years younger, but Jaime felt a decade older after everything had happened. Childhood fears were replaced by adult rage. When she thought about the man who took her sister, she pictured the many ways she would hurt him. While Jaime felt older, she wondered if her sister somehow didn't feel younger, like the pain had moved her back into the childhood perceptions of adult protections.

Jaime was tired of adult protections. Even though JB was supposedly hunting down the madman, she wasn't relying on that to solve everything. She had no doubt that the psycho would return, and when he did, Jaime would be ready for him. She wouldn't be hiding behind anyone. Jaime pictured the possible villains. Had Dexter become fully psycho after getting kicked out of Rabbit in Red last year? Was Daniel simply fooling them all? Who could it be?

"I don't know." Tara shrugged. "I don't want to be mad. I just want to hang with you guys. As long as I'm with you, I feel okay."

Jaime reached around and held Tara's hand. Together they sat against the back of the bed, and Jaime's thoughts drifted. *What am I really capable of doing? Am I capable of doing what I want to do? What I need to do for Tara?*

*****

Wes held Rose's hand in the commons as Donnie Chase greeted all of the first years and their parents. Wes sensed that his friends missed JB, but he felt a little lighter somehow with JB's absence. It felt like less could go wrong

*Yes, that's what it is,* Wes thought. *When JB is around, something bad always happens.* Wes wanted his parents and everyone to enjoy Hellfire as much as he did. With JB gone, hopefully they'd get to experience it just the way it was intended— no surprises. That would be refreshing.

"Good evening, everyone, and welcome to the ultimate event of our family week, a finale that you will never forget." Donnie lifted up her hands and ran one through the long, dark hair that had made her a perfect Samara. "I'll be your hostess this evening. Chester is helping oversee some of the technical operations of our Hellfire. JB called today with a message." She paused and smiled, making eye contact with several of the students. "He wants all of you first years to know how proud he is of all of you. He said, and I quote, 'Your Hellfire creation represents the epitome of creativity and is yet only the beginning of your future Rabbit in Red creations.' He's still out on other business, but hopes to return to say good-bye to all of the families before you depart." Wes noticed that Donnie had avoided eye contact with Jaime. "Now, to the moment we've all been waiting for! Parents, please come up front."

Wes looked over at his parents and smiled. "You're going to be great!"

"What the hell are you getting me into, Wes?" His mom looked at him as if he were making her jump out of an airplane.

"It will be okay." He smiled and tried to reassure them. He was thrilled to see his parents here, not just supporting but participating in something he helped create. He never had much to show them in high school. Although he had been a pretty good student, he was never involved in anything. Now was his chance to show them what all those days locked up in his bedroom reading books and watching horror films had really inspired.

From out front, Donnie continued, "You will all need to wear these." She held up a contraption that was part electronics, part straps. "This is called our Rabbit's Eye, a concept our first years helped create. The Rabbit's Eye is like a combination of a heart rate monitor, advanced Fitbit, and 4D technology. You will wear this as you explore Hellfire, and it will track a variety of data, including such things as your heart rate, the number of steps you take, how quickly you make movements, and much more. The Rabbit's Eye allows all of our images to come to life, much like in the game chambers you previously experienced. It is also how we will determine the winners, here and at the eleven locations nationwide. But we can't tell you exactly what it takes to win. Not yet. Just do your absolute best to complete Hellfire. That's all you need to think about. Are you ready?"

The parents looked at one another nervously as they put on the Rabbit's Eye, which consisted of a chest strap around the center of their body, a wrist band, and the 4D helmets they had worn in the game chambers. It looked like a laser tag device without the guns.

"Mom? Dad?" Wes asked. "One more event. You can do this, right?"

"I don't know what I'm doing, but I'll do it well," Mr. Pike said.

"Yeah, what your father said," his mom told him.

"Follow me, parents." Donnie waved, and Wes watched as they followed her past the game chambers, beyond the monitoring station, through the classic funhouse from last year, to the rows of studio rooms where the first years once battled the characters from *Misery*, *The People Under the Stairs*, and *Rosemary's Baby*.

Then a chill went down his spine. What was he making his parents do? He looked at Rose, then to Bill and the others. Everyone was smiling, but Wes felt something strange. They were about to watch their parents become truly horrified. *Should this be something they enjoy?*

Even further beyond those rooms existed quarters of this never-ending studio few had explored, but it was there that the first years, along with the help of a full construction and technical staff JB had hired, designed Hellfire, an eighteen-chambered haunted house.

The first years remained in the commons to watch each parent walk through on the giant screen. It was time to enjoy their creation, to see their horror come to life, and hopefully to get another good laugh or ten from the screams of their parents.

"Who is first?' Donnie asked the group. "You must only walk through one at a time."

Mr. Pike raised his hand.

"Very well, sir. Welcome to Hellfire!"

A giant gate covered in flames rose slowly, spitting fire at all directions.

"Is the fire real?" he asked, looking quite nervous.

"You can see it, right?" Donnie replied. "But you should know, just because you can see something doesn't make it real, and just because you can't see something doesn't mean it isn't there. That's all I can tell you as you begin your journey."

With a deep breath, Mr. Pike stepped through the fiery gate and entered the world of Hellfire.

Wes grabbed Rose's hand as he watched his father enter the first section, Wes's section. He held his breath.

Mr. Pike entered a library, a room full of books. Like all of the Rabbiteers, they escaped reality through fiction and film. Wes imagined all of the great stories of the world coming to life, not providing an escape, but rather trapping them in a world of horror. It was an extension inspired by the games they had experienced last Halloween. They all watched as Mr. Pike explored the room of books. A dull fire provided enough light for him to see various titles. He ran his hands across the dozens of books and walked around the room. Nothing had happened yet, and he looked confused.

Then he opened one of the books, and a shape of a demon appeared. A long black shadow with finger tips like a rake reached for Mr. Pike. He slammed the book shut, but the demon was free. It flew around the room and opened dozens of other books. A spirit arose from each one. Wes laughed when a clown popped up—because of course *It* was in Wes's section. Some books spit fire, some cast demons, and every book released a nightmare. Mr. Pike was surrounded now by spirits, clowns, and monsters of all shapes and sizes. The room moved, literally spinning, and Mr. Pike fell.

A clown with a mangled face and razor sharp teeth faced him. "There is no escape," it snapped. The first demon continued opening books and tossing them around the room as it spun in a circle. Wes lost his smile when he saw the horror on his father's face. Mr. Pike's hands trembled, and he stumbled when he took his next step.

"It's not real, right?" Mr. Pike asked to no one in particular and adjusted the Rabbit's Eye. Wes could see his father's chest expand and contract. Slowly, Mr. Pike moved forward.

A wolf approached and thrust out a lizard tongue that nearly slapped Mr. Pike's face. He screamed. "Wes! What in the hell did you get me into?"

Wes felt his own heart rate quicken. He bit his lip and cheered for his father.

"You can do it, Dad. C'mon!"

Horror's greats popped out of the many books in this room, and he was surrounded by monsters. A cheerleader with a skeleton face flipped toward him. Vampires flew in circles, and although Mr. Pike may not have recognized them, Wes smiled from the commons at the real images of Anne Rice's characters tormenting his father.

A resurrected Elvis Presley even appeared with a guitar and swung it at Mr. Pike, who ducked just in time. Zombies, devils, illustrated men, and women in black appeared from every corner.

They threw books at him, and with each book, a new evil appeared. Hannibal, Lestat, and Randal Flagg now stood directly in front of Mr. Pike.

"There is only one way out," Lestat said. "You must solve a riddle."

"Follow the rabbit," Randall Flag said. "Follow the rabbit to the book with new parents. When this young girl opens a door, she finds a marvelous new home with secrets not so apparent."

"Okay," Mr. Pike said aloud. "What book would that be?"

Wes held his breath as the monsters snarled and charged at his father. Mr. Pike dodged to the side, knocking over even more books, each one releasing another monster. Wes watched as he scanned the titles, searching for the right one. Mr. Pike's face twisted, and he sighed. *The Haunting of Hill House*, *Horns*, *Twilight Eyes*, *Something Wicked this Way Comes*: Wes had put a lot of books in this simulation.

Then his Dad's eyes widened, and Wes knew he had found it. It was another of Wes's favorite books, and he had hoped his dad would recognize it. From the corner of the room, one book remained closed. Mr. Pike ran for it, grabbed it, and held it up.

"Now what?" he yelled.

"Open it, Dad," Wes yelled from the commons.

His dad looked at the cover of the book, and then—almost as if he had heard—he opened it. Another demon arose from the story—Neil Gaiman's *Coraline,* of course. With a howl, it destroyed all of the other monsters in the room.

Then it glared at Mr. Pike. "Follow the fire."

Flames flickered on the ground, but Mr. Pike marched forward. A door had opened, and he entered the second section of Hellfire.

"Yeah, Dad!" Wes cheered. He turned to his friends. "Wasn't that awesome?"

"That's a freakin' incredible room," Bill complimented. "Amazing, man."

"Thanks," Wes said and grinned.

"Definitely very intense," Rose said. "Wow."

They watched as Mr. Pike started the next room, and then the next parent—Annie's mom—entered Hellfire.

"Go, Mom!" Annie stood up and cheered. "I hope she can get through it."

They watched her progress through Wes's conception. Wes's dad and now Annie's mom had made it through a few rooms, and everyone rooted for the parents. They watched as Annie's mom now walked through Rose's creation, the sixth room in Hellfire.

Wes sat up taller, watching Rose's creation come to life. He reached out and held her hand. When Annie's mom entered a new chamber, light revealed a long rectangular room. Hanging on the ceiling, making two rows from the front and back, were hundreds of nests. Bees, hornets, and wasps, nest after nest, waited for Annie's mom.

"Oh, Jesus!" she yelled.

Then the room turned to black.

"You know how much I hate flying, stinging insects," Rose said to her friends. "But the one thing I thought about is that they are all a daytime horror. They rest at night. What if they didn't? What if they were designed to initiate a full-on attack against people at night? Wouldn't that be terrible?"

Rose looked equally amused and haunted at the thought of her creation. Wes smiled at her. He couldn't help but love her all the more.

In Hellfire, Annie's mom was greeted by a swarm of buzzes. She screamed as the programmed sound projected deafening buzzing noises. Then hordes of insects lit up, sporadically like lightning bugs, and their stingers were enlarged to the size of syringe needles, long, sharp, and deadly.

"I always hated needles and shots," Rose said. "Ugh."

"It's a good thing you don't have to experience your own chamber," Wes joked. "You're sadistic." She squinted at him and curled her lip. "And I love it," Wes added. Rose smiled back at him.

He leaned in a kissed her quickly on the cheek. It was amazing to see her creation come to life. There was no other place he'd rather be than sitting by Rose's side and watching the horror they had created.

Annie's mom ran down the long hall, slapping at the flying terrors. "Get me out of this room!"

A small child appeared at the other end of the hall. Her pale face made her appear like a ghost. "Let's play a game," she said.

"Of course there's another game. What is it, bitch?" Annie's mom cussed at the girl.

"Hide and clap," the girl said. "I'll hide. You have to find me!" The girl vanished.

"I know what this is from," she said out loud. "Annie made me watch it a dozen times. Okay, one," she said, and she heard a clap from the beginning of this room. "Shit." She ran back through dreadful swarm of stinging demons to where she first entered the room, but she didn't see the little girl.

"Okay, two," she said, and a clap sounded back at the other end. "This is ridiculous," she yelled but ran back the other way. Once again there was no little girl.

"Three," she announced. The rules to this game stated that one must find the hider after three claps. The last one came from right behind her, and when she turned, there was a giant hornets' nest, bigger than a person.

"You've got to be kidding," she said, but she moved forward. She tore open the giant nest and stepped inside. Wes gasped at the screen—it showed her now standing in the middle of the nest. The hornets had cocooned her inside, rebuilding at lightning speed.

The little girl appeared inside the nest. "You found me!" She smiled at first, but then her mouth opened wide, wider than her entire face, and swarms of bees and wasps flew from out of her mouth. Annie's mom screamed.

The bees and wasps, in a radioactive-like glow, spelled out a phrase. *Follow the rabbit. Down the rabbit hole you go.*

Annie's mom looked into the large hole that was the mouth of the ghostly girl, wasps and bees shooting out like pouring rain.

"What the hell," she said and walked into the hole. She screamed as she fell down a fast, dark slide that dropped her into the next section.

"Yeah!" Annie yelled. "Dark and awesome, Rose. That room turned out perfect!"

There were many more chambers to explore and many more parents nervously waiting their turn to experience Hellfire. Wes kissed Rose again, his excitement and pride for his girlfriend at an all-time high. Then he put an arm around her shoulder and smiled.

*Now, let's just end the night without anyone getting hurt.*

He looked at Rose and then closed his eyes.

Wes's stomach hurt. It was too fun, too crazy, too cool. He leaned closer to Rose and took a deep breath, but he couldn't escape his thoughts.

*Something bad's gonna happen, isn't it?*

# Chapter Ten

Sally Wise had started to understand Hellfire's purpose. Each of these kids had put their fears into a virtual reality program. She had passed through several rooms, but not without a heck of a lot of cussing. Would she recognize her son's fears? What scared Bill the most? She was pretty sure she'd know the answer. It would be a stranger, a masked man, entering your home late at night to harm your family. It would be the same fear that she had.

But she knew Bill had other fears, too. He hated heights as much as he hated *Halloween III*. When she entered this new room and looked down through the Rabbit's Eye, she immediately thrust herself back against the safety of the room's wall. This was Bill's creation. The vertigo made her head spin and stomach churl. Below her, all she could see was the fast movement of cars and branches of trees waving as if warning her to turn around. She could feel the wind against her face, a freezing cold push, the kind of force one feels when literally standing on top of the world.

The door slammed behind her. There was no turning around now. From behind, a man entered wearing a black mask and carrying an axe. He swung it ferociously at Sally's head, missing her by inches. She pushed forward, but flames erupted from the floor in the only direction she could move. As she walked, the ledge on which she stood narrowed. Sally panicked—in this case, a fear of heights may have been genetic in the Wise family—and closed her eyes. Trying to stop the sensation of vertigo, she leaned back on the wall and slid forward. But the wall moved too, and Sally stumbled and screamed. The man with the axe approached quickly and swung it again at her head. Sally ducked, nearly falling off the ledge.

A voice in her head told her this wasn't real, that she could step off the ledge and she'd be on solid ground somewhere within these Rabbit in Red studios, but her emotions pushed out all logic.

She fell on her knees and crawled forward, trying her best to stay on the ledge, but now she was closer to the fire. Along with the wind, she could feel literal warmth each time a flame shot at her face. She crawled forward nonetheless. Fire was a better choice than the man with the axe. Reaching the other end of the room, she looked up and saw the exit was completely engulfed in flames. She looked behind just in time to see the man swing the axe vertically down upon her. She screamed and rolled off the ledge.

She should be on solid ground, but all around her was the most powerful dropping sensation. *What in the hell is this?* She kicked her legs and flailed her arms, but she couldn't feel solid ground. *Shit!* The night sky swallowed her, and the wind overpowered her screams. *Oh, Billy, what the fuck is this?* She was even more shocked at what she saw next. From above her, the man with the axe had dropped. He was flying at her, axe held firmly in both hands, the blade outward as if it would land right on her throat. She rolled forcefully at that thought, and she found she must have been on solid ground. She stood up, but the dropping sensation continued. It was as if she could float.

The fear of the simulations crushed all logical thought, and Sally snarled at the man with the axe. He was closer, almost upon her, but she lunged at him. Surprised, the man jerked back, and he lost the axe. Seeing it hover in front of her, Sally reached for it. Somehow she could control it, and without hesitation, she swung it like a baseball bat at her attacker.

The axe connected perfectly with his neck, but then she fell again.

She experienced the falling sensation in slow motion, and the sky appeared around her like a slow reverse waterfall. The man's head flew in the opposite direction of the room right into a huge, roaring fire. The falling had stopped altogether. Sally stood tall on her own two feet.

She turned around, gathered her thoughts, and brushed her hair out of her face.

"That was fucked up, Bill," she said to the empty room. Then she faced the fire and walked right through it into the next section.

*****

"Damn, Bill," Wes said back out in the commons as they watched on the big screen. "Your mom is fierce."

Wes took a closer look at Bill. Sure, Wes's simulation was pretty crazy—he loved the idea of lots of demons and horror monsters scaring people. But that was pure fiction, something any horror fan would love.

Wes worried Bill was out to genuinely terrify people, even his mother. Bill and JB may have more in common than Wes realized. There was a fine line between fun and fear. Did JB understand that? Wes didn't think so. He wasn't sure Bill understood it either, and that frightened Wes even more.

"I didn't know she had it in her." Bill looked around at the other first years. Their expressions told him they were both shocked and surprised at his mom. So far, the other parents had all fallen off the ledge too—that was a programed part of the simulation—but none had gone as far as chopping the head off of their attacker as he plummeted down at them.

"I like your mom more and more." Jaime grinned.

Wes flinched at Jaime's grin. He'd have to keep a closer eye on all of his friends.

"I'm sure she's had as many nightmares as I've had," Bill said. "Probably more. At some point, you just have to swing the axe. You know what I mean?"

"I know exactly what you mean," Jaime told them. Her eyes grew wider, and Wes felt a chill.

Then he turned his attention on Rose's dad, the next parent to explore Hellfire.

Mr. Dawn had progressed to the very end of Hellfire, and the one section that remained was Jaime's creation. He was inside what resembled a family room of a typical home. Picture frames formed rows of memories. The image in each frame was distorted and hard to see, an attempt to generalize the scene so that it could be anyone's family pictures up on the walls. Mr. Dawn moved forward, and with each step, a picture exploded. He stopped suddenly and examined the pictures up ahead. A screech came from his right, high pitched and piercing like Freddy Krueger's claws scraping along metal pipes. He stepped toward the sound, and another picture exploded.

Ropes fell from the ceiling. Giant, thick ropes, similar to those used to tie strong sails on a boat, wrapped around Mr. Dawn's body like an enormous spider web. The piercing sound intensified, and he tried to step again toward it, but the ropes had paralyzed him. He pulled at them, but they only tightened. He was bound and frozen in the middle of this room.

Then the flames reappeared. They slapped at the wall with the photos, and the remaining pictures melted, memories dripping like candlewax onto the floor. Mr. Dawn looked alarmed, his brow furrowed in confusion. Suddenly, the Rabbit in Red appeared before him. It spun, danced, and laughed manically. Then it sprinted across the room into the fire, leaving a trail of blood.

He couldn't move forward, but he could move in reverse. Walking backwards, the ropes worked with him. He stood within the flames and the wall that had held all of the pictures melted with them. A new room appeared. Mr. Dawn glanced at it and automatically tried to step forward, to escape where the ropes were taking him. But they tightened once again and he had no choice but to move into this new room.

At first, it looked like a funeral home lined with coffins, but at a closer examination, the floor was no floor at all. It was wet, thick mud, and the coffins slid into the ground as if it were quick sand swallowing them.

It looked like the only way out was to go down.

Mr. Dawn, the ropes pushing him in this direction, stepped toward the coffins and the gushing mud. It bubbled around his feet, a volcanic-like mesh that oozed. It must have reeked, too. Wes saw him try to cover his nose, but he couldn't reach his face with the ropes tangled around his body.

Something pulled him into the mud. His body turned as if he were on a slide, and he glided horizontally deep into the sludge that now surrounded him.

Everything around him went completely dark. He was shut in under the ground. Wes watched as the ropes appeared to tighten around Mr. Dawn's body even more. It looked like he was being buried alive. Wes reached over to hold Rose's hand, but she had thrust both arms up in the air.

"Tell yourself it's not real, Dad," Rose cried. "You can do this!"

Wes looked at Jaime and Bill. They each had smiles. Wes felt nothing like smiling. He felt like getting Mr. Dawn out of Hellfire and stopping this whole thing. It was getting to be too much.

But Mr. Dawn couldn't seem to catch his breath. The fire had returned. Wes stood up and opened his mouth but he froze. The fire had engulfed Mr. Dawn, and he yelled, the loudest, strongest yelp Wes had heard throughout any of the simulations.

Then the ground dropped again, and he fell. The ropes loosened. The lights slowly brightened his surroundings. He stood up, and the Rabbit in Red greeted him.

"Congratulations, you have survived Hellfire."

Jaime turned to her friends. "That was exactly what I wanted."

"Jesus, Jaime," Bill said. "It was . . . worse seeing it played out than when you talked about it."

"That was too much." Wes mustered the courage to say what he felt. "Too much, guys. What are we trying to do here? Kill someone?" His voice cracked, and he looked at Rose. Rose hadn't taken her eyes off the monitors and her father.

Jaime shrugged. "Too much? No. If we're going to really test people, we need to make them feel like they're actually going to die."

Goosebumps chilled Wes's arms as he looked in Jaime's eyes. Bill looked a bit pale, too, Wes was glad to notice.

"I wanted," Jaime continued, "to make someone feel completely trapped. Make them feel like there's nothing they can do about it. Nothing at all but to sit there and die."

Jaime looked away. Wes swallowed hard.

Then he turned to watched Mr. Dawn follow the Rabbit in Red to the exit. But Mr. Dawn still didn't look so well. His skin had become a ghastly white. Sweat glistened on his forehead, and he held his left arm as if it had been injured.

Then he collapsed.

# Chapter Eleven

"Dad!" Rose yelled. She ran to the back of the studio, and her friends followed.

They entered the first room of Hellfire and heard the rumblings of Wes's books come to life. Without the Rabbit's Eye, the room was more or less just a room full of props. They sprinted to an emergency exit that had been installed and circled around the chambers.

"Dad! Are you okay?"

Mr. Dawn pressed a hand against his chest and grimaced in pain. "Heart . . . attack," he mumbled.

Out of the corner of her eye, Rose saw Wes take out his cell phone. To Jaime and Bill, he shouted, "Quick! Get—"

"I've got this," Donnie told Wes. She shouted into the phone, "Get our medics here, now!"

Should she have called 911? Did JB have his own paramedic team, too? Rose wouldn't have been surprised if JB had a direct line to the President.

Donnie turned her attention on Mr. Dawn. "He's conscious. That's a good sign. We'll get him the help he needs."

It felt like the longest moment in Rose's life. There was only one other time in her life that she had felt like this—that camping trip, several years ago, when she had lost her brother. It was a difficult feeling to explain, a paradoxical pain. Everything hurt throughout her body, but it was an excruciating numbness, pins and needles in one's feet that never healed. As she watched her father grab his chest and moan, the pins and needles stabbed her again. This was no horror film. There were no witches in the background that would remove their makeup and thus their terror. This was a buzzing of bees on a summer afternoon all over again.

"It's going to be okay, Dad. Hang on." Rose choked out the words and forced back the tears. *Can this really be happening?* She looked up at Wes, who had his hands on her shoulders. Rose was on her knees, and she held her father's hand. He tried to speak, but only a gasp of air came out.

"Don't try to talk," Rose said. Her father blinked hard, as if to say, "I love you."

"I love you, too, Dad. But you're gonna be okay. You have to be." Rose turned her head sharply. A small tear that fell on her hand broke the dam, and she couldn't hold it in. *Oh, please, God, no!* She felt the pins and needles of pain all throughout her body, in her heart, her face, her arms and legs like hundreds and hundreds of bee stings.

Donnie called from behind. She directed the paramedics to a back entrance in the studio to have easier access to Mr. Dawn. Rose's mom was there now as well. Mrs. Dawn cried and yelled, then she hugged Rose tightly. They watched as a team of medical professionals put Mr. Dawn on a gurney and pushed him quickly outside of Rabbit in Red.

"Where are they taking him?" Rose asked. "Never mind, I'm coming, too." She grabbed her mother, and they chased the stretcher outside the studios.

"Let's gather back at the commons. He'll be okay," Donnie tried to reassure the remaining students. Rose turned around and briefly waved at Wes.

Wes ran up to her. "Can I come with you?"

Mrs. Dawn shook her head before Rose could answer. "Stay here, Wes. We need to be together now." She pulled at Rose, and before she knew it, Rose was outside of Rabbit in Red, riding in the back of an ambulance with her dying father. Her mother's arms were wrapped around her tightly. The sirens drowned out all of their cries and all of their thoughts, but the stabbing pain of the pins and needles never stopped stinging her.

*****

Back in the commons, Wes texted Rose. *Please keep us updated.* He paced back and forth, unable to focus on anything but his phone. *C'mon, Rose, please message me back!*

"Did he have a weak heart?" Jaime asked. "They shouldn't let anyone with any kind of medical condition experience Hellfire."

"I don't think so," Wes said. "Not that I know of." He tried not to show it, but Jaime's question shocked him. Was she really implying that it was somehow Mr. Dawn's own fault that he'd had a heart attack in her Hellfire chamber?

They took their seats back at the commons, and the rest of the parents gathered around.

Donnie looked flustered as she approached the microphone. "Um, okay. Hi, folks. That was unexpected, of course. We'll stay in contact with the hospital, Rose, and Mrs. Dawn. We'll notify JB, too. And as soon as we hear something, we'll let you know. In light of the current situation, I think it's best not to award the final prize or announce any winner. Let's just wish the best for Mr. Dawn and his family."

"Don't you think this is all too much?" Sally Wise stood up, straightened her shirt, and challenged Donnie. "You all have this idea that this is one big, funny thing, but something always goes wrong. You can't take Hellfire to the public after this."

"Mom!" Bill whined. "Please. This isn't the time." Wes saw the embarrassment on Bill's face.

"When is the time then, Bill? After someone dies?"

Donnie spoke up before anyone else could reply. "We appreciate your concern, and I promise we will take all of your concerns to heart." Donnie brushed the black hair out of her eyes. "No one is going to die."

Janet Stein stood up next. "You think we're safe here at Rabbit in Red? I thought maybe with some psycho out there that this may be safer than being alone. But we're no safer here. Not when you put people in harm's way."

Several of the other parents nodded and stood up to support Jaime's mom. Then Janet looked at Jaime and motioned for her to stand up. "C'mon. I've had enough. We're going home."

Jaime leaned back but didn't stand up. "No, Mom. I'm not going anywhere."

"Excuse me?"

"This is where I belong. You're crazy if you think you're safer elsewhere. Don't you dare take Tara. That would be the real harm."

She spoke firmly, and Wes just stared at them both. Jaime had such power in her voice, and her mother's face twitched as if she had been slapped.

"How dare you talk to me like that? You see what this place is doing to you? We're leaving. Now. That's not a suggestion."

Jaime looked at Bill for support, then briefly at Wes and the others, too. Everyone was staring at her. She snapped her head sternly back at her mother.

"No, Mom. I'm not leaving."

Janet glared at Jaime. Wes was sure his mother would have smacked him across his face had he talked to her like that. He wasn't sure what to think. He wasn't going to leave, not without Rose at least, but he certainly didn't want to have this fight with his family, in part because he knew that he'd agree with them. JB allowed them to create these simulations, but shouldn't he have checked them over? Or, more likely Wes thought, he probably had known what these simulations could do, and he didn't care.

Wes looked over at his parents, but they were quiet, entranced by the mother-daughter fight all were witnessing. He looked carefully around the room at everyone. All of the parents and first years just stared at Janet and Jaime, and all were completely silent.

Janet breathed hard, and her lips pursed tightly together. "I don't know what to do with you. But Tara is coming with me." Without giving Jaime a chance to reply, Janet stormed off in the direction of the sleeping quarters where Tara stayed. Wes knew that JB and his assistants wanted to protect Tara, but they limited her exposure to Rabbit in Red events.

"What do I do?" Jaime asked no one in particular, her head bowed down.

Sally Wise broke the silence. "You should listen to your mother. We should all go. Nothing good will come of this place."

The other parents and first years broke into murmurs, some angry, some confused.

"Look," Bill said to his mom, "I know you don't understand. But this place is . . . it's . . . it's not for you. It's for us. Oh-right? Don't you get that? These are our dreams. Our adventures. People get hurt in life. You can lock yourself inside your home and do absolutely nothing and someone can still get in and hurt you. This was an accident. That's all. What happened to Tara, that's . . . it's terrible. It's crazy."

The other parents and first years quieted down. Their eyes were focused on Bill.

This was the leader Wes had grown to admire last Halloween. He hadn't seen much of that leadership yet this summer, but God knew there were too many distractions. *Tell them, Bill. Speak up.* He wanted to believe in Bill, even if he doubted some of Bill's beliefs at times.

Bill stood up and spoke even louder, as if hearing Wes's thoughts. "I don't know where I'll be in four years, but I know I don't want my nose stuck in textbooks surrounded by people who don't get me. I'm lucky, Mom. Yes, lucky. Here in this world, I'm surrounded by others who understand me. Who share my passions. I mean look at Hellfire. We did that! Tell me where else in the world we'd be able to combine our passions to make something like that. People fall off merry-go-rounds. People trip over their own feet. I don't mean that I don't feel bad for them, but I'm not gonna stop just because it was too much for you or anyone else. You don't know JB like we do. You think he wants to miss all of this? This is his number one passion, so you know the only reason he's not here is because he's out there."

Bill swung his arms wildly, pointing outside of the studio. "He's out there because that's where the crazies are. He's out there to protect us. Outside of those doors . . . Jaime's right. That's what's not safe."

Wes saw the hottest flames of the entire day in Bill's passionate eyes. Bill sat down then and lowered his head into his hands. He pulled at his golden blond hair. Sally sat down next to him and put an arm around his shoulders. She didn't say anything. All of the words had been said.

Wes's cell phone went off. "It's Rose!" He answered quickly, and his mouth and eyes widened. He nodded a few times, and then slowly a smile formed on his face. He exhaled deeply and then announced to the group, "Mr. Dawn is going to be okay! It wasn't even a heart attack. It was a big panic attack. Panic, that's all. Rose said JB got them immediate access to help at a private care facility. No hospitals, no waiting."

*No witnesses or media or police reports, you mean?* Wes tried to shake the question from his thoughts.

"They're going to keep him for observation. But he's gonna be okay."

It felt like the temperature in the room dropped a few degrees, and everyone heaved a communal sigh of relief. They listened to Wes's repeat "uh huh" and kept quiet until he hung up the phone.

"Rose says that her dad's not only okay, but in good humor. He says that he deserves the final prize, and he's coming back to collect it." There were a few chuckles throughout the room, but Wes saw some parents still looked worried.

"You're too old for me to control you," Bill's mom said and sighed. "I want a phone call every single day. Do you understand? To let me know you're safe. There's a whole school year to come. If this was only a summer project, I just can't even imagine . . . so you'll call. *Daily*. Okay?"

"Oh-right." Bill smiled. "We'll be fine. I promise."

"I better find my mom and talk to her," Jaime said. "In private this time."

When Jaime took off, Wes sat down. There was a lot to discuss with his parents, and everyone had a lot to get off their chests. But he didn't want to do any more talking. He only wanted to wait for Rose to return.

*****

Rose walked back into the commons several hours later. It was late, and it appeared everyone had already gone to bed. Everyone but one, that was. Wes's head rested on folded arms on a table in the commons. Rose heard the slightest snore and smiled. She walked closer to him, coughed gently, and his head popped straight up.

"Rose!" Wes shouted. She smiled wider, and when he hugged her, for the first time since she saw her father fall, the pins and needles went away. The tighter Wes hugged her, the better she felt. "I'm so glad your dad is okay. That was terrible. Are you okay?"

She hugged him back, softly and gently, smelling the familiar body spray to which she had become accustomed. Rose put her head on his shoulder. She could stay like this all night, and if she knew Wes, he wouldn't pull away. Not soon anyway. Maybe not ever. She rested and let herself recall that conversation when he officially asked her out. She wanted to think of a happy memory.

"I have something I wanted to ask you," Wes had said, shuffling his feet on the concrete outside of Rabbit in Red before everyone else had arrived.

Rose had felt her cheeks warm. It was the first time they had seen each other in person since Halloween last year. She had had a feeling this would happen, or at least she had hoped. She had told herself that if Wes didn't make it official, she'd have to say something to him, but she wanted to give him a chance.

"I like you." Wes's head had shrunk in between his shoulders and he kicked at the concrete. "If it weren't for you, I don't know if I'd be here. I mean, I like all this stuff, you know that. But it's pretty crazy, too. I'd risk it all to be by your side. These last several months have been . . . well, amazing and terrible all at once. I love our chats, but I hate that you're so far away. So I promised myself . . ." Wes paused and took a deep breath, his chest blowing up like a balloon. "I promised myself that I'd do whatever it takes to be close to you. I don't ever want to be far away again. So will you . . . will you be my girlfriend?"

She felt even warmer, and not just because of the California sun. Looking him in the eyes and taking his hands, she said, "Yes. Absolutely yes."

Then she leaned in and kissed him. They went for a walk outside after that, waiting to see when Bill or Jaime would arrive. They found a private corner and lost track of time getting to know one another in new ways. No words were needed.

Now as Wes held her, Rose felt even more grateful to have him in her life. He was the sweetest, most genuinely caring person she knew. He wasn't really the competitive type, not like Bill, and Rose liked that about him. He was strong and talented in his own ways. As she pulled away from the hug, Wes leaned in and kissed her, not as passionate as they that day outside of Rabbit in Red, but somehow this was even better. She felt more than passion. She felt the touch of someone—the first someone ever outside of her parents—who genuinely cared about her.

When she finally pulled away, she said, "I'm okay. Quite well, actually." She kissed him again. *There's something about the fear of losing loved ones that brings you closer to others*, she thought. *Maybe that's another reason why we all like horror so much.*

"And your dad?"

"Yeah, he's going to be fine. The docs gave him a big lecture about diet and exercise. His heart is weaker than it should be, and that may have played a part in his panic attack."

"Good. I mean . . . well, you know what I mean."

"I do." Rose smiled at him and took his hand. "Where are Bill and Jaime?"

"They left to help Jaime's mom and sister check in to a hotel. Her mom wanted to leave, but JB I guess made a compromise to get them a hotel room with private security guards stationed outside their rooms all night. I guess he wanted them close still. You missed quite the fight between Jaime and her mom, and everyone and their parents." Wes rolled his eyes.

"I bet." She frowned. "Everything was going so well, too. Wasn't it?"

"Hellfire is amazing, but I wouldn't be surprised if JB wants to advertise it by using what happened to your dad."

Rose shook her head. "I don't think that would be very cool."

"No. No, I guess not." They sat down at their table in the commons. "We were told JB had an announcement to make before the night is over. Donnie said he'd be returning after everything that happened today. No one is actually sleeping yet. They'll be back here soon."

They sat in a beautiful silence for several minutes while they waited for everyone else to return and for JB to make his announcement. Rose held his hand and leaned in close. She enjoyed the quiet, and she closed her eyes until everyone else came back.

"So that's the big guy himself, eh?" Mr. Pike asked as he approached Wes and Rose. JB had now walked to the main part of the stage, and the parents and first years were all gathering.

"Rose, sweetie, we're so glad everything is okay. How are you?" Mrs. Pike asked. Her eyes flicked to their clasped hands, and the smile on her face widened. It made Rose smile, too.

"I'm okay. Thank you for asking. Looks like JB is getting ready to talk."

They straightened in their seats and watched JB shuffle around up front. He was talking to his assistants and kept checking his phone. There was an ominous feeling about it all. JB, who almost always appeared strong and confident, looked nervous. After a couple of minutes, he approached the microphone.

"Hello, everyone. My name is Jay Bell. Parents—I am so happy you have joined us for this week, and I only wish I could have been here for more of it. I would very much like to get to know each of you. We'll have a special dinner for our last night, and I'd like to make the rounds and chat with each of you."

JB cleared his throat and took a sip from a glass of water. "Let's talk first about what will happen next. We will continue with Hellfire as planned. Teams will be building the set at eleven select locations throughout the U.S. We will advertise it and select one new recruit from each location. You must be wondering how we are evaluating contestants."

JB looked warmly at Rose and tried to smile. She stared at him. Would she ever really know if it was madness or genius inside his head?

"The Rabbit's Eye provides detailed analysis about your heart rate and many other factors. It can, in short, give us comprehensive analysis about an individual's amount of fear and how well they were able to control that fear. Our new recruits will be chosen from among those who are able to control their fear the while completing Hellfire. We expect to have some very brave new recruits."

Finally JB truly smiled, and Rose felt some relief. It was a return to normal, or as normal as Rabbit in Red could be. To see JB discuss horror and his creations without that slightly sadistic smile was like seeing a child walk away from an ice cream truck. It wasn't natural.

"Oh, yes, we will always have surprises," he continued. "First, we have some final modifications to make with the Rabbit's Eye. We should have been better able to detect what was happening with Mr. Dawn. Rose," he said and looked her directly in the eye. "I'm so sorry. I'm happy your father will be all right, and I promise to all of you that we will make modifications for the Rabbit's Eye to shut down Hellfire if it detects that it's too much and could cause actual injury."

His eyes were empathetic, and, for better or worse, Rose trusted him.

She smiled and nodded. JB continued. "While our teams build and promote Hellfire at its various locations, we will also begin the next part of our program for first years. I have recruited some of the most talented geniuses in our industry. They will provide a course of study for all of you. And here's a pleasant surprise, something I am sure your parents will appreciate. I have been able to collaborate with UCLA. My team has proposed their course of studies, and you will receive official college credit for your participation here. I'm not the biggest believer in needing a formal degree to be successful, but for your sakes—and for your parents' sakes—I wanted to make sure you'd leave here with an official degree, too."

A short burst of enthusiastic conversation took place between parents and first years. Rose watched the others, thinking that JB had had this up his sleeve the entire time. He played the card when he needed it the most: to keep people here.

"I'd like to introduce you to three of your professors now. First, meet Victor Cunningham." Victor walked out to JB's side. A short man with a distinctly sharp and pointed jaw, he had blonde hair that was gradually turning white. "Victor will teach you all the tricks you can possibly imagine with a camera. Next, we have Shirley Rice."

She was a stocky, heavier set woman, with curly gray hair, something that looked like an old perm out of the 1980s. "Shirley will teach you everything about writing. She is a master of her craft. Finally, I want to introduce Curt Waggner."

An older bald man walked out next. He wore a buttoned up shirt and webs of chest hair poked through. He may not have had any on his head, but it was obvious the rest of his body was like the Wolfman. "Curt is a master of technology. He's actually one of the game programmers for many of the things you've experienced, but he can also do anything with a computer when it comes to editing.

Now, I do have one piece of unfortunate news that I have been reluctant to share."

Here JB scanned the crowd before him. Clearly, he didn't want to say anything to scare parents and first years any more than necessary.

"It's best you hear about it from me first as the media will no doubt spin its version. I had a fourth professor who was supposed to be here. She was going to work with those of you interested in acting. But earlier this week, she disappeared. That's why I wasn't here. Among other things, I was out looking for her." He paused again. He looked over to the new professors, who nodded gently with encouragement.

"Her name was Emma Williams. I was, actually, able to find her. Unfortunately . . ." JB paused and looked around. Rose felt the pins and needles return. She squeezed Wes's hand, and braced herself for what she thought was coming. JB's eyes narrowed and his face tightened. As he paused and formed the words, Rose saw the color of his skin pale. He scanned the room and looked them all hard in the eyes.

"Unfortunately . . . she's dead." Silence. In that one word, it was as if all of the air in the room had escaped.

*First, someone kidnaps Tara? Then my dad almost has a heart attack. Now one of our would-be teachers is dead?* The pins and needles stung more sharply, and Rose didn't know what to think.

"The police are investigating the cause," JB continued, "but it appears that foul play was involved. I don't want to scare you, but I would bet that whoever was behind Tara's abduction was also behind the death of Emma Williams. Now, please," he stated more sternly, "before you ask questions, I want you to know that when I'm done talking, I will visit with each of you personally. But by now I hope you know this: inside Rabbit in Red, I can protect all of you. Outside of here, my reach is limited, as is all too obvious with the unfortunate loss of Emma Williams. First years—and parents, your children—you are safe here."

Rose squeezed Wes's hand harder at JB's words. They looked at one another. They didn't need to speak to understand one another's thoughts. JB would keep trying to convince the parents that Rabbit in Red was safe. The first years wouldn't say otherwise. Rose knew they didn't want any more arguments, and even if it seemed illogical, they wanted to be here. Perhaps they were all crazy, but they weren't leaving. They'd rather be on the inside, next to JB and their friends, than alone on the outside. They were safe on the inside, right?

*Yeah, real safe. Kidnappings, emergency trips to the doctor, death . . . no, murder!*

Well, she tried to convince herself, two out of the three had happened on the outside. It had to be safe on the inside. She scooted closer to Wes. *Yeah, we'll all just stay right here, forever, if that's what safest.* Wes released her hand and put his arm around her instead, but this time it didn't make the pins and needles go away.

# Chapter Twelve

Daniel Lloyd had remained largely quiet during the summer term. He hung out with Leroy and a few others, but he was mostly content to observe. Family week had been the real nail in a silent coffin. He wasn't going to invite his father. Not a chance in hell. Daniel had moved out of his dad's house the moment he could. Their relationship had never improved. His father had read about some of the Rabbit in Red events, and when Daniel returned home after Halloween weekend last year, he wasn't greeted warmly.

He sat by himself in his Alien pod bedroom. He was looking through pictures on his phone when he stumbled across one of his father in a hooded sweatshirt. Daniel's body shook with chills. He didn't even know how or why he had that picture in his phone. Did he take it and forget? It brought back memories of last Halloween, and he thought about the day he saw his father when he returned home from the contest.

"What a loser," Mr. Lloyd had chuckled when Daniel came home on a rather chilly November day for southern California.

Daniel had forcefully locked his teeth together, and a snarl ripped through his face.

"Got somethin' to say, boy?" His father stared at him, an alpha dog looking at his pup. "That's what I thought," he said to Daniel's silence. "You think this shit is gonna do anything for ya? Wastin' your time like you always do. It's no wonder your mother left us."

Daniel's stomach churned just thinking of the memory. Acid shot up causing a sharp burn in his chest. He hadn't wanted to be there at all, much less talk to his father about his experiences. When he was forced to be home, he spent as much time as possible at school or in the gym. When that wasn't possible, he stayed in his room and watched all the horror he could find. He'd be lying if he said that he didn't sometimes fantasize about killing his father in some of the gruesome ways he saw on the screen.

Daniel's mom had walked out on them years ago. His dad hadn't talked to her or abuse her the way he abused his son. Daniel was the lucky recipient of his father's charm. But his mom did see it. She saw it, and she didn't do anything about it. He didn't think she liked what she saw and heard, but she wasn't strong enough to do anything. So she left.

Flipping through more pictures he had stored on his phone, Daniel remembered the last time he saw her. He had just entered high school, and one warm September morning, she woke him up about an hour earlier than usual.

"I'm leaving." She said it matter-of-factly.

"What?" Daniel, who at age fourteen was just beginning to build the muscle he had hoped to use against his father one day, sat up in bed.

"I can't stay. I can't take you with me. I'm here to say good-bye." She leaned forward then and kissed him on the cheek, but it wasn't affectionate like a mother's kiss. It felt like the kind of peck one would give a stranger in a country where such greetings are appropriate etiquette.

"I don't understand. You can't leave me with him. Not alone." Tears burned in young Daniel's eyes. He clenched his fists, his knuckles turning a ghostly white.

"He doesn't love me anymore, Danny, and I can't watch what he does to you." She stood up, evidently ready to depart at that exact moment.

"Wait! Why can't you take me with you?"

"You're too young to understand. I'm too old to tell you. One day, when you get out of this house, I'll find you, okay?"

"Where are you going?" His voice was hoarse now, shaky with tears.

"I can't tell you. If you don't know, he can't beat it out of you."

"But he'll try. You know he'll try anyway." His face was stone, but his mom's was harder.

He didn't recognize her. Her emotionless features made her more like an alien than a parent he had lived with for the last fourteen years. She placed a hand on the bedroom door knob and turned around. The sun was now beginning to rise, sharp blades of light stinging the room.

"You have to stand up to him, Danny. I can't take watching you cower in fear any more than I can take him." She snapped her head back to the door then, took a step outside, and without looking around again, she said, "Good-bye."

Daniel sat there in bed and let the tears pour down his face. After a minute, he wiped them away with the palm of his hand. Then he did as many push-ups on the floor of his bedroom as he could. On the last one, he collapsed, his face slamming against the floor. He didn't flinch though. He did all of this to prepare for what would happen when his father found out that Mom had left them.

Daniel pulled himself from the memory. Now he was living at Rabbit in Red. His bedroom of terrible memories had turned into the sweetest *Alien*-themed room. Bill still looked at him like he was a monster. They had spoken maybe five words to each other the entire summer. Bill was obsessed with Jaime. Wes and Rose were obsessed with each other. Everyone was obsessed with whoever abducted Tara, with Mr. Dawn's panic attack after Hellfire, and with the alleged murder of the would-have-been professor.

And so Daniel listened to everyone's theories. He observed their reactions. He learned everything he could about every single person at Rabbit in Red, and he kept himself in the shadows as to not give away anything else about himself. With all of the crazy events that had already happened, who would have thought to give Daniel a second glance?

It allowed Daniel to obsess on his own goal, and that suited him just fine. Everyone, so far, had appeared to be oblivious to his true ambitions.

*****

Rose held Lester the rabbit up in the girls' sleeping quarters. It was now September, and they had enjoyed a rather news-free month or so since the end of summer term. They focused on new projects, learning from the professors JB had introduced.

Jaime sat in a bed next to Rose, working on one of their projects. "Those Hellfire commercials on TV are pretty sweet. I wonder how many people will participate."

"A ton," Rose said without much enthusiasm.

"Why do you say it like that?"

"Oh, I dunno." She paused. "I think it's because I feel like we've finally found our groove. We're working and studying. It's all really awesome stuff. No one has been kidnapped, rushed to the hospital, or killed recently, you know? And soon there will be a new bunch of people here. I kinda like it the way it is." She sighed and sat Lester down on her bed.

"Rabbit in Red isn't just for us. It's going to get bigger every year," Jaime said.

"That's what worries me," Rose confessed and stroked Lester's fine hair.

"Halloween will be here before we know it. It's crazy, if you think about it. This time last year we were solving riddles on our phones. Now we're creating sets and scenes of horror movies and building a new round of games for whoever is selected after Hellfire. We've come a long way." Jaime worked at the computer monitor of her bed, and Rose smiled. The monitor was touch screen, and Jaime enthusiastically swiped and pressed with her fingers. "This is what science-fiction flicks used to look like."

Rose nodded, then looked down at her phone and laughed.

"What?" Jaime asked. "Oh, you're on your phone. You know, Wes is just a minute away. Even when you guys aren't together, you're texting."

There was a little annoyance in Jaime's voice that Rose picked up on.

"It's not Wes. It's your sister."

"Why is Tara texting you?"

"She wanted to show me a pic. Look!" Rose sat Lester down on her bed and walked over to Jaime. Tara had sent Rose a picture of her hair. It had grown in and looked more like a boy's crew cut, but Rose thought it was nice to see her with a head full of hair again. Tara had continued to buzz the rabbit in the side of her head, but the reason she texted Rose was obvious.

"She dyed her hair red!" Jaime shrieked. "That crazy kid. Tell her I love it."

"I will." While she texted Tara back, she asked Jaime, "So, you and Bill? You two official or what?"

Jaime's hands finally stopped moving. Rose knew Bill and Jaime were close, but wondered if there was more the two of them talked about when no one was listening.

"He's my best friend," Jaime stated.

"Nothing more?"

"What more could you want than a best friend?"

"Well," Rose started and then stopped abruptly. She wasn't exactly an expert on relationships. "Well . . . Wes is my best friend. But we're also more than that. You know?"

"I *know!*" Jaime said, rolling her eyes dramatically. "You do realize I have my head phones in and the volume turned all the way up and can still hear you guys sucking face, right?"

Rose giggled at that image. *Sometimes when you're in love—is that what this is?—it's easy to forget everything else.* She tried to interpret the expression on Jaime's face. Was it jealousy? Or pain?

"I'm sorry. Or should I say: sorry, not sorry." Rose gave Jaime a friendly smile. "Seriously now, you and Bill have never talked about being more?"

Jaime stopped what she was working on completely now and faced Rose with undivided attention. "I see something in his eyes now and then," Jaime said. "Sometimes I think it's love. But I don't know if it's more than a best friend kind of love. Then sometimes I see something else, particularly over this past summer. I see . . . I see fear and confusion. Like he's scared of me." Jaime swung her feet off the side of the bed and looked Rose straight in the eye. "Does he have reason to be scared of me?"

Rose literally bit her tongue. They had all sensed a change in Jaime since Tara was kidnapped, but no one said anything to her about it. JB had arranged for a team of counselors to be available, and Jaime had been talking to one on a regular basis. Once they started actual classes, Jaime seemed to get better. The work kept them all busy and focused.

"If I'm being honest," Rose began, "yeah, maybe. Sometimes, Jaime, you get this look in your eyes that you really want to hurt someone. I don't think anyone is going to get over their sister being hurt like that in just a couple of months. You have reason to be angry, but I would also guess it keeps Bill from getting any closer to you."

"Hmmm," Jaime mumbled. She frowned and looked away, and Rose wondered if Jaime even realized the darkness in her eyes.

Was this really the first time anyone had told her this? How much had Tara's kidnapping messed Jaime up inside her head?

"I guess I never thought of that. Thanks for being honest, Rose." Jaime turned back to her computer, swiping and editing images on screen for a current project. Rose watched her, hoping that maybe her words would help Jaime. But the only thing she noticed is that Jaime hit the screen with her fingers with a forceful anger of some kind that wasn't there before their conversation.

Rose went back to Lester, fed him a nice snack of alfalfa, and texted Tara again.

*Wish you were with us here. Really love ur hair.*

She replied with a picture of one of the security guards JB had hired to watch over Tara and her mother. *Wish you were here. This guy is HOT.*

Rose laughed to herself this time, not wanting to distract Jaime. *At least one of them seems okay,* she thought, *and it's ironic that it's Tara.*

Maybe it was time she had a good talk with Bill, too.

*****

Daniel followed Wes and Bill. Although he tried to watch everyone very closely, he kept the two of them even closer. He didn't have to speak to observe.

In the front of the studio, Wes and Bill walked through the *Hellraiser* hall and into the school-themed wing adjacent to *A Nightmare on Elm Street*. Perhaps this wing was intended as a tribute, but it was also put to practical use. This was where they had their classes.

Bill and Wes sat with several other students who were attending a discussion by Professor Victor Cunningham. Daniel took a seat right behind them and grinned. Bill and Wes didn't even seem to notice him. Their professor wore a blue blazer over a white t-shirt and jeans. He ran a hand through his once blond but now mostly white hair, and when he spoke, his sharp jaw line moved in a way that reminded Daniel of Dracula.

"Art inspires art," Cunningham stated. "That's a theme JB admires, as do I. As you create your projects for the soon-to-be new recruits, let us use that as our motivation. What do you think of when it comes to horror and fire?"

"*Carrie*," Wes shouted out. "The story ends with her setting everything on fire telepathically. King used it as a motif in several stories, including *Firestarter*."

"Yes, but JB used Carrie's stage as a design last year. We haven't used the other. What else will you turn to for inspiration?"

Daniel decided to join the discussion. When he spoke, Bill glared at him. "*The Wicker Man* would be a powerful thing to experience. Trap people and let them burn."

"Yes, good, Daniel," Cunningham complimented.

"I've always been a fan of the end of *Halloween II*," Venus Bowers said.

"Yeah!" Leroy jumped in. "Michael gets burned. That could be a good theme to use."

"I agree, and JB alluded to that film last year in the very wing we now sit in," Cunningham said. "Do you think fire would be the most painful death? What is the worst way to die?"

"Fire is slow," Daniel spoke up again. "If your entire body is on fire, then you feel pain everywhere. That has to be the most powerful death."

"I've always thought drowning or being buried alive would terrible." Venus shuddered. "If you're drowning, you may not feel pain right away, but you feel all the fear of what is about to come. Same with buried alive. Isn't fear worse than pain?"

"Is it?" Cunningham challenged. "What is worse? To experience pain in every single part of your body or to anticipate death, knowing it's coming?"

"Fire doesn't give you time to think," Bill said. "It may be more painful, but it would at least shut up the brain."

Cunningham nodded. "Your Hellfire creation brilliantly plays on many fears. The new recruits will have experienced all of that and passed your test, yes? So what will you to do them once they are here?"

"Since they will have faced many of their fears already," Daniel said, "the next step is to make them feel pain."

"Pain is as much a part of horror as is fear," Cunningham said. "The passive reader or movie-goer experiences fear, yes. But they don't experience pain. Is pain a necessary experience?"

The students were quiet, and Daniel noticed the discomfort on Wes's face.

"But we can't inflict real pain on people," Wes said. "That wouldn't be right."

Cunningham's eyebrows came together as he examined Wes. "No, but what can we do?"

"We can trick their brains and senses into thinking they are experiencing pain," Daniel said.

"Wouldn't that be a test in genuine terror?" Cunningham laughed. "Now how do you propose we do such a thing?"

Daniel was surprised when Bill spoke up next. "I have a perfect idea," Bill said.

Daniel smiled.

# Part II: Hellfire

"Would you mind getting inside the oven to clean it?"
- Grandma from *The Visit*


"The only thing that keeps you from being a monster is killing."
- Carol from *The Walking Dead*


"He's trying to force you to like more normal things, and you shouldn't like things because people tell you you're supposed to, okay?"
- Jonathan Byers from *Stranger Things*

# Chapter Thirteen

The man watched all the stories on the news. Hellfire haunts had been built throughout the country. He studied everyone and everything, recorded news stories on his DVR, and bookmarked hundreds of YouTube videos about Hellfire. He didn't want to miss a single detail.

"We're standing outside of Hellfire," a reporter stated. "The infamous Rabbit in Red horror studios have created a national haunted house competition. I'm here reporting live in front of the New Orleans location, but there are ten other models throughout the country. This week, horror enthusiasts have been invited to a special challenge. On the frightfest4D.com website, the same one used last year to announce the first Rabbit in Red challenge, participants have been invited to test the their abilities to overcome fear."

The reporter turned to one of the contestants. "This is Carol Fisher, an eighteen year old girl from Alabama who made the long drive down to experience Hellfire. Tell us about yourself and why you want to do this, Carol."

The girl tossed her long blonde hair and looked into the camera. "I've been obsessed with JB since I learned about last year's contest. I've read everything he's written. I know the kind of people he wants to work with, and I'm that person. I'm going to walk through Hellfire with my head high and await my ticket to Rabbit in Red."

In addition to her long blonde hair, Carol also had an athletically tight body, like that of a runner or kickboxer. She also had a large chest, perfect for a horror film.

"What draws you to horror?" the reporter asked.

"Let's say you're driving down the road," Carol said. "On one side is a young couple, happily in love. Further ahead, one of the funniest comedians in the world is telling some jokes. On the other side, a couple is breaking up. And up ahead from them is a dead body of a person brutally slaughtered. Which are you going to pay attention to?"

"That's rather morbid," the reporter said.

"Life is morbid." The girl shrugged gracefully. "Comedy, romance, drama, all of that is nice. But horror—horror is the train wreck that captures our attention no matter what else is happening in our lives. I want to be a part of that."

*And I have a feeling you will,* the man thought as he watched Carol's interview.

The reporter faced her camera. "Well, folks, JB and Rabbit in Red have given us permission to record a few of the scenarios. Stay tuned, and we'll show you what Carol experiences first hand. Let's go to our affiliate in St. Louis to see what's happening at the Hellfire location there."

"Yes, here outside the beautiful Midwestern city of St. Louis, the gateway to the west, is another opportunity to experience Hellfire," a new reporter stated. "The great master of horror, Jay Bell of Rabbit in Red studios, has opened the door to his infamous horror lair, but only for those who pass the Hellfire test. Looking out at the long line, I see mostly older teenagers and young adults. Whoever wins will be given a golden ticket to attend a weekend at JB's Horror College. I'm standing with Brandis Dern, another Rabbiteer hopeful. What draws you to this contest, Brandis?"

Brandis had short, dark hair and a lean, muscular body. He stood with confidence, but the smile on his face made him look like a young boy.

"You saw some of the games last year. That was amazing. And those contestants are now learning at Rabbit in Red. Man, who would want to go to a traditional college when you could be learning horror directly from the master?"

There was something about this kid's eyes that the man noticed. Something dark. Something that reminded him of himself. He rewound the news broadcast and watched it again. *I'm gonna have to keep an eye on this one,* he thought.

"Speaking of the master," the reporter said, "JB has been awfully quiet as to how winners will be determined. What do you think you will have to do to win a ticket to Rabbit in Red?"

"Well, sir, I don't want to say my thoughts on that publicly as it may help someone else out and I want to win. But I will say this: if you've read JB's many thoughts on horror, you know what he wants. If you haven't read that stuff, you don't deserve to be here anyway."

"Good luck to you, Brandis." The camera shifted away from the young man and zoomed in on the reporter. "Our cameras will be following along in the rooms JB has granted us permission to film in. Speaking of JB, he is still surrounded by trouble. His first official year of turning Rabbit in Red into a college of horror has been rocked by controversy. Back to the station for a full update."

On the TV screens across the nation, the Rabbit in Red logo appeared: an innocent bunny trapped in a bloody red box protecting an axe.

A news anchor spoke. "The elusive Jay Bell—so private in fact that we don't even have public photos of the horror master— has been working with a group of college students to study and create horror. The students worked together with JB's team to design Hellfire, but they aren't just living in a fictional world of terror. Literal horror has found them over the last several months. Stay tuned for a full report as we tell you about the abduction of a little girl, the near heart attack of a parent, and the murder of a would-be professor—all connected to Rabbit in Red."

Yes, the man had watched all of these news stories and more. Now, it was his turn. Dressed in all black, he traveled and now waited in line along with everyone else at a Hellfire location outside of Las Vegas. It was still warm out, but he wore black dress pants with a black button up shirt. He adjusted his face. He knew the best costume and makeup shops in Hollywood, and he also knew he might find himself on TV. If nothing else, he was certain JB would see him as he walked through Hellfire. Part of him wanted JB to see. He wanted to look into a camera at the end of Hellfire and stick up two middle fingers. But no, now was not the time.

He needed to beat Hellfire and earn a ticket to Rabbit in Red.

They were calm now, he knew, back at the studios, but only because he let them be calm. They hadn't taken his warning seriously after he had burned Tara Stein. They kept on going at Rabbit in Red. He had thought he had gotten lucky when one of the parents suffered that attack, but unfortunately the damn fool survived. If he had died, perhaps they would have shut down Rabbit in Red. Then JB would be alone, with no one to mentor and nothing to create. He'd be at his most vulnerable then, and that was exactly how the man had wanted him.

JB might have thought he was pursuing the man, but it was really the other way around. *I have been chasing you*, he thought. He knew who JB had hired to teach the students. Emma Williams was a brilliant woman, perhaps the smartest of the four teachers JB had hired, and that was why the man had chosen her.

He had watched as JB left her northern California home, just outside of San Francisco. When JB got into the back seat of one of his fancy automobiles, and when the driver pulled away, the man had knocked on Emma's door.

"Did you forget something, Jay?" Emma said as she opened the door. When she saw it wasn't JB, her expression changed. "Who are you?"

He marched forward into Emma's home. He didn't touch her or anything in her house. He simply stared into her eyes, a dark, deeply evil stare. She backed up, but the man knew where he wanted her. He had done his homework of course and studied the layout of the home. He walked toward her in a way that would make her back up to the kitchen of her home, where a long staircase to the basement connected.

"What do you want?" Emma yelled as she walked backward. She wasn't thinking. She was falling perfectly into his trap.

"Wait!" she cried. "Wait! I know you. How could you do this?"

She was at the edge of the stairs. The man still hadn't touched her. He had mastered the power of his mind and the power of his eyes. They were truly powerful components if one only learned how to use them to their fullest potential.

"Only through a fiery death can they be purged." He jumped at her then, still not touching her, and she lunged backward. Of course, that was exactly what he wanted. She threw herself down the basement stairs, a long, winding fall. He walked down the steps slowly, a wide smile on his face.

Her head was turned in such a way that was only natural to an owl. She wouldn't be getting up today or ever again.

"One down," the man had said.

JB and his team hadn't reacted the way the man wanted them to react to his threats. So the man had decided he had to step up his game. If one death didn't make JB listen, then there'd have to be more.

Many more.

The man had resolved to make them all pay. If they were dumb enough to sleep in the center of horror, if they were dumb enough to keep going after someone had been murdered, then they deserved what was going to come their way.

And it would start soon, oh so soon, but first, he had to complete Hellfire. *You want someone who can control their fear, right, JB? I know that's what you're looking for. So that's exactly who you will get.*

The man dressed in all black stepped into Hellfire and laughed at their creations. They didn't know what real horror was, but he'd show them soon enough.

# Chapter Fourteen

Bill watched as the new recruits entered the commons. The looks on their faces took him back to exactly how he had felt last year. He had gotten to see *The Shining*, *Halloween II*, *It*, *Carrie*, and *Psycho* settings and more. But best of all, as he walked through those, he had gotten to see Jaime for the first time.

The new recruits now walked through *Hellraiser*, *A Nightmare on Elm Street*, and *Candyman* settings, among others, and Bill wondered if any of them had someone just as special waiting to meet them for the first time.

He certainly had noticed that JB spared no expense celebrating the arrival of new recruits. It was the week before Halloween. As promised, one contestant from each of the Hellfire locations was invited to join Rabbit in Red for an entire week's worth of festivities this year. Unlike last year's contest, JB wanted to give new recruits a complete taste of what a horror college would be like. So they followed first years to classes, participated in discussions with the professors, looked at some of the projects they were working on, and of course eagerly anticipated the follow up to Hellfire, a special contest designed just for them. Like the parents, they were able to play in the game chambers and re-enact the simulations from last year's event as well, and the new recruits were eating it all up.

Eleven new recruits in total joined Rabbit in Red for Halloween week. They joined with select individuals or pairs of first years to mentor and guide them throughout the week. The first years greeted them upon arrival, gave them a brief tour of the surroundings, and awaited the official welcome from JB to take place that evening.

There was something about Brandis Dern that Bill immediately didn't like. Brandis had an aggressive demeanor that contradicted his boyish grin and short, crew cut dark hair. It was the way his brown eyes widened whenever he talked to Jaime. Bill thought of offering him a towel to wipe the drool.

"I read all about Tara," Brandis told Jaime. "You've got an amazing sister. She must get it all from you." Jaime turned away from the compliment, but Bill saw her cheeks turn the color of Rose's hair, and he didn't much care for that.

Taking a step closer to Jaime, Bill said, "So what's your favorite horror movie?"

"*It Follows,*" Brandis said immediately. "It has all the nostalgia of a horror classic put in a disorienting modern setting. It's quite intelligent."

Bill grimaced at the smug way Brandis talked. He didn't like how smart the kid sounded.

"It could have been scarier," Bill said, reaching down to pet Falcor, the pup who followed loyally by his side.

"I thought the suspense and intrigue were refreshing. Too many films rely solely on blunt in-your-face scare tactics," Brandis replied matter-of-factly.

*You could use a good fist in your face,* Bill thought. Then he slipped an arm around Jaime, but she inched away from him. He didn't like that at all either. He hadn't been as close to Jaime as he would have liked from day one this year. But it wasn't his fault, was it? Whenever he talked with her, there was something different. She had an anger. He understood that. So he never made a move, never tried to be anything more than a friend, really. *She's got to figure out all of this other stuff first, right?*

"I agree," Jaime said. "We need movies that create haunting atmospheres, where the horror the viewer creates in her mind is more powerful than any thrill on screen."

"Exactly!" Brandis cheered. "My thoughts exactly." He smiled at Jaime, and Bill felt sick to his stomach. *If I puke, please let me puke right in his face.*

"What about you? What's your favorite movie?" Bill asked Carol Fisher, who was paired up with Jaime and Rose. He desperately wanted to put the focus on someone else.

"Anything by JB," she grinned. "He's a genius. I could never pick just one." Carol wore a tight white tank. Bill's eyes dropped to her chest. Carol reminded him a bit of Annie, but she had a tight body to go with those large . . .

Just as he was thinking about that, Jaime moved closer to Bill. Their sides touched. It was as if Jaime knew where his eyes went and suddenly got jealous.

*Well, isn't that interesting?*

Wes worked with a boy named Ricky Thomas. Ricky appeared to be half white, half Latino with the slightest of accents. His dark hair was short and buzzed, but something about it was odd, like it didn't quite match his face. He looked like he tried to grow a goatee, but the hairs were fine and nearly invisible. For just a second, Bill thought Ricky was wearing makeup, but he didn't want to say so. The poor guy, apparently, had other problems. Ricky had received a room with a private bathroom, and he often had to leave and use it. Quite a lot, actually. He had told Wes it some kind of digestive disease, and he shit all the time. Bill didn't need to know any more.

"What about you?" Wes asked him.

"I like *It Follows* too, I guess." Ricky shrugged. "I get why Brandis likes it. It's artistic. But I get why Bill thinks it could be scarier. It's not exactly the kind of movie that gives you good jump scares, not like Hellfire."

"So, you have a favorite?" Wes pressed again.

Ricky shrugged. "It's hard to pick just one." Ricky looked like he wanted desperately to fit in, to the point where he was cautious about forming too much of an opinion on anything. Wes simply nodded.

*That's a good pairing,* Bill thought. *Wes can help him gain confidence. Anyone who has to run to the bathroom as much as that is bound to have some self-esteem issues.*

They walked from a classroom to the commons and tried to get to know all of the recruits. Daniel and Leroy were assigned a guy named Jimmy Cyphers.

Bill watched Jimmy interact with Daniel and Leroy. Jimmy was thin with brown hair and wore tight fitting clothes, much like Daniel. Then Bill saw something very interesting, and he couldn't help but smile. Daniel bent over to pick something up, and Jimmy's eyes went straight to Daniel's ass. And they stayed there. Jimmy smiled.

Rose must have noticed, too. "Keep an eye on that," Rose told Bill. "Daniel can be cruel. Jimmy ought to be able to be himself, you know?"

Bill nodded. Could it be karma? Daniel always seemed like the kind of jerk who'd also be a homophobic asshole. Bill hoped it wasn't the case, but he agreed with Rose that it was something to definitely keep an eye on.

Bill, Jaime, Rose, and Wes all took a seat at their usual table, waiting for the assistants to appear. The lights in the *Candyman* commons went off, and the theme song from *American Horror Story* played loudly in surround sound. The assistants appeared in the corners of the room, a soft spotlight on each of them. They had reprised their roles from last year for Halloween week. Chester Malcolm sported the Captain Spaulding clown outfit, Michael Quinn walked out as little Sam with a pumpkin mask, Thomas Lance appeared as Pumpkinhead, which ironically didn't have a pumpkin for a head at all and more closely resembled the creature from the Black Lagoon, and lastly Donnie Chase walked out with the long, endlessly wet, dark hair as Samara from *The Ring*. The first years cheered and applauded. It was like watching the opening credits of *Halloween* or *The Shining*. The way those classics opened would always make Bill smile.

Their spotlights dimmed, and a powerful light illuminated the front of the commons near the big screen. The music shifted to that of a great rumbling like an earthquake. A hole in the ground formed, and from the bottom, a small elevator lifted JB. He didn't wear a Freddy costume this year. Perhaps he had heard some of the first year jokes about his appearance, and now JB had decided to fully own it. He was dressed as Frankenstein's monster. Falcor cowered close to Bill as the crowd screamed with excitement.

"Greetings, friends!" JB shouted. "Welcome to Rabbit in Red's second annual Halloween celebration!"

After another round of applause, he continued. "I am pleased to have eleven new recruits, all very talented in unique ways. You are our Hellfire survivors, and you will be rewarded with a week of challenges. For those who survive this week, you will be invited to join our team as full-time horror students!"

"This is so cool," Brandis said to Jaime as he moved closer to her at the table. Falcor growled lightly, and Bill rolled his eyes.

"Good pup," Bill whispered and petted the dog on the head.

"Our first years have designed the next round of challenges for you," JB said. "This year, new contestants will work in teams to complete a variety of tasks." The screen behind him lit up, and the Rabbit in Red logo danced. He pointed to the screen as it previewed a portion of the new contest. "Our on-location Hellfire has been remodeled with all new challenges. You will complete it with partners or small groups this time instead of individually. The theme of our week, as is no surprise to you, is fire. It will be a more *intense* experience. To complete each new section of Hellfire, you will need to think quite quickly. The longer you take, the more pain you will *feel*!"

He chuckled in that manically sadistic manner and the first years laughed with him. The new recruits however did not cheer this time.

"Pain?" Carol asked Jaime.

"You'll see." Jaime smiled.

"I see by your expressions that you are concerned. I ask you this: Isn't the fear you felt a form of pain? I can promise you something. You will not be physically harmed, not really. But here's the twist, which you must agree to if you wish to continue and to have a chance at joining us: during these challenges, you will in fact think and feel as if you are being physically harmed. There are so many things we look for in a team. One of those things we are focusing on this year is your ability to understand and overcome pain. Those experiences will help you create the best horror!"

"I don't understand," Carol told Jaime. "What does he mean?"

"I can only tell you what JB already said," Jaime said. "It's not real but it will feel real."

"How is that possible?" Ricky, who had sat close to Jaime, asked.

"Anything is possible here," Wes told him.

They looked back up at JB on stage. The Rabbit in Red logo changed. The rabbit was now trapped in its bloody red box as flames engulfed it. It screamed, and the new recruits jumped back.

"Now, I thought you were all here because you had control of your fear." JB laughed. "You may not have known it at the time, but one thing we measured during your initial run through of Hellfire was your level of fear. You proved yourselves to be the best of the best at managing and controlling your fears. So now we raise the stakes—both in what you will have to do and in what it will earn you if you succeed. So let me ask you: ARE YOU READY TO *BURN* THE RABBIT?"

# Chapter Fifteen

Jaime watched the new recruits discuss their strategies and ideas, and she smiled.

"This is about survival," Brandis told Ricky, his partner, as they stood outside of the remodeled Hellfire. The first years walked them to the entrance to wish them luck before turning around to watch their performances on the big screen in the commons. Brandis faced Jaime. "How about a kiss for good luck, gorgeous?"

Jaime laughed, mainly because she saw Bill's fingers curl into a fist.

"Classy," Jaime replied. "How about I just tell you good luck." She saw Bill's hands soften, but he rolled his eyes. *I know what you're thinking, Bill. HashtagDoag2.0. But I wouldn't be too sure about that.* She did find Brandis attractive, even if he was a little cocky. Maybe it was the cockiness she liked.

Ricky stepped closer to Jaime. "Hey, what about me? If you want to drive either one of them jealous, I'll take a kiss." His eyes told Jaime he was completely serious. Then he smiled, and she couldn't help but flinch a little. His teeth were stained yellow, and she wondered if he smoked. Maybe that was why he actually took so many bathroom breaks. "Maybe another time," he said and winked at her. She took a step closer to Bill.

"Any final words of wisdom?" Carol asked Rose.

"Mind over matter. The mind can create any kind of reality. That's what we're counting on, too." Rose giggled softly. "But tell yourself it's not real. It helps. Kinda."

Daniel's mentee, Jimmy, stood in a group of three. He was paired with a girl named Diane Willow and a guy named Kent Callahan. Diane was a larger girl with thick, curly, dark hair, and Kent's hair sported a series of tight cornrows. It was cool to see so many different people together to celebrate a passion for horror, but something felt off. Like one of them didn't belong. Jimmy appeared effeminate at times, and she wondered how honest he would be. Kent looked overdressed, like he was trying too hard to look a certain way. She didn't understand that either. Who were these guys? Who were they really?

Jimmy held out his fist to Diane and Kent. "You ready, guys?"

Diane tapped it back. "Ready." Kent looked at the two of them as if they were aliens and shook his head.

"You guys just better not slow me down," he said. "My choice next year is this or nothing. I ain't got the grades for college. I need this."

"This should be a very interesting event," Wes said.

"Oh-right, everyone. Good luck." Bill extended his arms in a wide gesture. He looked a bit like JB, speaking to the entire room this way. "We'll be watching from the commons and cheering you on. See you on the other side! Consider this your hazing."

Bill reached for Jaime's hand, but she subtly folded her arms across her chest. Wes and Rose, who had no problems holding hands, led the way out.

"Hey," Daniel said to Jaime from behind, taking her out of her thoughts. Daniel hadn't spoken much to anyone. She still didn't completely trust him. At first, his quiet was comforting, but the longer he was quiet, the more she suspected that he may be up to something.

Jaime looked at Daniel with curiosity. "Hey back."

"So how are your mentees?" Daniel asked.

She hesitated, and Bill jumped in and answered. "Brandis is kind of an ass, if I'm being honest."

"He's not an ass," Jaime snapped. "He's just . . . confident."

Bill rolled his eyes. "More like arrogant. Reminds me of you," he told Daniel.

"I'll trade you mentees," Daniel said, ignoring the insult. "I think . . . I think my guy has a crush on me. Have you guys noticed anything?"

Rose laughed and turned around. "I thought you'd be flattered."

"Well," Daniel smirked "don't get me wrong. You can't blame the guy. But I don't swing that way."

"Are you sure?" Jaime asked.

"Hey!" Fire flickered in Daniel's eyes for a second.

Jaime just laughed. "*Anyway*, other than that, how is Jimmy?"

Daniel eased up. "He's smart. I think he'll get through our riddles pretty easily actually. He seems to have that kind of mind. When his mind isn't in the gutter, that is."

Jaime almost laughed again, and then caught herself. Was that the first time Daniel had said something to make them smile? It was a strange feeling.

"Um, listen you guys," Daniel continued. "There's something else I've been wanting to say." Wes and Rose put on the brakes, and everyone stopped to look at Daniel. "Is it just me or is there a little something off, something different about JB this year?"

"What do you mean?" Jaime asked. She thought for a moment. Was JB different? Well, of course he was different. Everything was different this year. *We didn't get to start with a celebration. We started with a manhunt for my sister, and it's not exactly been downhill since then.*

"One day he's here. One day he's not. And even when he is here, he doesn't seem to be . . . all here, you know?"

"He has reason to be distracted," Jaime defended. "Have you forgotten there is still someone out there trying to sabotage him and scare us away?" She surprised even herself with the anger in her voice. Should she even be defending JB?

"I know that, of course," Daniel said. "It's more than that though. Just look in his eyes when he's talking, okay? There's something else going on."

Jaime squinted at Daniel, trying to figure out his meaning and his intentions.

"And, I also wanted to say," Daniel continued, "something I should have said a long time ago. I appreciate you guys inviting me back. If I were in your place, I probably wouldn't have invited you back."

"Thanks for the honesty," Wes said facetiously.

"Yeah, well . . . I'm just saying . . . but seriously, keep an eye on JB. Something doesn't feel right to me." Daniel walked ahead of them. The four stayed behind for a second and exchanged puzzled looks.

"That was odd," Rose whispered.

"That's Daniel," Jaime stated, but she wondered if Daniel wasn't on to something here. JB had plenty of reason to act stranger than normal, but could Daniel be right? Could they all have been blinded to a mystery simply because of all of the tragedy surrounding Rabbit in Red this year?

*****

Back in the commons, they watched as Brandis and Ricky entered the first Burn the Rabbit challenge. The first years had designed this project together, and with the support of JB's highly advanced technical team, they had made some special modifications to the Rabbit's Eye. It still read heart rates and enhanced the surroundings to have full 4D special effects, but they did something that earned JB's praise.

Perhaps they had all been living in this alternate, questionably ethical horror reality for too long, Jaime thought. If the public—or the new recruits' parents—knew what they were doing, certainly even more people would try to shut down Rabbit in Red. But the new recruits were legal adults, had signed their contracts, and had of course skipped the fine print at the bottom of the release of liability forms.

Jaime thought it was all quite clever.

The Rabbit's Eye had been re-programmed to send electrical impulses to the heart and the brain. Previously, they'd only seen the 4D effects. Maybe they'd feel the effects if the floor moved or if the temperature suddenly increased, which of course were effects JB already used. But with the enhanced Rabbit's Eye, the electric impulses would trick the brain and the body into feeling actual pain. They weren't getting hurt physically, not exactly. It was a trick, like mental magic, a perception of pain that would feel real but wasn't. Their brains would perceive the pain through electric impulses, and the human brain could trick itself into feeling anything. That was the magic behind the new challenge this year.

They joked that this was technology JB could sell to the highest bidder in the government. It would allow, among other things, for people to be tortured without actually being tortured. The moment the device was removed, they could look around and see that all of their limbs were intact. With the device on however, they could make the person think that anything was happening. JB's team would monitor heart rates, and they had agreed that if the heart rate reached unsafe levels, they'd stop the program. But that would mean the contestant would lose the game. After all, these new recruits had demonstrated out of thousands nation-wide that they were able to control their fear the best. They went through Hellfire with the lowest heart rates as monitored by the Rabbit's Eye. They possessed a unique, nearly frightening ability to control fear.

In other words, it was only natural that the first years spent the first part of their studies determining how they could scare the shit out people who didn't scare easily.

The answer was pain. And when Jaime thought about it, it made her smile.

*****

Brandis and Ricky entered the first room. The Rabbit's Eye was strapped to their chest and faces. The room was completely dark. Gradually, the rabbit appeared in the middle. Large, white, and grinning with sharp pointed teeth, the rabbit cackled. An axe illuminated in the corner and shot straight at the rabbit, cutting off its paws. The rabbit screamed, and then the room started to rain down fire. It looked like large snowflakes, but they were flames instead. When they hit the rabbit, it screamed.

Looking over their heads, Ricky and Brandis saw the fiery flakes slowly come toward them. Ricky reached out his hand to catch one. When it touched his palm, he yelped.

"Oww! What the hell?"

Brandis looked confused, then reached out a hand too at the fiery flakes. "That hurts!" He brought his hand back quickly. "I can't believe this actually works."

The fiery flakes fell slowly. Brandis and Ricky still didn't seem to completely understand what was happening, but as each flake hit their body—their head, a shoulder, their back—a burning pain would shoot through their body. It literally felt like they had been burned.

"Don't touch them!" Brandis shouted. "We have to avoid all the flakes."

The rabbit spoke. "If the rabbit burns, you burn. Solve the mystery before you turn to ash. You must find and give me the correct film. Are you ready for your riddle?"

"Yes!" they both shouted, dodging more flames.

"Burn the rabbit. Burn the rabbit in red. She sat on a hospital bed. She knew what she was. She told the orderly to open the blinds. That way she could truly be dead."

The room shifted into a video store. The flames continued shooting down from above.

"Okay," Ricky said. "It's a riddle for a movie. We have to find it here and give it to the rabbit. Oh, shit. Look!"

It was hard to see at first, but the flakes were dropping more quickly. "Oh, man. I bet it's programmed to pick up speed the longer we take," Brandis said. "Okay, any ideas?"

"Damn!" Ricky shouted as a couple of flames landed on his arm. "Why does it hurt so bad?"

"I don't know," Brandis said. "Just think! It's gotta be a vampire story, right? What else dies when you open blinds? It died from the sunlight, yeah?"

"Makes sense to me. But there are so many vampire stories. Woman on a bed. Orderly. Must be a hospital. She knew what she was. Owww!" Ricky was hit by more flames. "Jesus. Okay, umm, whoever it was didn't want to be a vampire. I dunno. I can't think with these damn flames!"

"Fuck!" Brandis shouted. He leaned over, searching the rows and rows of movies. The flames were dropping quickly now. If he stood still, he'd get hit immediately. They skipped around the room, trying to dodge the flames. "This is nuts!"

"How are the movies even arranged? Genre or alphabetically?"

"Looks like alphabetically. No separation of genres. Any ideas?" Brandis swirled to the side to avoid the increasingly quick fire drops.

"Start throwing any vampire movie you can think of at the damn rabbit and see what happens!" Ricky threw *Blade* and the *Buffy the Vampire Slayer* at the rabbit, but nothing happened. Brandis picked up *Salem's Lot, Shadow of the Vampire,* and then *Underworld.* Still nothing happened. Ricky grabbed *Dracula* and ran toward *Interview with the Vampire,* tossing both at the rabbit. The flames dropped more quickly. It was now impossible to even dodge them.

"Jesus, man, I can't take this!" Ricky shouted as he was hit with flame after flame.

"Don't give up! Keep looking! Wait. Here! I know what it is," Brandis said. He picked up *Let the Right One In,* a Swedish film that had an American remake called *Let Me In.* He tossed it at the rabbit, who was more than half engulfed in flames. When the video hit the rabbit, the flames vanished and the fiery flakes stopped falling.

"Congratulations, you were successful," the rabbit announced. "You may move into the next room."

Brandis and Ricky examined themselves closely and then each other. "I feel okay now," Ricky said. "Can you see anything?"

"No. What about me?"

"Nothing, man. Weird."

"I feel okay now too, but that hurt! How many more of these do we have to go through?"

"A lot." Ricky sighed. They moved into the next room to await instructions. And more pain.

*****

Carol Fisher entered the second room with her partner, Julie Clarke. After the first room, Carol was happy to be paired with Julie. She was incredibly well-read and understood the *Let the Right One In* riddle immediately. She hadn't seen the movie, but fortunately it was based on a book.

Julie looked either half-Asian or maybe Native American. She had long dark hair and a pale face, but always wore a smile full of energy. That was until she started to feel as if she had been burned.

In the second room, Julie grabbed Carol's hand. Carol's blond hair was tied tightly back into a ponytail, and she looked ready to fight. She stood with her chest out and chin high, ready for the next challenge.

The rabbit appeared in the middle of the room once again. "If the rabbit burns, you burn. Solve the mystery before you turn to ash. You must destroy the enemy before it destroys you. Are you ready for your riddle?"

They nodded, but even if they had said no, they were certain the rabbit would continue regardless. "Who goes there? If it reaches you, it will consume you. Find the tool to test me, then destroy me or forever despair."

They looked up at the ceiling expecting more fiery flakes to fall, but this time they felt the flames from below. Gradually, the floor was catching on fire. Small flickers of fire greeted them, but they knew these would soon intensify.

"Who goes there? That's the first clue," Julie said. "That's the name of a book that this popular movie was based on."

"Just tell me!" Carol shouted. "What are we looking for?"

"I don't quite remember. This is about John Carpenter's *The Thing*. I know that much."

"Yeah!" Carol said. "The thing is like a monster that can assimilate other people, right? In the movie, a crew discovers it somewhere in the Antarctic or something. Then one of the guys finds a way to test to see if the people are real or if the Thing has *consumed* them. How did he do it, though?"

"Look around," Julie said. "And of course be careful of the fire."

Flames rose up to the rabbit's knees, and the bursts of fire around the room were the size of campfires.

"Oww!" Carol yelled as one suddenly popped up under her feet.

"Needles in haystacks! Look at all this junk!" Julie yelled. The first years had programmed the room to include lots of red herring items, things designed to throw the contestants off track. That plus the fear of fire and sporadic pain they felt when it hit them created quite the challenge.

"I see knives, guns, bats, rope. Anything ring a bell?" Carol jumped over a couple of fires on the floor.

"He tests their blood! I remember now. But how?"

"Yes! Choosing *The Thing* isn't just random. Think about it! In the first game's reference, it was fire that killed a vampire. In this, it wasn't exactly fire but it was *hot*!"

"That's right!" Julie cheered. "It was heated wire. Copper wire, I think. When the wire is put into the blood, the blood flees from whoever the Thing possessed. Do you see any wire?"

"Over there," Carol said and pointed. There was a batch of copper wire, and it was heated all right. It was in the middle of a fire that stood up to their waist.

"Grab it!" Julie commanded.

"You grab it!" Carol snapped back.

"Fine, you wimp!" Julie reached in and her face twisted. She looked like she had just grabbed a hot pan without an oven mitt. She pulled her arm out and cried. "I can't!"

More fires burst up through the floor. The rabbit was consumed up to its chest. "We don't have much time," Carol said. "If the rabbit burns, we lose, right?"

Julie nodded, but held onto her arm and grimaced. "You have to try, too."

Carol approached slowly. The fire grew larger.

"It's only gonna get higher," Julie warned.

Carol opened her mouth and screamed before even touching the flames. She thrust her hand in, grabbed the wire, rushed to the rabbit, and tossed it.

The flames vanished and the room cooled. "Congratulations, you were successful," the rabbit announced.

"This is crazy," Julie said.

"No. Not crazy. Genius. We're learning how to understand pain," Carol told her. She smiled wide. "JB is brilliant. We get to experience pain!"

# Chapter Sixteen

Jaime focused her attention back on the contestants.

The big screen in the commons rotated out among the pairs or small groups of new recruits. First years now watched as Jimmy Cyphers, Kent Callahan, and Diane Willow tried to complete a section. Jimmy stood in the center of the three, and he nearly hopped in place, obviously excited. He wore a bright blue button-up shirt and tie, which looked a little out of place for this event. On his left stood Kent, the look on his face as tight as the cornrows in his hair. On the other side, Diane's dark curly hair dripped in sweat. All of their faces held panic and confusion. Studying each of them, Jaime still thought something was off about this group of new recruits.

The rabbit reappeared in the center of this room, its paws already on fire. The challenges were getting harder and they had less and less time to complete them.

"If the rabbit burns, you burn. Solve the mystery before you turn to ash. You must find and give me a model. Are you ready for your riddle?"

The rabbit paused for a second, not giving them any option to decline. "What a perfect setting for a fire, but watch the floor. All the melting makes the fire even harder to ignore. Find the image that connects this scene to the remake of our Camp Crystal Lake killing machine."

After the rabbit spoke the riddle, the floor around them immediately sank. "I feel like I'm sinking," Jimmy yelled. "How is that possible?"

"It's hard to move," Diane said. "Like we're stuck!"

"Shit, the room is already completely on fire!" Jimmy cried.

"Keep your eyes on the prize," Kent shouted with authority. "Do you know what you're looking for?"

"I wasn't sure at first," Diane said, "but we're definitely in *House of Wax*. This room is melting quicker than any candle I've ever seen."

All around them, the walls, the ceiling, and even the floor, dripped gooey wax. It was hot too, like the flames from previous scenes, and when they touched the wax, Jaime knew they would feel the pain all throughout their bodies. She leaned back in her chair and watched.

"So what connects *House of Wax* to the remake of *Friday the 13th*?" Kent asked.

"Oh, that's easy you guys!" Jimmy said. "Ouch! Dammit, this wax is hot! You have to find a model of the one dude! Remember in the movie that they made wax models over real people? There was one actor that was in both movies! Shit, better look fast. All the models are melting!"

A series of mannequins surrounded them, but Jimmy was right. Several had already lost limbs, and a few faces had caught on fire. If they didn't find the right one quickly, they would surely lose this particular section.

"I don't remember who the guy is!" Kent shouted.

"He is also the guy in *Supernatural* and *Gilmore Girls*!" Jimmy said. "Like, what hasn't he been in? C'mon!"

"I haven't seen any of those!" Kent yelled back.

"Jared Padalecki is his name. I've seen them, Jimmy. Love *Supernatural*." Diane forced a brief smile at him before getting attacked by dripping wax. They glanced back at the rabbit, which acted as a timer of sorts. If the fire reached its head, they were all in trouble. It was only waist high at the moment.

"I don't know what he looks like!" Kent growled. "You two better look fast!"

"Yeah, yeah," Diane said. "He's got long dark hair. Quick!"

They ran around the melting room as fast as they could, which was really like an uncoordinated march. Watching on the big screen in the commons, Jaime knew exactly what they must be thinking. They didn't understand how the technology here could change the way they physically moved or how everything worked so perfectly together, but this was the most technology advanced system in the world. Of course, she was sure they didn't understand how they felt like they were actually on fire at time either, but she couldn't help but smile a little when they screamed.

Tossing around models and mannequins, they struggled to find the one that matched the character Padalecki played.

"What if it already burned? Shit!" Jimmy spun around the room. He turned so fast, Jaime got dizzy watching.

Giant globs of wax fell, creating splashes as if boulders were crashing down into water. The wax splattered the room like it had been shot out of a cannon, and the three recruits shrieked. Each time even a bit of wax hit them, it burned. It was more than a little glob of wax now. Wax-sized basketballs attacked them. Diane fell over after one smacked her in the head.

"Jesus, this is too much!" she cried. "Guys, we're losing."

"We cannot lose!" Kent roared. "Find the goddamn model!"

"They're all melting," Jimmy whined. "What do we do?"

They looked back at the rabbit. The fire was at its neck, and in the blink of an eye, it engulfed the rabbit's entire head. The rabbit screamed louder than it had all night, and then the ceiling of the room crashed down upon all the three. It was pure, fiery wax.

"Sorry, you have failed," a voice called.

The lights went on. Jimmy released a long sigh. "The pain. Wow! Just like that, it went away." He took off his Rabbit's Eye.

Kent followed suit, and then they both screamed. The simulation was over, or so they thought. But Diane stood right in front of them. They looked at her without any special effects distorting their vision. And what they saw was worse than any special effect they could imagine. Because this was real.

Diane Willow was completely on fire, and her wails were even louder than the rabbit's.

Still watching on the big screen in the commons, the first years all jumped on their feet. Jimmy pushed Diane on the floor, and she started to roll around. A sprinkler system went off and soaked all three of them. Jimmy and Kent stared at a now motionless Diane on the floor.

Then the heart-pounding electric music blasted throughout Rabbit in Red. It was the music they had heard early last summer, the alarm that was to warn them of danger. The rabbit appeared in the commons in front of the first years.

A deep voice announced throughout the studio, "Follow the rabbit." It hopped back toward their *Alien* rooms. Several of them covered their ears at the deafening music, but they followed the rabbit.

"Shouldn't we get the recruits?" Jaime yelled.

"Yeah!" Bill tried to shout back. He grabbed Venus and Leroy. "You guys lead everyone into the safe room. We're gonna get the recruits and make sure they know where to go!"

Venus and Leroy nodded. The first years followed except for Rose, Wes, Jaime, and Bill who ran in the opposite direction to help the recruits. Daniel stood for a moment in between the two groups. Jaime saw hesitation on his face, but then he turned and followed the others to the safe room.

The four first year leaders sprinted past the individual game chambers. They crashed into the new recruits in the middle of the old funhouse. Brandis was leading them out.

"Where are Kent, Jimmy, and Diane?" Jaime asked.

"Still inside," Brandis huffed. "We didn't know what to do. This music is so loud. We're just following that rabbit!" Off to the side, another image of the rabbit appeared, waving the new recruits forward.

"It will lead you to a safe room," Bill said. "Go! We'll get the others and be right behind."

"What's happening?" Carol asked.

"We don't know," Bill said. "Just hurry!"

Brandis, Carol, and the other recruits followed the rabbit, and the first year leaders marched ahead. As they approached the redesigned Hellfire, Kent and Jimmy walked out, and Kent had carried Diane in his arms, one arm around her upper back and the other supporting her legs.

"Oh, God! Is she okay?" Rose asked.

"She's passed out," Jimmy said. "That was a real fire. Look at her. She's got burns all over her body!"

"Jesus!" Wes cried. "Where's JB? Where are the assistants? We need to get her help!"

"We haven't seen anyone," Kent said.

"Let's get them to the safe room," Bill said. "Then we get her an ambulance and find out what's going on!"

They ran back to the first year sleeping quarters, Kent still carrying Diane. They stared at the ladder that would lead them up.

"There's another way," Jaime said. "The way I took with JB when I first arrived last summer. Follow me."

She ran back into the commons and stood over the part of the staging area where JB rose up from the ground to greet them. "Last summer, he met me at the front of the studio. You guys were already down in the safe room. He walked over here, knelt on the floor, and activated some kind of switch."

They dropped to the floor, the music still booming, a terrifying alarm system. "What's this?" Bill said. They looked at what he had found, a small, silver square in the corner of the floor paneling adjacent to the movable platform. He pushed on it with his finger, but nothing happened. Jaime crawled toward him.

"Let me try." She pressed and held her finger on the silver square, and suddenly the floor started to move. "Quick—you guys first," she told Kent, Jimmy, and Diane.

"Jaime, how?" Bill asked. She looked at him and sighed. She had learned a few secrets from JB when she first arrived here last summer after Tara had been kidnapped. But there was no time to explain all of that now.

"I'll tell you later. Now, move!"

The movable platform could fit all three if they squeezed close together. They lowered to the floor below, and when they reached the bottom, Jaime pressed on the silver square again, which brought the platform back up.

"You guys next," she told Wes and Rose. They were lowered to the bottom, and once again Jaime pressed the button and the platform returned.

"Let's go," Jaime said.

"Oh-right." They were lowered down too, and Bill reached out for Jaime's hand. She gave it willingly. "What do you think is happening?"

"I wish I knew," she said.

All of them were now on a level directly below the commons. They took out their cell phones to use as flashlights, and Jaime led the way.

"There was another slide. Somewhere back here," she said, as they all followed. They went as fast as they could, but in the dark and with Kent and Jimmy carrying Diane, it was like a slow jog.

Then Jaime tripped. "Oww!" she cried, as she fell hard on the floor. Rose and Wes, who were right behind her, stumbled next.

"Careful," Wes said. "There's something on the floor."

They used their cell phones for flashlights to see what it was they had tripped over.

"Oh my God!" Rose cried.

"No!" Bill yelled, over the screams of the others.

They had tripped over a body.

It was Donnie Chase, JB's assistant, dressed as Samara. They shined their phone flashlights directly on her face. A pool of blood had formed around her head.

"Is this real? Is she dead?" Wes asked.

Jaime leaned over, feeling for a pulse in Donnie's wrist. There was too much blood around her neck. She listened for breathing next. She put an ear close to her mouth and watched her chest.

"It's real," she said finally. "She's dead." In that moment, everything froze and went numb. Jaime looked at Bill, Wes, and Rose. Then she looked down at Donnie's dead body.

*What is happening here? Who did this?*

She remembered what it felt like last year to be attacked by a woman with a sledgehammer, shot at by a man in leather, and chased by a dog. In each of those moments from the past, she had thought she could die. But then they had turned out to be a game, a real life simulation led by actors.

Jaime checked for a pulse again on Donnie. No, this was no trick. Donnie Chase was dead. And that meant that any of them could die and that no one was safe.

The alarms continued to sound. Jaime blinked hard. "We better get down to the safe room," she said. *That's certainly an oxymoron,* she thought. *Nothing here is safe. Not anymore, if it ever was.*

They marched ahead once again, a new dread weighing on their shoulders. Jaime looked around, trying to remember where to go. She felt along the walls, pushing and feeling for anything that might resemble a door. She felt like a walker, a zombie. Just going through motions now, she didn't know if she could think or feel any more.

"Here," she called, finding a small door knob. She pulled open a door. A slide, just like the ones from the first year sleeping rooms, awaited them.

They slid down into the safe room. When they entered, the music finally quieted. JB stood in the center, and the first years and other recruits surrounded him.

Monitor after monitor lined the walls, and everyone looked around, trying to find anything out of the ordinary.

When everyone had arrived and the music completely stopped, JB said to them, "We have an intruder. Someone sabotaged the game to hurt you. They succeeded with Diane. An ambulance is already on its way."

"JB," Jaime said, "that's not all."

"I know," he muttered. "We watched you come down on that monitor." He pointed to one behind them that recorded the level underneath the commons.

"I'm afraid that one of our own has been murdered," he said. "And I think . . ." JB looked around the room, scanning each of them. Jaime held her breath and couldn't take her eyes off of him. He knew something they didn't, she thought. He had to, right? She studied his eye contact, trying to see if he stared at any one of them longer than another.

"And I think," JB continued, "whoever did it is here with us at this very moment."

# Chapter Seventeen

Bill watched the police, fire department, and ambulance arrive moments later. JB, the assistants, and the professors spoke to the first responders. Chester Malcolm went with the paramedics as they took Diane to the emergency room to be able to keep an eye on her and report back directly to JB.

After several long minutes, JB spoke to the first years and new recruits. "We will be conducting a full investigation and working with local authorities to find the person or persons responsible for today's tragedies. You will be quarantined to your rooms until we've interviewed each of you. Once that is done, you may make the decision to return to your homes if you wish."

JB's eyes were swollen and his shoulders slumped. He looked . . . defeated, Bill decided, which was no surprise considering he had promised them that they'd be safe on the inside. For now, they all remained in this safe room while police did a thorough search of Rabbit in Red. JB watched on the monitors. Even he was asked to stay put. Everyone was a suspect.

Bill, Wes, Jaime and Rose moved quietly into a corner of the safe room where they could talk. Bill didn't know what to say. Wes was the first to speak up. "What are we going to do?"

"Is it possible this could be a game within a game scenario?" Jaime asked. Bill studied her face. He knew her well enough to understand that she didn't think this was true. Maybe she was asking it solely as a way of comforting the others, even if it was false hope. "I mean, last year we were convinced we were being attacked. Could this be similar?"

"That sure would be better than the alternative," Bill said. "But you said it yourself. Donnie was actually dead. And how do we explain the army of police here?"

"She's a professional actress," Rose said. "We all know what they are capable of when it comes to simulations."

"These are real cops." Wes shook his head. "And what happened to Diane was real, too. We saw that up close."

"I don't know what to think." Bill looked around the room. JB, the assistants, and the professors looked genuinely worried. *They wouldn't put all of us through this to only make it some kind of sick game, right?*

But then Bill remembered how last year he was ready to call the police and storm out of Rabbit in Red when a woman attacked him with a sledgehammer and a man in leather shot a gun at them. That turned out to only be an act. Maybe there was hope that was all this was, too? But he didn't think so. Everything felt different. The looks on the assistant's faces. JB's tone of voice. Everything.

They waited for hours as the police thoroughly searched the studios. Then they were escorted to their bedrooms. The new recruits would stay with the first years. They wanted everyone to be as close together as possible.

"We'll be calling you down one at a time to interview you," JB said. "I'm getting interviewed first, then my team, and then each of you. It's going to be a long night. Rest when you can."

Up in the *Alien* bedrooms, they all gathered in the guys' sleeping area. Many of them had their cell phones out, texting or talking to families back home.

"What should we say to our parents?" Carol asked. "They're gonna make us come home, won't they?"

"Can they *make* you?" Jaime said. "Do what you want. I'm telling my mom that it's only a game within a game. A sick, twisted mystery that we have to solve as part of the contest."

"Is that what it is?" Jimmy asked. "Diane was really hurt. I can't believe that's part of the game."

"Maybe that was only an accident," Jaime said. "We've been through this before. If it is a game, then JB wants us to find out who is responsible for Donnie's murder. If it's not a game, well . . . then we'll find the real murderer. Either way is a win-win situation, don't you think?"

"Unless one of us ends up dead," Brandis said. "Is that a risk you're willing to take?"

Jaime didn't answer. The recruits looked terrified and worried. They fidgeted with their phones. Bill stood up to address everyone.

"Last year, I was ready to kill JB for some of the things he put us through. I don't know if this is a game in a game. I do know he won't tell us if it is, but I agree with Jaime. If you want to go home, you should go home. If you want to stay, then we'll figure out who did this. We're here because we want to create horror, right? We know that JB thinks the best way to create horror is to have experienced it. So whether it's real or not, this will make us stronger. If you want to stay, then tell your parents it's part of a bigger game, and that it's *only* a game."

The recruits mumbled to one another. Wes leaned in and whispered so only Jaime, Rose, and Bill could hear. "Do you really think that's true? That this is another test?"

Bill stared coldly at no one in particular. "No, I don't. But if we stay, we can help find who did this. If we leave, we go back to what? Nothing? Take some boring classes somewhere? We've survived crazy before. I don't want to go home. I want to find who did this, get him or her out of our lives so that we can actually enjoy what we're doing here."

Rose held Wes's hand. They all looked frightened. Bill sighed. He didn't know what was really happening. But as crazy as it might sound, he really didn't want to go home.

"Let's find who did this," Rose said. "Let's start right now. Look around the room. JB said that he thought the murderer was with us. We know more about everyone here than the police do. Where should we begin?"

All four of their heads turned and examined Daniel. He was sitting next to Leroy. His face was way too calm for Bill.

Quietly, they scooted over to Daniel's side. Could he be the one responsible? Did he snap somehow and decide to get revenge on Rabbit in Red by killing Donnie and burning Diane? Bill thought it was possible.

"So what do you think about all of this?" Bill asked, studying Daniel carefully.

"Let me guess," he said. "You already think I had something to do with it." He lifted his eyebrows and looked at each of them individually.

"We're just wondering what you think," Bill said, trying not to let Daniel know what was really inside his own head.

"I think you're crazy if you still think this is a game within a game."

"So what would you do?" Jaime asked.

Daniel shrugged. "You all found shit by exploring the studio last year when people went missing. That's as good of a strategy as any."

"We're stuck here," Wes said.

"When it's *over*." Daniel sighed. "The interviewing can't last forever. When it's done, we explore. But keep it quiet and stay in small groups. I don't know about you all, but I just need to move. Walk around. Check things out."

"Okay," Jaime said. "Let's make a couple of teams to help us. These recruits are smart. Fresh eyes and new perspectives may help."

"But remember that any of them could be responsible for this," Rose whispered so no one else would hear. "We need to pay attention to their behavior as much as we pay attention to our surroundings."

"Sounds like a plan," Wes said. "Let's create some teams."

Bill nodded. He wasn't sure he wanted to be working with the new recruits, especially if it could be one of them responsible for this. But that wasn't the only reason, he knew. The real reason was that he'd have to deal with Brandis. He didn't like how close Brandis had been getting to Jaime.

Not one bit.

*****

The interviews took all evening. It was close to midnight when Chester Malcolm came up to their sleeping quarters to address them.

"It's been a long one for everyone," he started. The fatigue darkened his eyes, and he looked about a decade older from the last time Bill saw him, just earlier that day. "The good news is that Diane is going to be okay. She has several burns, and some will leave scars for life. But she's alive and will heal."

"What caused the fire?" Bill asked. "Did the police or JB find anything out?"

"That particular room of Hellfire was definitely tampered with," Chester said heavily. "They found the remains of an intricate wiring system, something we never installed. That makes all of this even more bizarre. How someone could get in there and set something up without us knowing it is something we cannot understand. The wiring appears to have been triggered by a remote device. It was an intentional act of violence, of attempted murder actually."

*Attempted murder*. Those words sucked out what little hope Bill had left.

Wes rose his hand hesitantly, even though he didn't need to. "So . . . it's not part of the game? It's real?"

"Very real indeed, Wes. Very real indeed."

"The same for Donnie's murder?" Rose asked.

"Unfortunately." Chester rubbed his forehead and sighed heavily again. Shaking his head, he continued, "Right now, JB and the police are viewing the video feed. They'll watch as long as they have to in order to find some clues as to who tampered with Hellfire and hurt Diane and who murdered Donnie."

"Do they have any leads?" Jaime asked.

Chester shrugged and started to walk away. Before leaving, he turned and said, "I know it will be hard to sleep, but we're asking you to get a full night's rest. In the morning, perhaps we will have discovered something on the video feed. Then we can move on. Remember, guys. Strength in numbers. No one should be doing anything alone."

"Diane wasn't alone," Bill muttered.

"I know." Chester looked at Bill. "That was clearly premediated. I don't think anything spontaneous will happen to anyone if you stick together." He left the room then, and a dozen whispered conversations ignited in the dark.

"There's no way I'm sleeping," Jaime said. "We search tonight."

"Won't they see us?" Wes asked. "On the video feed?"

"Maybe," Jaime answered. "But I'm thinking they will either be too distracted by watching old video feed to notice or they won't care because they'd be happy if we discovered something."

Overhearing the conversation, Brandis jumped in. "I want to help."

"Me too," Venus said, and several others, most notably Jimmy and Kent, stood up with them.

"What's the plan?" Brandis asked.

Bill looked at Jaime, and she nodded. He stood up and addressed the group.

"Okay, let's divide ourselves up," Bill said. "At least three to a group. More if you want."

"So far, the victims have all been girls," Rose said. "So I'd say each group have a mix of guys and girls, too."

"Yeah, that makes sense," Bill told her. He took a deep breath and addressed everyone in the room. "From there, we'll take different sections of Rabbit in Red. Just, uh, no one explore Hellfire. Not tonight."

He looked around at the gathered students. "And, of course, some stay here, too. We have to keep an eye on everything."

Everyone nodded, and Bill sat down to think for a moment.

*When did all of this start?* Bill thought back to graduation. He got into a fight with his mom because someone left a burning axe outside his house. Who could have done that? Any one of them would have been available. Daniel could have travelled to do it. Dexter certainly could have, but Dexter wasn't here, and JB had thought whoever was responsible was here.

Surely, the axe outside of his house was a warning. Then, before he could reunite with Jaime last summer, before he had any chance of telling her how he really felt about her, Tara was kidnapped. Bill scanned the room. Who is responsible?

*Then the parents come visit. Mr. Dawn has a panic attack. That was accident though, right?*

After Mr. Dawn's accident, everything had been going okay until the recruits showed up. So is it one of them? Then they learned of a would-be professor that had been killed, and Diane got burned for real. Then Donnie was actually murdered.

*Who in the hell could be responsible for all of this?* Maybe it was even bigger than one person. It was so much to digest. Bill shook his head.

"You all right, Bill?" Wes asked, putting an arm on his shoulder.

"I dunno. I really dunno." He looked up at everyone. "I was just thinking of everything. From Tara to . . . to today. Okay, you guys ready? We'll make our groups and go."

They nodded, and Bill led them all out of the bedrooms and down the ladder. The teams split up in the commons. The first team consisted of Bill, Jaime, Brandis, Carol, Julie, and Daniel. A second team consisted of Wes, Rose, Venus, Jimmy, Ricky, and Kent. It seemed they were more comfortable with slightly bigger groups, after all. The others divided into more teams, with some staying behind to guard home base.

"Good luck, you guys," Jaime said. "Text or call if anything happens, okay? Cell phones are still working, right?"

"Let's do a quick test," Bill suggested. He messaged Jaime a short *hey J*. All it took was that simple text to remind Bill of innocent memories. A time when he would stay up all night texting Jaime. Those nights were over. Would he ever have them again?

"Got it," she said. "Let's go."

*****

Bill and Jaime led their team through the commons up into the *Hellraiser* hall.

"Last year there was a game within a game," he told Brandis, Carol, and Julie. "We found an axe that led to other clues, all part of one bigger mystery. If this is some kind of twisted game in a game, no matter what Chester says, we may find similar things. If not, well, maybe we'll find something to help figure out what's going on."

Bill was sure this was no game, but he wanted the recruits to understand the whole picture. After all, they had been fooled before.

Brandis nodded, and Bill observed that he was walking awfully close to Jaime, nearly touching her shoulder with his arm. Then Bill looked back at Daniel, who had positioned himself pretty comfortably between Carol and Julie. It was a terrible time to be feeling any kind of jealousy, and Bill tried to shake the emotion from his gut.

"What are we looking for?" Julie asked.

"Anything out of the ordinary," Daniel told her.

They examined the *Hellraiser* hallway, but discovered nothing.

"Which next?" Jaime asked. "The Freddy hall or the classrooms?"

"The Freddy hall," Bill said. Then he spoke to the new recruits. "Last year this was a hall that resembled the hotel from *The Shining*, but that's where we first discovered the axe."

They examined the walls carefully. Each section resembled a part of a boiler room, Freddy's domain from *A Nightmare on Elm Street*. JB had installed real pipes. Speakers emitted sound effects of fire burning and nails clawing. That all led to the boiler itself, a giant furnace that projected real flames.

"The detail is so real," Carol said. "I mean, it is all real. JB can do anything."

"Remember that," Daniel told her.

"What does that mean?" she asked.

"It means he can do anything." Daniel shrugged. "I don't know if we should all so easily trust him."

"I don't think that's fair," Carol said.

"I do," Julie said.

"Just have an open, unbiased mind," Jaime jumped in. "And open eyes. Anyone see anything?"

"Nothing. Should we check the classrooms now?" Daniel asked.

"Wait," Jaime said. "Did anyone look inside Freddy's boiler?" They shook their heads.

"We should check inside, then," Bill said.

"Yeah? Who wants to stick their hands inside?" Daniel asked sarcastically.

Carol and Julie shook their heads. "We had enough of getting burned," Julie said, "even if it was only in our heads."

"I'll do it." Bill approached the boiler. The flames spit sparks, and the heat intensified as he got closer. He took a deep breath. Nothing was easy, that was for sure. Then he carefully looked inside.

"Do you see anything?" Jaime asked.

"Oh, shit. Yeah, there's actually something there. Looks like a black box."

"How is it not ashes?" Carol wondered.

"Must be a fire proof box," Bill said. "Like the ones they have on airplanes or something."

"Reach in quick, dude," Daniel said. "It will be like running your hand over a candle's flame. Quick and it won't hurt."

Bill sighed and pulled open the metal door to the boiler. He gasped painfully as he touched it. "On three," he said aloud, mostly for himself. "One, two, three!"

He darted his hand in quickly as if punching someone. Instead of grabbing onto the box, he pushed it outside of the boiler and it crashed on the floor.

"You okay?" Jaime asked.

"Yeah. I'm okay. Like a candle, as Daniel said. One big ass candle." He tried to laugh.

Daniel looked sideways at Jaime. "You know, I kind of find it funny that Jaime knew there'd be something inside."

"It was an educated guess, D-bag," Jaime snapped. "If I were hiding a clue, I'd put it in there."

"Quite a coincidence. That's all."

Jaime rolled her eyes at him.

"Wait! Does this mean it is a game within a game?" Julie asked hopefully. "Maybe nobody was really murdered?"

"We can only hope so." Jaime sighed. "For now, let's see what's inside the box."

Bill frowned. Something more had to be going on. Who the hell would be leaving clues around the studio again?

*What the hell is going on?*

The fire-proofed box, about the size of a large shoebox, opened easily.

"What are those?" Carol asked.

Daniel laughed. "For someone who knows a lot about horror, you don't know much about film history. Those are called video cassette tapes. They were used in something called a VCR. Maybe you've seen one in a museum or something?"

"I know what they are, jerk," she replied. "I was just . . . wondering what they could be for. What could be on them, I mean."

"Uh-huh," Daniel said.

"How will we watch them?" Julie asked.

"We're inside the largest film studio in the world." Daniel shook his head. "I'm sure there's a VCR somewhere."

Bill studied Daniel. He was sure eager to see what was on this video. Could he be up to something? *How do video tapes, old tapes by the looks of it, have anything to do with what is happening now?*

To be honest, though, curiosity certainly had the best of him, and he was just as eager as Daniel to see what was on them.

"Let's go find a VCR, then," Bill said, and they took off back toward the commons, where they ran smack into Rose and Wes's team.

"Guys, you remember that trap door in the funhouse? We looked in there, and this is what we found!"

Rose held out a large, rectangular box. Inscribed on the top was another riddle. It read, *Ashes to ashes. Dust to dust. They lit the matches. Who can you trust? Take your chances. Understand the past, you must.*

"Jesus!" Jaime cried. "Have you looked inside that box?"

"Yeah, it's a—"

"A VCR!" Jaime interrupted Rose.

"How did you know?"

"We already stumbled on the riddle's solution. Ashes, dust, matches—all clues to Freddy's boiler. Inside, we found these video tapes. So, understand the past we must? Guys! What do you think is on these tapes?"

"Only one way to find out," Bill said and looked around. *It is a game then, right? It's all happening again.* Or was that just wishful thinking? He decided they better see what was on the tapes first. "Let's watch in one of the classrooms. Maybe this isn't for everyone's eyes just yet."

They nodded in agreement and ran to the empty classroom section of the studio.

Rose and Wes connected the VCR to a monitor in one of the classrooms. Bill took a closer look inside the box of video tapes. There were multiple tapes, all labeled in numerical order.

"Here's the first one. Let's see what's on it."

# Chapter Eighteen

A young boy, maybe about ten years old, appeared on camera. Sporadic squiggly lines distorted the picture. In the background, a little girl rested on a twin sized bed. A small wooden desk sat next to the bed, and a few shelves above the desk housed monster toys. Wolfman, Frankenstein, and Dracula faced one another as if preparing for a great battle.

"This is my best friend Nancy," the little boy said. "We watched the greatest movie I've ever seen. It was called *The Exorcist*. I'll never sleep again, I don't think, and that's okay because it was incredible. Nancy and I are gonna make horror movies! This one is called *After the Exorcist*."

The boy walked toward the camera, which he must have placed on a dresser or desk across from his tiny bed. He turned to Nancy and asked, "Are you ready?" She nodded. The boy looked back into the camera and said, "Action!"

Nancy moaned on the bed, then tossed in a series of convulsions. The boy giggled off camera, and then he walked toward the bed.

"You have a demon inside of you," he tried to say in his most serious voice. "We must terminate the demon."

"NO!" the girl shouted and sat up in bed quickly.

"Be gone, demon!" the boy demanded. He pressed his hand against her forehead and the girl began a series of awkwardly funny spasms once again. "I said BE GONE!"

The girl collapsed back on the bed. She moaned as if in pain and sat up slowly. "You saved me, Jay! Thank you for saving me!"

"And cut!" He pointed at the camera, but it kept recording. "That was great! Okay, what do you think we can get to look like green vomit? Let's do it again and have you throw up on me this time. Wouldn't that be great?"

"Gross!" Nancy laughed. "But okay. I'll puke on you."

"Yay!" Jay cheered. He ran to the camera. "I need to find some vomit. Be back soon." Then he shut it off.

Wes glanced at all the others who were watching. This wasn't right. It was like reading someone's journal without permission. Exciting, but wrong.

"So that's JB as a boy," Bill said. "This is weird."

"Why do you think we have these?" Jaime asked. "I mean, what does that tell us?"

"Let's try the second video," Rose said. "There's gotta be something in here that we're supposed to see."

"Oh-right," Bill said and put in the next video.

Wes folded his arms on his chest and inhaled heavily.

A slightly older JB greeted them on camera, maybe eleven or twelve at the most. He was dressed as a mummy, but his bandages were dirty and hanging on very loosely.

"Happy Halloween," he said to the camera. "I went trick-or-treating tonight. I don't have anything to show for it though. Those stupid eighth graders took it all." His eyes were wet, and he tried to brush off some of the dirt on his mummy bandages.

"They took everything, and then they shoved me on the ground. Look. They ruined my costume." He stared into the camera, and his red, wet eyes blinked hard.

"I have a movie idea though. I want to record it so I don't forget it. I thought about it the entire walk home. I'm calling it *Hang Those Who Shame.*"

He walked back by his bed, his bandages dragging along the floor with him. He lowered his head as if thinking and then he slowly straightened up and stared hard at the space in front of him, as if someone were standing right there.

"Give us your candy, Jay!" The pitch in his voice was startling, a high piercing sound of a young boy nearing puberty.

He stepped forward and turned around. "It's my candy. Why should I give it to you?" His voice was calm as he played himself.

Turning back around into the other character, he yelled, "Because you're a loser! Losers don't deserve candy! Losers like you deserve nothing! You and your books and your stupid movies and your stupid ideas. You're a weirdo! A WEIRDO! No one likes you. Don't you know that?"

The little boy spun around again. "But why doesn't anyone like me? I didn't do anything to you or anyone else. Why do you have to be so mean?"

The high pitched piercing voice of the other boy screeched, "Shut up Jay Smell Slime! You stink, Smell Slime! You stink like your mother, and she stinks because she pooped you out from between her legs. She'll never be able to clean up that stink!"

As the little JB spun around into himself, he charged his imaginary abuser, his arms straight out—just like a mummy in old horror films—and pretended to choke the other boy. He fell on the bed, his arms still straight, and thrust up and down on the bed, choking the pretend boy. He breathed hard but did all of this without making a sound. Then he stood up. He looked around his room. Not finding what he needed, he imagined he had a rope. He tied the rope around the other boy's head, then he took the other end and tossed it up at the ceiling. He pulled at the make-believe rope, as if pulling up the unreal boy to hang him over the bed.

Then young JB took a step back. "You get what you deserve," he snarled. "Hang those who shame."

He breathed in and out, like ocean waves beating against the shore.

"Hang those who shame," he repeated.

A chill shot through Wes's bones. He unfolded his arms and stood up. "Guys, I don't know how much more of this we should watch," Wes said. "It feels wrong."

"Yeah. That was intense," Bill said. "You remember what he told us all last year about making friends with one another?"

Jaime nodded. "I remember because I greatly admired it. He said, 'Don't hang with those who shame.' This puts a whole different spin on it."

Rose turned to Wes. "Don't you think it's possible JB put these tapes out there himself for us to find?"

Wes shook his head. "But why? It doesn't feel right. This is too personal."

"Then who wanted us to find these?" Daniel asked.

"That's another mystery," Bill said, already holding another tape.

"That nickname," Carol added, "is so cruel. Smell Slime. I hate it."

"Kids can be as bad as the villains in horror movies," Wes told her with a frown. The new recruits hadn't been introduced to everyone's pasts. He looked at Bill, who lost a father. Then to Jaime, who lost an uncle. Then to Rose, who lost a brother. Out of the four of them, he was the only one who hadn't lost someone to murder, suicide, or accident. He remembered something Rose had told him from last year, when they shared what their fear simulations were all about during that dreadful second round of games. Rose had told him to never compare his pain to that of another. That all pain was unique. He didn't think he'd ever forget that advice.

When he saw JB's bullying story, Wes instantly felt sick. No, Wes had never lost anyone. But for years he had lost something. Self-esteem? Self-confidence? Maybe this was why—as crazy it might be—he actually kind of wanted to be at Rabbit in Red. It was the first time he felt confident and respected. He looked over at Rose and smiled. Maybe she had the most to do with it. But when he watched JB's video, Wes connected immediately to what the young Jay was feeling. It was also at least partially why he didn't think they should keep watching such videos. Didn't they get it? This was like watching a murder. A murder of one's self-esteem.

*And God knows what that could lead to,* Wes thought.

"Smell Slime is a little odd though," Bill said, interrupting Wes's thoughts. "Why not just call him Jay Smell? How does the Jay Smell Slime fit?"

"Who knows?" Jaime shrugged. "Kids can be as stupid as they are cruel."

Just as the new recruits didn't know the tragic pasts of many of the first years here, Wes realized that they certainly didn't know everything about the new recruits and their pasts either. What horrors had they experienced? Were they here for a reason? Or was it as simple and random as whoever "won" the Hellfire on location contests?

He had wondered before if there wasn't a reason behind who JB chose. Not just winners of a contest. Although he didn't say it, he suspected that each of them was here not only because of a deep enthusiasm for the horror genre but also because of a shared history of personal horror. Everyone had their stories and their secrets. He looked at the new recruits and wondered what haunted their pasts.

Not all of the new recruits were there watching, and Wes thought that was definitely for the best. The other half were with the rest of the first years keeping watch from their sleeping areas in case anything happened. Wes took his time looking at each of the new recruits, wondering what their pasts were like.

There was Carol, blond, beautiful, someone who seemed to love everything about JB and Rabbit in Red.

There was Julie. He knew from watching her in Hellfire 2.0 that she was brave and strong, and also a bit cynical about what was going on. He liked that about her.

There was Brandis. What was his past? Wes sure didn't know, but he guessed Brandis and Bill would have an interesting future. They both appeared to have a crush on the same girl.

Then there were also Jimmy, Ricky, and Kent. Had any of them lost someone? If Wes had to guess, he thought that all three looked like those who could have been bullied like him. No matter how progressive the world may seem, a gay teenager was always going to face some challenges. What challenges had Jimmy faced?

And every time Wes looked at Ricky, Ricky looked different. It was as if this place was making him older. Or that digestive disease had really taken a toll on him, which Wes thought odd, too, as Ricky was nearly as heavy as Wes. Wouldn't someone with a digestive disease be skinny? How old did he say he was? A teenager, right? At times, Ricky looked old enough to be twice that, but who knew what all he had been through before Rabbit in Red.

And then there was Kent and the cornrows. Wes and Kent were both African-American, but that didn't mean Wes related to him. Kent had a very different style, and Wes wondered who he really was. Wes thought of all the baggy sweatshirts he had worn to cover up his weight. Wasn't all that style a way of covering up something about yourself, too?

Wondering what the past was like for each of these new recruits, Wes wanted to be careful. There could be anything on these videos, and seeing that could change any number of things.

"I get where you're coming from, Wes," Bill said, "but there must be something on these tapes that we need to see. Don't you think?"

"Maybe we should take these to JB and ask him directly," Wes suggested.

Bill didn't argue with Wes's logic, but Wes thought he saw something change inside Bill. Bill wanted to see the tapes. Wes saw the determination in Bill's eyes. No amount of reasoning would change that.

"Wait," Bill said. "JB put us through hell last year. Assuming this place doesn't get shut down, we could potentially be spending a lot more time with him. Who knows what else he'll put us through? Donnie's murder—that could still be a twisted component of this game, right? I say we learn as much about JB as we can."

Wes shook his head. Bill didn't think Donnie's murder was in any way part of a game. "I don't like it, man."

Daniel jumped in. "I'm with Bill on this one. The more we know, then the more we can understand."

Wes wanted to tell Bill that if Daniel agreed with him, it probably wasn't a good idea. Instead, he turned to Rose and Jaime. "What do you think?"

"If we see anything we really feel is inappropriate, we can always turn it off," Rose said.

"So you think we should watch these, too?"

Wes could tell she was trying to respond very carefully. "Not necessarily, but what if there's something here we should know?" Rose asked. "I'm not saying I like it. But there is power in knowledge."

If there was anyone here Wes fully trusted, it was Rose. He had hoped she'd be completely on his side. Maybe Wes wasn't seeing the full picture. He nodded in defeat. He just worried that once they fully opened this door, there was no turning back. Anything could come back to haunt them.

"Go ahead then." Wes gave in. "Put in the next tape."

The difference in JB's appearance was about two feet of height. He had dramatically jumped to the stature they knew now. He was incredibly thin though and had the darkest of hair, long, almost down to his shoulders. The video showed the same bedroom as before, but the walls were covered in a variety of different posters. *Dawn of the Dead*, *The Omen*, *Alien*, and—no surprise—*The Exorcist* posters lined the walls they could see on camera. He pulled up a chair and spoke. His voice wasn't quite as deep as it was today, but it was eerily similar, a familiar voice spoken from a face hardly recognizable.

"Tonight's the big night," he said. "It's the Halloween dance at school. I'm going to tell Veronica that I love her. Wish me luck."

He turned the camera off, and a second later on tape they were transported to a new setting. JB had set up the camera inside a high school gymnasium. The basketball court was decorated with streamers, and several tables held pumpkins, candles, random Halloween decorations, as well as drinks and snacks. A stage lined the basketball courts, and they saw long, thick maroon curtains before JB turned the camera back to face the court. He must have placed the camera underneath one of the curtains. Early eighties music blasted through the gym, and several teenagers, all dressed in various costumes, danced ridiculously on the court.

JB was dressed as a vampire, and not a cheesy dollar store kind of costume either. He had a long black cape that looked custom made. The makeup on his face displayed a perfectly pale complexion, and his long fangs looked incredibly sharp. He motioned at a girl, and someone dressed as witch approached. He stood close to where he had placed the camera, and then he spoke to the witch.

"Nice costume," she said.

"Thanks, Veronica. Listen, I . . . I came here alone tonight because I wanted to talk to you."

"About what?" She narrowed her eyes.

"You must know . . . you must have detected that I have feelings for you. Tonight I wanted to tell you directly. I've . . . I've been infatuated with you all throughout high school. Your beauty is unlike anything else. I think I'm . . . that I'm in love with you. I want to ask you formally to be my girlfriend."

She stared at him as if she were completely clueless. "Is this a joke?"

"This is no joke," he said. "Will you go out with me?"

"Have you looked in a *mirror* recently?" she snapped. "Take a good hard look at yourself. And then take a good look at me. We are a total mismatch. It's not gonna happen, Smell Slime."

He looked hard into the camera and shut it off with such force that everyone watching jumped back. But the video wasn't over. The next part of the tape showed JB sideways and only his legs. It must have been the same night, as the vampire cape still draped over his legs. When the video continued, there were other voices, but they couldn't see any faces.

"Loser!"

"What a creep! You think Veronica would go out with you? You really are a big day dreamer!" The insults were followed by laughter, about five or six voices coming together.

It was obvious now that the camera had fallen on its side somewhere along the street. These other teens must have knocked it out of JB's hands or he dropped it, and then somehow the camera turned on, capturing this pitiful moment.

"Why do you take that stupid camera with you?"

"Hey! His life is a living horror movie. That's why!" More laughter.

"Poor, Jay. You'll be a virgin for life, won't you?"

"Who would want to touch Smell Slime's dick? Your hands would fall off from disease!"

"Let's see the Smell Slime dick," another voice shouted. "I bet it's deformed!"

"Like a creature from one of your stupid movies! You got a creature living in your pants? Let's see!"

All they could see on video was JB taking a step back. Someone had lunged at him and pulled at his pants, trying to take them off.

"ENOUGH!" It was JB's voice. "Get off me."

"What are you gonna do Smell Slime?" The kid went after JB again, and this time he roared.

"Don't TOUCH me!" They heard an awful sound next, the sound of something snapping. A kid screamed and fell on the street. The camera showed a mangled arm, twisted in the wrong direction. JB roared again and they all heard thumping sounds. One at a time each of the kids that had laughed at JB fell to the ground. Five bodies altogether. Some with mangled limbs, others with blood and bruised bodies. JB picked up the camera. He pointed right at all of the kids. They were breathing hard, holding their bodies in serious pain.

"I should kill you all," JB said. "Touch me again, and I will." Then he walked away and shut off the camera.

# Chapter Nineteen

Jaime gulped and looked over at Wes. She stood up and was pretty sure she was saying exactly what Wes was feeling. "That's enough for tonight, I think," she said. "It's late. Let's sleep on what we saw and talk in the morning."

They all looked uncomfortable, but Wes was sweating.

They crept back to their bedrooms, climbed up the ladder, and glanced to see if anyone was awake. Everyone had stayed on the guys' side of the sleeping area, even though many simply crashed on the floor. The bigger the group, the better, everyone had thought.

"Go ahead, guys. Get some sleep, if you can," Bill told them but reached out for Jaime's hand. "Hey. Can we talk?" She nodded slightly but didn't answer. "In your room?" She nodded again but even less enthusiastically.

Rose faced them both before walking away. "Don't stay too long, okay? It is better if we all stay together." She had a sweetness and an understanding in her voice, but Jaime saw something else on Rose's face. *It's about time you two talk.* Jaime nodded.

"We won't," Bill replied.

Jaime let go of his hand and led the way. The girls' sleeping area was empty and was dimly lit by a few screens in the *Alien* like pods that had been left on. She sat on her bed and looked up at Bill. He appeared as tall as ever standing over her, and a certain maturity had aged him over the year.

"Are you okay?" he asked.

"Are you?" she followed up.

"No, not really. I don't know what's going on or if we should even be here. Sometimes I question our sanity." He tried to smile, but Jaime didn't reciprocate. "That last video," he continued, "shocked me. It's hard to see JB as just a kid who got picked on hard instead of the leader we see today. But there was something else that bothered me."

Jaime lifted her eyebrows. "Yeah?"

"Can I sit?" Bill asked, gesturing at the bed. When Jaime nodded, he sat next to her and continued. "It took a lot of courage for JB to tell that girl how he felt, you know? I want to be able to be brave like that, too."

Jaime felt her heart skip a beat. There were many things she had thought about over the past year since meeting her best friend in person. She had always been an avid proponent that a girl doesn't need a boyfriend for happiness. But Bill did make her happy. She had told herself that she could still be a leader even with a boyfriend, but she often worried about being overshadowed by Bill. She'd be lying though if she didn't admit that a part of her frustration was that Bill never spoke up about how he really felt.

"I like you a lot, J. I'll be honest. Seeing the way Brandis flirts with you pisses me off. Seeing JB, even younger than me, risk embarrassment for a girl he liked was inspiring. I just don't know what I really want."

He paused and looked into her brown eyes. She felt her heart and her mind race. What did she really want? Was she scared of what he might ask her? Or scared of the words he wouldn't say? She had felt more in the last year than most people do their entire lives, from the epitome of anger to the epitome of excitement. At one time, the answer was so easy. She had wanted Bill. She had loved Bill. But now? Were those feelings still there or had something changed?

"No matter what I do or what we do," Bill said, "I'm just scared of losing my best friend."

"What do you mean?" she asked. Was this the moment? Would he finally ask her to be his girlfriend? She felt the adrenaline pumping through her veins.

"What if we try to be more and it doesn't work? I know things have been awkward recently, but what if you didn't ever want to be around me again?"

She reached out for his hand this time, the first time she had done so in weeks. "I can imagine a lot, but I can't imagine that ever happening." Maybe this was what she wanted.

"What do *you* want?" Bill asked, as if reading her mind.

She pulled her hand away and looked out at the empty room. That was the million dollar question, wasn't it? And when she really thought about it, the answer had nothing to do with Bill. She faced him and spoke.

"I want to find the man who attacked my sister. I want to find the person who hurt Diane. I want to find whoever killed Donnie. That's what I want."

"Do you think this could all be a trick?"

"What happened to Tara was no trick. That's all I know for sure. Someone is out there, Bill. Maybe right in that other room. Someone who is really fucked up."

"Are we fucked up?"

Jaime crossed her arms and bit her lip. "Who isn't? But at least we have a reason to be." She paused, turned to him, and put an arm around his back. She pulled him in close, and he leaned his head down upon hers. "I wish I had memories like you did of your mom and dad when they were together. I don't have that. I've never seen my mom happy, and you know all she does is watch sappy romantic movies longing for a man in her life. My Uncle Tim and Aunt Megan though. Now that was a happy couple."

"Tell me about them."

Jaime relaxed a little. "Tim had such a playful spirit. He was always smiling. He was like a big kid, really. He used to pick me up and spin me around in circles. God that was fun. To be so little and to see grownups like powerful gods."

Without thinking about it, she reached out for Bill's hand again and held it. She smiled at him and the memory. "But you know what? He'd try to do the same to Aunt Megan. Now he couldn't spin her by the arms, but she'd laugh when she saw him spin me. He'd put me down and say 'Oh, you want some too?' Then he'd run at her. She'd scream and pretend to try and run away. But he'd always catch her. He'd pick her up in a giant bear hug and spin around. They'd fall to the ground, and he'd kiss her."

"You've always described him as such a happy man. What happened?"

"We don't know. Or at least no one's told me."

"Does your dad ever try to talk to you?"

"I've gotten a few cards here and there. Mom has an e-mail address, and she says she keeps him updated." She paused and remembered the Skype call she received the day of her graduation. "You know, he called me on Skype to say congratulations the morning of my graduation. I don't think I told you that. Everything happened so quickly after we graduated. Tara's kidnapping. Us moving out here. I hadn't talked with him in four years before that. Just cards and an occasional email. Then that call. Isn't that weird?" Then a terrible thought entered her mind. Her father had said he loved her and Tara, missed them both, and would get home soon to see them. He promised. And then Tara got kidnapped. Could her father actually have something to do with all of this?

She shook it from her thoughts. *That's insane, right?*

"What happened between your parents?" Bill asked.

"Mom says that he fell out of love with her and she lost her best friend. So he moved away and never came back. Not even for me or Tara."

She breathed hard through her nose, her mind dreaming up dozens of possibilities. Maybe she and Tara really did have a crazy father who for some reason wanted to stop Rabbit in Red? But no, that had to be crazy. No parent would actually hurt a child, not like Tara was hurt.

And no, her father couldn't be a murderer. She made a mental note, though, to check in with her mother and find out where he was. Maybe it was time for another Skype session. Did he even know that Tara had been hurt?

They sat in silence for a while, and finally Bill said, "Do you remember the first time we talked like this?"

She smiled, happy to think of something different. "Of course. Our first night at Rabbit in Red. You had nightmares, woke me up, and we fell asleep talking in the commons. That was a good night."

"I hope we have more nights like that."

"Me, too."

She knew they should go back to the group, but it felt good to have such quiet. The calm after the storm, they say. Sometimes it took a great eruption to bring an inner peace. Bill hadn't asked her out, but maybe that was for the best. There were too many things going on, too many thoughts to process. What Jaime needed most right now was a best friend and nothing more. She closed her eyes, and they fell asleep in her bed. It was the most peaceful night's rest she had gotten in a long time.

*****

Chester Malcolm paced nervously.

He and JB were wrapping up a long night's discussion from the safe room below.

"This is quite frustrating," JB said.

"How would someone be able to tamper with the surveillance equipment?"

"There are plenty of people out there smarter than you or me. The gaps in our surveillance feed of course directly correlate with the times of the murder and the sabotage on Hellfire that burned poor Diane. How are our kids?"

"They are questioning the authenticity of everything. Wondering if it's all part of a game again."

"Good. That may be the only way they stay with us."

"Sir, do you think it's a good idea that they stay?"

"They are safer here than on the outside." JB slammed his fist on a desk as Chester nearly interrupted him. "Don't you tell me that these things happened inside of our studios! I am most aware. But look at it this way. If those things can happen inside Rabbit in Red, then a lot more and a lot worse could happen outside."

"I . . . that's exactly what I was going to suggest," Chester mumbled.

"I want 24-7 surveillance on our list of suspects. That starts immediately, do you hear me?"

"I've already contacted the appropriate agencies. We'll be receiving hourly updates."

"Good."

"Sir, do you know who it is?"

JB glared at him, and Chester felt his muscles turn to JELL-O, but JB didn't answer.

"Is it Dexter?" Chester looked for some kind of reaction. "Is it . . . my brother? You were the last person to speak to either one of them."

JB looked at him but didn't blink.

"Is it one of the new recruits?"

"We don't have time for speculation," JB said.

That wasn't any kind of answer, Chester thought.

As if reading his mind, JB said, "What I know and what I can prove are two different things. The police are tired of my theories. They won't listen without evidence."

JB clenched his fists. Chester didn't see him frustrated like this very often.

"What do we do with all the kids?"

"We'll suspend the final part of their contest until after the current situation has been resolved. They need a distraction. Let's send them off location for the rest of the semester as part of a filming project with the professors. That will give us time to prepare their end of year challenges, too."

"You're still going through with those?"

"Absolutely." JB looked surprised at the question. "That's what they're here for."

"You're not worried about another injury?"

"Does a coach worry about his players getting injured? Sure, but it doesn't stop them from playing the game. The coach does his best to make sure the players are prepared. They will be."

JB marched away like a general off to battle. Chester sat down and rubbed his forehead. He had the worst headache possible, and he knew the pain was only going to get worse.

Chester always had the utmost confidence in JB to accomplish absolutely anything, but this had been going on far too long.

He worried that someone was outsmarting them all.

And it terrified him. Because what this person seemed to want was blood.

Real blood.

*****

Daniel pretended to be asleep so he could watch everyone. Bill and Jaime had been absent a long time. He figured they must have slept together, maybe just sleeping, maybe more. His eyes had adjusted to the dark enough so that he could make out the faces of those sleeping nearby. Rose slept in Wes's bed. How disgusting, he thought. Why a pretty girl like that would date a fat guy like Wes, he would never understand. On his right, Leroy was snoring softly. Daniel examined those on the floor, mainly the new recruits. Brandis tossed and turned in his sleep like Bill. It seemed to Daniel that Brandis and Bill had a couple of things in common. It would be interesting how those things played out if Brandis stayed with them for the long term.

Next to Brandis, Carol Fisher slept silently. Daniel was keeping an eye on her. If his plan was truly to work, she would be important. She had so much faith in JB. If he could do something about that, then his plan would work.

Then something strange caught Daniel's attention. Ricky rolled to the side, and there was something about his face, something about his whole body that was odd. Ricky had a private bathroom, they knew, supposedly because of a disease that made him poop all the time, and no one questions poop, Daniel thought. I wonder . . . no, it can't be. Can it?

Daniel squinted and took a real close look at Ricky's face and body.

Is he a *she*?

Daniel had heard people talk about transgendered individuals, but he had never met one. *That's what this is, right? Maybe he doesn't have to poop all the time. Maybe he's just covering up his . . . I mean her boobs.*

Weird, but whatever. *Maybe I'll ask someone about it tomorrow. Or maybe I'll keep Ricky's little secret all to myself.*

*Secrets come in handy, especially at a place like this.* With that thought, he finally drifted off to sleep.

# Chapter Twenty

Bill groaned at the sight of Brandis. He just couldn't help it.

"This isn't fair," Brandis complained. He wore a sleeveless shirt, rubbing on his bicep, and then ran a hand through his short, dark hair. It was sticking up in spots. Bill hated that Brandis somehow still looked good even after a long night, and he hated it more that he caught Jaime staring at the boy. He was the one who'd slept with Jaime last night. Well, not *slept* slept with her, but it was great.

"We never got to finish," Brandis said. "Are we gonna be invited back?"

"You do realize a murder has taken place, right?" Kent questioned. "I'm okay leavin' this place."

"I want to stay!" Carol whined. "I'm with Brandis. It's not fair."

"I understand your objections," Chester told them. He had woken everyone up early this morning to discuss the plans. First years would be flying out to a filming location in northern Minnesota to help with a movie project. He joked that they had all experienced enough heat. The cold would be good for them. New recruits would return home.

"I'm legally an adult," Brandis said. "Most of us are. If we want to stay, we should be able to stay. We could help."

"JB thought some of you would be upset," Chester said. He took a deep breath and smiled. "All right. For those in school or who have work responsibilities, as long as you can organize it on your end to be with us, you may come."

"I'm graduating early," Brandis said. "I have more than enough credits already."

"Me too," Carol said. Bill saw an eagerness on their faces. *They must be crazy if they're so desperate to return*, he thought.

"I don't," Kent said. "And that's okay with me."

"You all work it out with your families and schools and jobs." Chester lost his smile and looked around the room. "This is our last night here for a while. Pack your things and make arrangements. Let us know if you're staying with us or returning home, and we'll arrange the travel."

The exceptions granted to new recruits pissed off Bill. They had only stayed for a weekend last year and had to wait almost an entire year before returning. Why would JB grant exceptions to them? It wasn't fair. What would be perfectly fair is if Brandis never returned. Then there'd be no one else that Jaime would look at the way she looked at Brandis sometimes.

While the recruits rushed to discuss the situation with whoever they could, Bill gathered the first years together. "It's time you guys all know what we found last night. If we're leaving tomorrow, we should finish watching the rest of the tapes." He told them all about seeing young JB goof around as a boy filming an *Exorcist* scene, how JB reacted to getting bullied one Halloween, and of course what happened with to the guys who harassed him after a high school Halloween dance.

"There are more tapes?" Annie asked.

"A few more." Wes sighed.

"What are we waiting for?" Annie questioned. "These sound important, guys. It's insight to the guy who made me stay in a basement room last year chained to a goddamn wall while you were 'attacked.' We need to see these."

"Yeah," Leroy said. He'd also been one of the so-called missing students last year, forced to keep quiet in the basement of *The People Under the Stairs* themed room as part of JB's plan. "Think about it. The dude's a genius but clearly has issues. Let's figure out what those issues are."

"Didn't he say something really bad happened to him?" Annie asked Bill. "Last year, when he showed the footage of your dad's murderer getting caught?"

"Yeah. I remember. JB told us he had his own scary story to tell us one day." Bill's felt a lump in his throat and his arms turned cold. How much of JB's personal horror was on those tapes?

"I remember, too" Rose said. "He talked about how each of us had dark pasts. That our pasts were one reason why we were chosen. Then he told us that he had quite the dark past of his own, perhaps the scariest of all."

"Shit, how could I have forgotten that?" Wes asked.

"I think I did, too," Jaime confessed. "There have been so many . . . distractions. It's hard to remember everything."

"I think we better watch the rest of those tapes," Bill said. If they were going to understand the big picture, then maybe they did need to know everything that had happened to JB in the past. After all, Bill thought, it was JB who said he perhaps had the scariest history of all. You couldn't tell someone that and not expect them to be curious, right?

*****

Rose considered the best way to comfort Wes when watching the rest of the videos. She agreed that they needed to see what was on them, but she also understood Wes's concerns. Somehow she'd try and be the balancing act.

Attempting to be inconspicuous, the first years left individually or in small groups to walk to the classroom wing of Rabbit in Red.

"How do you feel about these tapes?" Wes asked her. The two of them walked together, hand in hand, pretending to be simply on a leisurely stroll throughout the studios. They paused to examine some of the art in the *Candyman* commons and the *Hellraiser* hall.

"I'm telling myself that JB knows pretty much everything that goes on here. Maybe this is part of his game," she said. "And 'game' isn't the right word. Not anymore. Purpose, maybe?"

"If the world were to ever see my fear simulations from last year, I'd be mortified," Wes said.

"But you overcame it, right? You're so much stronger than those bullies." She squeezed his hand tighter. Wes was looking better every day. Today he wore a *Resident Evil* t-shirt over a large pair of khaki jean shorts, and she liked it. Initially, she had found herself attracted to what was inside Wes. He was gentle, caring, and smart. He knew what it was like to be a wallflower, just as Rose did. But the more confidence he acquired, the more physically attractive he became, too.

"Were you ever picked on?" Wes asked, squeezing her hand.

"I think you'd be surprised how mean girls can be." There were stories she hadn't told him or anyone. Not yet. "Not to say what you experienced wasn't absolutely terrible, that's not what I mean at all. But sometimes I think boys at least bully directly to your face. Girls are quiet about it, you know? They paint a picture of you behind your back and spread it. Before you even know what rumors are flying around, it's already a wildfire you can no longer control."

"That happened to you?" The look on Wes's face was pretty much the same expression he wore whenever something absolutely disgusting happened during a horror movie.

"They used to draw pictures of me and my red hair. It started pretty uncreatively at first. Across my face, they'd call me Satan."

"You're the sweetest person in the world. How is that even possible?" The genuine shock on his face made her smile. *He* was the sweetest person in the world, she thought.

"I kept to myself and always had a horror book I was reading. They joked that I was obsessed with the occult."

"Seriously?"

"People criticize what they don't understand." Rose paused for a moment and embraced Wes. "I know that it's crazy that we're even here. I can't imagine what my family would say if I didn't try to convince them that everything happening was all part of a game. But you know what? Not once has anyone criticized our relationship here. Well, maybe Daniel last year. He seems to have less hashtagDbag in him this year. But I think of my high school days. Had we been together at my high school, those jerks would have teased us every day."

"Cuz I'm black and you're a white little Satanic demon?" Wes tried to joke.

"Exactly." She smiled and kissed him. "I'd like to think I wouldn't care. But I think I would, you know?"

"It's got to be harder to be in love when you're surrounded by jerks," Wes stated. He bit his lip right after he said it. They had never said anything about love, not yet. Rose just smiled and kissed him again. She couldn't get enough of it.

"The Satan jokes were pretty junior high," Rose said, after pulling away. "High school got worse. Technology made it worse. Some asshole took one of my pictures and created a meme. At first, it was just more ginger jokes. Then it became crude. I think the most popular meme was one where he drew an arrow from my hair to my . . . well, my groin. He wrote, *if you think she's red up there, you should see down here.* It got over a hundred likes on Instagram." She sighed and shook her head. "And again, no one said anything about any of this to my face. But I could feel their stares and hear their laughter as I walked by. What's so funny about red hair anyway? I never did anything to them."

She caught Wes's eyes drop below her waist when she told him about this. He looked so shocked when she told him, but she saw a little boyish curiosity on his face, too. They hadn't made love yet, but Rose was ready. She knew he was a virgin just like her, and when the moment was right, she'd let him explore whatever he wanted.

"It's like . . . it's like it doesn't matter that anything is right or wrong," Wes said, his eyes meeting hers again. "People still pick on differences. That's why I hated Daniel at first. He's calmed down this year though, don't you think?"

"He's a hard one to read. I hope so, but I also worry he could be hiding something. Like he's just got a really good poker face this year and is shutting the hell up because we invited him back."

"I just hope there's nothing on these tapes that we can't un-see," Wes said. "Maybe we already crossed that line, but if it gets worse . . . I just don't like it."

"I know, babe," Rose told him. "That's why we need you here with us when we watch though. Speak up if it feels like we're seeing something we shouldn't."

He nodded, and they reached the classroom wing. Several of the first years had already gathered inside. Rose saw him take a long, deep breath to counter the nervousness, and they sat down as Bill set up the next video to watch.

The next video showed JB in what appeared to be a college dorm room. There were two twin beds along opposite sides of the walls. JB had turned on the camera, walked backward into the middle of the room, and spoke directly into the lens.

"The essence of art, of horror in particular, is to see the world through someone else's eyes. Unlike other genres, horror gives us the opportunity to see through the eyes of the darkest of villains."

He sat on his bed, looked out at the doorway, and called, "You can come in now."

A young, nervous-looking woman stepped inside. "Are you sure about this, Jay?"

He nodded. "Over there."

"Why do you want to do this again?"

"It's . . . it's a project for my psychology class. Please. Take your pick. Over there."

The woman walked to a corner of the room, which the camera didn't pick up. When she returned, she held a wooden paddle. JB took off his shirt and rolled onto his stomach.

"Hit me. Hard."

The woman gasped. "I don't know if I can do this."

"Please! I trust you. I need . . . . I need to get an A on this project."

"Remind me not to sign up for that class," she said. She stepped closer to him, lifted the paddle over her head, and smacked him on the back.

"You have to hit harder than that."

She sighed and lifted the paddle again and brought it down with a sickening whomp on his back.

"Again!"

She hit him a third time and then a fourth. By the fifth, a black and blue spot had formed on his back and blood trickled out from the center.

"Good. Pick something else," he demanded.

"You're bleeding, Jay. That's quite enough, don't you think?"

"No. I need to feel the pain. I need to know what I can take. Please."

The woman stepped off camera, and this time approached with a long, heavy belt. JB rolled over. "On my chest," he said. She smacked him. "Harder." She whipped the belt at him again. "Now across my face."

Rose winced and grabbed Wes's hand.

"That's enough!" Wes shouted. "What are we supposed to be learning from this?"

She saw how uncomfortable he was, but she didn't say anything. She couldn't help but wonder what was on all of these tapes, too, and she wondered what all JB would do. And why he would do it.

"Let me at least fast forward then," Bill said. "You're right. This is sick. But I want to make sure we don't miss anything."

As Bill fast forwarded, the woman moved from one object to the next. JB had taken quite a beating, and the woman left in distress. Then the video jumped to a new scene, and Bill let it play.

"Thanks for coming," JB told a man who walked in the dorm room.

"Money, please?" The guy held out his hand. "Now nothing perverted, right?"

"This isn't about sex," JB assured the man.

"What's it about then?" the guy asked as JB handed over a wad of cash.

"I'm studying the psychology of horror. I need to know what it feels like to be both victim and villain. You can stop at any time, okay? But try to hold out for me." The guy nodded. "Take off your shirt and pants and toss them on the bed." The man did as instructed and stood in the middle of the dorm room in only his underwear. "Now, pick your poison." JB pointed to a part of the room once again that was off-screen. The man pointed at something they couldn't see.

"Ahh. One of my favorites." JB walked off camera for a second and came back with a giant, thick rope. "Slap my leg two times when you can't take it anymore."

JB tossed the rope around the man's throat and squeezed. The man gasped for air and thrust his hands up at the rope. He looked as if he were trying to pull it off, but he didn't slap at JB to stop.

Then JB pulled him on the ground. The man was on top of JB, JB's back on the floor, the man's back on JB's front side. It looked like a sick wrestling move. The man coughed, his face started changing colors, and finally he slapped JB's leg twice. JB released him immediately.

Red, rug-burned marks appeared on the man's throat now. He coughed and sat down on the bed to catch his breath.

"I appreciate the easy cash, but what the fuck is wrong with you man?" the guy asked after several minutes.

"I'm just trying to create the perfect horror. I want to be a filmmaker. I can't imagine creating from only one's imagination. I want to experience it all, as much as possible."

"Yeah, sounds totally normal," the guy said and rubbed his throat. But then he added, "Next week, same time?" JB nodded. "Okay, see you then."

Rose could feel the panic in Wes's body. He was shaking, but then again, she was shaking, too. The leader, the mentor, the man they all looked up to: was he just a monster? It was like every time they thought they found a logical reason behind JB's craziness, then they'd discover some new and even sicker thing he had done. Were they just believing a lie this entire time? And again, who gave them these tapes?

"This is bad, you guys," Daniel said. "It's like what JB did to us in the simulations, but this stuff was real."

"Thank God he has technology now," Bill attempted to joke.

"Do you guys think this is okay?" Daniel asked.

"No," Rose said after seeing the terror on Wes's face. "No, not at all."

"But these people knew what they were doing," Bill said. "He even paid the dude. It's not like he was really trying to kill him. It's like . . . like what an actor might do to fully understand a dark role."

Rose tried to study Bill. Why was he trying to defend JB?

"That's how you become really messed up in here though," Jaime said and pointed at her head.

"Messed up enough to put people through real danger?" Venus asked. "To perhaps really set someone on fire? Or to actually kill someone?" Several people nodded in agreement.

"You guys think JB would have sabotaged this place himself?" Jaime asked. "That he'd really kill one of his assistants?"

"I don't know," Annie said. "But look. Why hasn't JB caught the killer? Or whoever took Tara? If he's so smart and resourceful, then why doesn't he know who did this?"

"Are you saying he could be the one that hurt my sister?" Jaime's face turned beat red.

"He found her pretty easily, didn't he?" Leroy asked.

Jaime looked over at Bill for support, then to Rose and Wes. Rose studied her, too. No one seemed to know how to respond. It couldn't be JB behind the murders, could it?

Bill finally spoke up. "There's no doubt JB is messed up. You don't become a horror visionary without some part of your brain being crazy. But I can't believe he'd really hurt someone."

"You just saw him choking a guy on camera!" Daniel argued.

"Yeah, but . . . but that's different. The guy knew what he was getting into. He wasn't a victim."

"There's one more video," Wes said slowly. "I hate to say it, but I think we better see what's on it."

Rose nodded hesitantly. Last year, JB had put her in a giant crib and surrounded her with witches. There had been a room full of clowns, spiders, a hanging noose, not to mention the buzzing of bees just for her. JB was certifiable, she thought. There was a breaking point last year where she could have punched JB right in the face. But at the end of a very long weekend, he had brought them all closer together. They had overcome fear. He even discovered Bill's dad's murderer. So was JB really a madman?

She didn't know, but she watched with trepidation as Bill picked up the last tape, put it in the VCR, and pressed play.

# Chapter Twenty-One

Jaime sat next to Bill on the bus to International Falls. She stared out the window, and little was spoken between them. There was so much to digest and understand. Jaime thought they should be discussing it, but she didn't want any of the professors or Chester to hear. The first years, a few of the new recruits, the professors, and Chester all had landed at the Minneapolis/St. Paul airport and boarded a bus for their road trip up north. They were headed for International Falls, which fell right near the Minnesota and Canada border.

Pairs sat next to one another on the chartered bus. Wes and Rose sat in the far back next to Jaime and Bill, then Daniel and Leroy, Annie and Venus, Dennis and Brandon, Emily and Caitlin, Gage and Noah, Helen and Laura, and Gary and Claire. Eighteen first years in total, and all had stayed at Rabbit in Red. Up front, Brandis sat with Carol and Jimmy sat with Ricky. Jaime thought about how they started last year with nineteen. Only one of the original nineteen was no longer present: Dexter Lange. They might not have spoken his name, but that didn't mean they had forgotten about him.

From the moment Bill and Jaime watched Dexter's interview prior to the first Rabbit in Red Halloween contest, they knew he was troubled. His fascination with *American Psycho*, the cold, apathetic expression on his face, and of course the violence. Many of them had been on the receiving end of that physical violence at the end of the games last year. For that, JB had expelled him from Rabbit in Red.

Now that the first years had seen the videos of JB, they wondered more about Dexter. They had seen JB take and give pain, but it was all under controlled situations. Dexter didn't care about that. He cared only about winning. He had no empathy.

Jaime remembered something JB said last night before they departed. She was certain it wasn't the first time she had heard JB say this. The master host had commented on the loss of Donnie, on Diane's progress, on Tara's, too. JB had told them, *"If we can't feel sadness for others, then we aren't fully human. Denying our feelings is the only thing not real. It takes away from our humanity."*

It was as if he was giving everyone permission to feel, to be sad, and to question all of the emotions they had experienced.

Jamie thought back to her experience with Dexter last year. He certainly didn't have those kind of emotions. But still, could the same be said about their master host? Was there a hypocrisy here? A conflict that hadn't been resolved?

Like Voldemort, it was almost as if no one liked saying Dexter's name out loud. She thought back to the first time she had seen him. He was being interviewed on TV and she told Bill that something looked off. Then, at Rabbit in Red, Dexter had hung out with Daniel mostly, but he never exactly bullied or joked in the way Daniel did. There was something deeper to Dexter, and not in a good way. Dexter used Daniel to get to the end of the game last year, and then Dexter used actual violence.

And was Dexter the one behind all of this violence at Rabbit in Red?

He certainly possessed the brains for it. He also possessed the will, she thought. But did he have the resources? To think that Dexter could outsmart JB, though, was insane. Who could outsmart JB?

That was the million dollar question at the moment. They had seen the rest of the tapes, and they knew what JB was capable of. Maybe this wasn't exactly a game within a game, but that didn't mean that JB wasn't behind it all somehow.

Jaime had been trying to study everyone closely. She noticed that Daniel had been doubting JB for some time now, and Bill still tried—even if it was rather weak—to defend JB. Something was changing in the way Jaime thought about everything. She had nearly lost her sister. She saw Tara right after some monster intentionally hurt Tara. *If you're around evil long enough*, she thought, *you're destined to go a little crazy*. As she stared out the window, she pictured what she would do to Tara's attacker, whoever it may be.

She pictured blood, lots of blood. There would certainly be a knife. She had always admired the use of a knife. Simple, small, no need for the theatrics of something like a chainsaw. And just for a touch of irony, maybe she'd use a rope, too.

In her reflection on the bus window, Jaime caught herself smiling. She drifted away in her thoughts. It was all rather relaxing, actually. Before she knew it, they had arrived at their location at International Falls, and everyone was quick to get off the bus and stretch their legs.

"Tara!" Rose was the first to cheer and run off the bus when she saw the mini version of Jaime waving outside of the lodge where they would be staying. After a hug, the others wanted their turns, too.

"Get over here," Wes said, giving Tara a giant bear hug and swinging her around.

"And me, of course!" Bill called. He took off her winter hat and traced his finger along the shaved rabbit in her head. "You kept it up? It looks cooler than ever." Tara's hair had grown out now to a point where no one would have known just six months ago that it had all been burned off. It was still short, but it had resumed a fullness of normalcy. Still, she buzzed the rabbit outline on the side of her head. It was as if she never wanted to forget what had happened, like she could, and as if she wanted to be a part of the Rabbiteers.

"Hey, Sis," Jaime greeted and hugged her tight. She wrapped her hands around the back of Tara's head and pulled her close. "Glad you're here. Mom, too?"

"Mom said she'd prefer the warm California weather and would be happy with JB's security staying close. She thinks one of them is hot." Tara rolled her eyes.

"Well good for her, I guess."

"Yeah," Tara said. "But she wouldn't let me go until JB promised to surround me with security. I felt like a celebrity being escorted everywhere with bodyguards. So what are we gonna do out here? It's so cold."

"JB had a film crew out here working on a current project," Jaime said. "We get to help or observe or do whatever we can. I think JB wants to keep us all very busy."

"Cool!" Tara said. "Let's go inside."

They grabbed their bags that had been stored under the bus and followed Tara. There were guards by the main door of this lodge, out in the driveway, and around the sides.

She turned to Daniel. "Hey, if there is so much security wherever we go—guards hired by JB—then how could it actually be JB who is behind this?"

Daniel thought for a moment. "That's just it though. He hired them. Doesn't it sound like the perfect defense? And who would better know the guards or the hours they worked than the guy who hired them?"

Jaime frowned. "He's thought of everything. *If* he's really the one behind it all."

"You'll see." Daniel smirked. "I have no doubt."

Bill must have been listening to their conversation, and he jumped in. "So if JB is responsible for everything, then what's the purpose of it all? What happens to us?"

Daniel raised his eyebrows. "Haven't you ever wondered if *we* are his next horror movie?"

*****

For a week at the lodge, it was all work and no play. Late one night, Wes, finally alone in a room with Rose, shut the door.

"Are we ever gonna talk about what we saw?" Wes asked Rose. They had been there over a week, and Jaime was right: JB was keeping them incredibly busy. They woke up before sunrise to help film crews get the shots they needed in the snow and freezing cold. Sometimes in the middle of the day, they'd be able to take a nap, but the moment the sun went down, they were back outside filming night shots. They were averaging about five, maybe six at the most, hours of sleep a day. Work certainly had kept their minds off of everything else. Wes couldn't shake the cold from his bones.

"What's to talk about?" Rose replied. "I mean, we don't know what it means."

"There's something very disturbing about that final video. It means *something*."

"I'm too tired to think." Rose yawned. She leaned against Wes, and he wrapped his arms around her.

"And why were we supposed to watch them in the first place? I still don't get it."

"I know, baby. We can talk about it in the morning." Just the feel of her body often eliminated any thoughts and worries Wes had.

Wes kissed her, and then the door opened. No knock, either. It was Bill. "Oh, sorry, guys."

"It's okay." Wes yawned. "What's up?"

"I was just looking for Jaime."

"Oh," Wes said and frowned.

"What?"

"Nothing."

"What? Tell me, please," Bill demanded.

"She's out on a walk."

"In this cold?" Bill paused for a moment, his face turning red. Wes could almost see steam spray out of Bill's ears. "She out with *him*, isn't she?"

"Bill, come here," Rose said. He walked over to her slowly and bit at his lower lip. She sat down on the bed and patted the space beside her for Bill to take a seat, too. "I know, like, none of us have barely had time to talk this week with all the work they've been putting us through. But have you . . . have you tried to talk to Jaime? About, you know, being more than friends?"

"I tried," he said.

Rose put a hand on his knee and looked him straight in the eye. "Try harder."

"Is that what you want, man?" Wes asked.

"I thought so. I don't know." He sat there looking at the floor, and Wes sat next to Bill. Wes just didn't understand this. Bill was their leader most of the time. He had confidence that no one else had. At least he used to. So why didn't he just go for it with Jaime? He tried to find the right words to say all of these thoughts.

"You know, I couldn't *not* go after Rose. And I don't have half the guts you have. So what is it, dude?"

Bill shook his head. "Don't sell yourself short, Wes. You have a lot more than you give yourself credit for." He looked up. "It's just . . . every time I get close to really saying it, something happens. It's like . . . I'm wondering if it's just not meant to be."

"We've all gone through a lot of shit," Rose said. "But why not just say it anyway? Maybe it would help you both deal with this shit."

Bill chuckled. "You know, the first time I was going to ask her out was at the end of our weekend last year, and then I saw you guys making out. I couldn't top that." He smiled and shrugged. "But no, it's not that simple. I just . . . I just wanted the timing to be right. I was gonna do it when our summer session started, and then of course . . . everything happened with Tara. But it's more than that, too. She's . . . I don't know if she's the same Jaime I met last year. Have you noticed that?"

Rose nodded. "But that's to be expected. For all of us, really."

Bill sighed. "Yeah, I guess." He looked from Rose to Wes. "I don't mean to interrupt you guys. Believe me, I know we haven't had much time on our own. I'm gonna go for a walk. Clear my mind. Thanks, guys."

"You sure you're okay?" Wes asked.

Bill nodded, gave a weak smile, and walked out of their room and down the halls down to a small lounge. He sat on the couch for a moment, and within seconds, he was asleep. He might have had a lot on his mind, but these long work days took absolutely everything out of him.

His nightmares, though, were as bad as ever.

*"But I thought you captured the murderer? You're the murderer?" Bill asked in his dreams.*

*Jay Bell stared back at him, a sinister smile on his face. He had slowly removed a black ski mask. Bill was crawling on the hallway floor in between his bedroom and his parents on that dreadful night many years ago.*

*JB was the home intruder.*

*"Twists and turns, my boy. I needed to know what it was like to rob. I wasn't expecting to kill that night, but you know—two birds, one stone. It felt good to have that experience. And then I saw you. I got to look into the eyes of a little boy who watched a parent murdered. That's an emotional experience you can't fake on camera."*

*"No! How could you?"*

*"You talk as if I had a choice. I am who I am, Bill."*

It wasn't the first time he had experienced that nightmare. He sat up on the couch in the motel lounge and wiped at his forehead. It was a cold sweat, something that often accompanied his nightmares.

Thankfully, the lodge supplied limitless hot chocolate. Bill walked over to a small kitchen area just adjacent to the lounge where he had fallen asleep. He poured a cup and looked out the window of the dining room.

Outside he saw Brandis and Jaime.

Bill instantly felt the hot chocolate come back up in his throat.

He wasn't a fool. He had seen the way she had been looking at Brandis. And Brandis was far less discreet in how he had been looking at Jaime.

Bill wanted to run right out there and punch Brandis in the face. He wanted to throw his hot chocolate at the window and scream.

"I'm such an idiot," he said through clenched teeth. *If only I had just said what I felt. If only I wasn't so stupid. So cowardly.*

Brandis stepped in closer to Jaime. *Is he who she really wants?* Bill couldn't believe what he was seeing. It was worse than any horror film he had ever seen. Brandis turned his face slightly to the side, put one arm behind Jaime's head, the other around her waist, and kissed her. Bill's stomach burned. Then he saw Jaime put her arms around Brandis. She was returning the passion. Bill could only stare.

It was no small kiss, either. He watched them both lose themselves in one another, until he couldn't stand the sight any longer.

He threw away the rest of his hot chocolate and returned to his room. Slamming the door, he didn't care who he woke up. He stared at the ceiling the entire night, not sleeping a wink. When a professor knocked on the door right before sunrise, he thought to himself, *all work and no play make Bill a dull boy.*

*****

After ten days of filming, everyone was learning what it was really like to shoot a massive movie: early days, long nights, and brutal weather. The film crew was finally taking a day off. With no one to wake them up, not a single person awoke before noon. Even Bill slept in until Wes woke him up.

"I'm arranging a meeting. We need to talk about what we saw. Rose and Jaime's room in fifteen minutes. By invite only."

Bill nodded groggily and got out of bed to get dressed. Even hearing her name made him feel upset, but he went to Jaime's room as instructed. They had bigger things to think about.

Wes also had gathered Daniel, Venus, and Annie. "What's he doing here?" Bill asked when he saw Brandis next to Jaime.

"I invited him," she told Bill sternly. "I trust him." Bill rolled his eyes and took a seat next to Wes on the opposite side of Jaime and Brandis. Daniel grinned as Bill walked past, and he had a momentary thought of punching Daniel in the jaw. He wasn't in the mood.

"I don't know how long we're gonna be here," Wes started, "but when we get back to Rabbit in Red, we need a plan. Now what do you think that last video is all about?"

Bill sighed, but it was time to talk about it. He thought back to their final night at Rabbit in Red before they left for International Falls. That was just a little over a week ago, but with all this work, it felt like it was months ago. Bill had put in the last tape left in the box they'd discovered in Freddy's boiler. The first thing Bill had noticed was that JB was clearly older. His hair was still obnoxiously long, a retro hairstyle from decades past. He recognized his body. It was thicker, bear-like. That was familiar but little else was.

*When JB spoke into the camera, his voice was nervous. "I've done something unforgivable," he confessed. "Someday I'll show you this video and you'll understand. I hope. That's why I need to record this. I fell in love with the most beautiful woman. She took away my pain. I felt nothing but pleasure when with her. She took away my desire to learn about pain." JB shifted and cracked his neck. "We had many great years together, you and I. But I realized I need to feel that pain. I can't create without it, and for a few years now, I've been unable to create anything. I lost a part of me when I found you. I have to find that part again, or I'll go through life like a zombie. I don't want dinner served at six or a routine date night. I need to experience the world, all of its sights and sounds. And all of its emotions, including the pain of leaving you."*

*He stood up and looked in a mirror. "I don't recognize myself." He took scissors and started cutting his hair. He turned it into an uneven mess, but suddenly the JB they recognized began to appear before them.*

*He looked straight into the camera. "I can use the monster in me to create. Or I can let the monster die and do nothing at all. The latter is not an option. I'm sorry. I hope one day you'll forgive me." He picked up a long, sharp butcher knife. He faced a direction off-camera, something they couldn't see. Then he lifted his arm high up over his head, and just when he was about to bring the knife down, the video feed became disoriented. Lines squiggled throughout, and the sound cut off. Then the screen went to black.*

*Bill gasped. Had JB just killed someone? And of course— why was that the one thing not on these tapes? Another mystery in a mystery, he thought.*

*But it was clear that JB had a knife and that he had used it on something. Or someone.*

*The first years said nothing, but after a minute, JB walked into the classroom. Everyone jumped.*

*"I'd like to talk with all of you back in the commons. Now, please." He left the room without even looking at the TV, the old VCR, or the video tapes in the box Bill had in front of him. They panicked, convinced that he must have known what they were doing.*

*But back in the commons, he simply reported on what they would be doing in Minnesota, told them to go to bed, that they would be leaving early in the morning. He gave them no time to talk about the video.*

*****

Jaime was glad they had finally decided to speak about it. Maybe it was too shocking to deal with at first. Maybe they needed a good week's worth of work to process everything.

"Do you think JB killed someone?" she asked. "Whoever it was that he supposedly loved?"

"That's what it looks like to me," Daniel stated. "He asks for forgiveness, he cuts his hair. It's all a bag of craziness, if you ask me. Then he slashes something off camera we can't see. I bet he killed his girlfriend."

"I can't believe that," Bill argued. "He's never hurt anyone outside of a controlled environment."

*You know that's not true*, Jaime wanted to say. *The kids outside the school dance? Sure, he was just a kid, too, but it was still brutal. No normal child hurts someone else like that, right?*

"We're talking about an entire lifetime though," Brandis countered, and Bill rolled his eyes again. "Throughout his entire lifetime, you don't think he could have hurt someone for real? Or even murdered someone? Outside of his experiments or whatever you want to call them?"

"If that's the case," Rose said, "then what do we do?"

"Maybe we need to get these video tapes to the police," Wes suggested.

"Then what happens to us?" Bill asked. "Do we just go home and say good-bye to Rabbit in Red and to each other forever?"

"We have to do what's right," Wes said. "So what's the right thing to do?"

"We have to know what's real," Brandis added. "I don't want to go home. Why do you think I'm here? But we can't work with a murderer. We need to know if it's real or not. If it's not, then we have nothing to worry about, right? And if it is, then why would we want to stay?"

Jaime saw the way Bill looked at Brandis. It was a look she had never seen on his face before, and it scared her a little.

"Did you bring the tapes with you?" Jaime asked Bill.

"Yeah. They're in my bag, back in my bedroom. You want to call someone now?"

"I know we're in the middle of nowhere," Jaime said, "but we have to start somewhere."

"Oh-right. I'll get the tapes. Then we'll call the nearest authorities and see how we start this investigation."

"I'll go with you," Jaime said.

They walked together quietly, and Bill looked straight ahead, never once making any kind of eye contact with her or saying a single word. *He knows, then, huh?* Yeah, he must know, she thought. *How, I don't know, but he does.*

Bill went into his bedroom and pulled out the bag that was under his bed. On his knees, he looked like he was praying. Jaime remembered the feelings she had for Bill when they first downloaded the Rabbit in Red app and solved horror riddles. She breathed hard through her nose and remembered the feeling she had when Bill first shared the news of the contest with her. Everything would change now, wouldn't it? Officially, she may never have been Bill's girl, of course, but now she was sure officially *not* Bill's girl. She felt the difference in the air. It was palpable, and Bill's lack of saying anything just added to the tension.

She tried to dismiss these thoughts. After all, they had something much bigger to deal with. Was JB a murderer? Now they had finally made a decision to involve authorities. Would that change everything, too? Brandis was right. They needed to know what was real. They had to know. Jaime hoped that JB wasn't *that* crazy, that he hadn't committed murder.

Bill reached in for the video tapes he had brought.

He turned around and looked at Jaime. She thought there were tears in Bill's eyes. They looked red and painful. Then he spoke. "Um." A big sigh. "They're gone. All of the tapes. Every single one. Gone."

She laughed out loud.

Of course they were.

## Chapter Twenty-Two

Professor Cunningham gathered all the students in the dining area of the lodge. They had completed their twentieth and final day of filming. During that time, they only had one full day off to themselves.

*There certainly is something to be said about keeping busy, Jaime thought. There's no time to feel anything else.*

"You've all done great work here," he complimented. "It's important to see what filming in all kinds of settings actually requires. Now that you've been in the cold for nearly a month, maybe fire doesn't sound too bad." The joke received a few small but uncomfortable laughs. "You have the night to relax. Tomorrow, everyone goes home. To your actual homes, that is. You'll be invited to return to Rabbit in Red after the New Year."

"Everyone?" Bill asked.

Cunningham nodded. "Everyone who can make arrangements, first years and new recruits. JB wants everyone back." Bill sighed and looked over at Jaime, but she didn't meet his eyes.

It was close to Thanksgiving, not even December yet. For Jaime, the idea of being stuck at home alone for over a month was not appealing.

"That long?" Wes asked.

"Spend the holidays with your families," Cunningham replied. "You should cherish those days."

"Is there any news?" Jaime asked. She didn't want to say the word murder, but she wanted to know, as they all did, if anything had been resolved.

"JB wants you all to know that he is working diligently to pursue all evidence related to the sabotage of Rabbit in Red and the murder of Donnie Chase."

"So, no news?" Jaime demanded. "Is that what you're telling us?"

"If we had anything else to report, I wouldn't hesitate to share it with you," Cunningham said with a weak smile. "Now enjoy your evening together. Our bus will take us to the airport in the morning and you'll all fly out to your hometowns."

Dinner was served, and for their last night, the Rabbit in Red team prepared a special pizza for them: Freddy's pizza. The pepperoni and cheese was designed in a way to represent the mangled face of Freddy Krueger. Ordinarily, they would have enjoyed this. The first actual Freddy Krueger face was actually designed on a piece of pizza in a random act of inspiration. But tonight, no one was in the mood. Jaime had gotten used to living with others, to the constant company and work, and the thought of going home to do nothing was depressing.

After Cunningham left, it was only the first years and recruits in the dining hall. Wes stood up and called for everyone's attention.

"I think we need one final discussion to determine what we're going to do when we get back after the New Year. This is our last night together for a while. I don't want to spend it talking only about depressing things, but we should have a plan, don't you think?"

The noises from eating and talking transformed into nothing more audible than a whisper.

Jaime stood up next. "I agree with Wes. I think the first question is: do we trust JB?"

Daniel interjected. "I think the first question is: did JB murder Donnie and damage his own studio?"

They'd started this discussion over a week ago, when Bill returned empty handed with no video tapes to show. Last time it erupted into a series of arguments and nothing was resolved. Then they were all back to work, morning, noon, and night. The discussions were limited to brief talks in between shoots or short walks around the lodge. By now, everyone was aware of what the tapes showed even if they weren't there to see them first hand.

"I trust him," Carol said, standing up and brushing her long, blond hair out behind her head. "He would never kill someone. I don't know how you all can think that."

"We saw him with a knife, slashing, right after he looked like he was losing his mind," Daniel argued.

"We can't jump to conclusions," Bill finally said. "We can't crucify a guy because of something we only think could have happened."

"Based on what we did see, he's not to be trusted," Brandis countered. "Anyone who would create pain and take pain like he did—something's not all there."

"I don't understand why this continues to be an issue," Bill snapped. Jaime could tell that Bill was clearly even more annoyed by the fact that it was Brandis challenging him. "It's what JB does. He tries to get into the mind of the victim and the villain. That's what our simulations and studies are so often about."

Jaime's eyes shot back and forth between Bill and Brandis. Bill hadn't spoken to her directly in over a week. She didn't want to hurt Bill, and she did like him. Brandis simply possessed the assertive personality she was hoping for from Bill, someone who confidently and passionately expressed his feelings for her. Bill had been evolving into something more like a brother, and if that was all he wanted to be, then what could she do about it?

There was something else Jaime was discovering about herself, too. She didn't want to be anyone's sidekick or number two. Bill had been their natural leader. In that context, he was confident, but when it came to her, he was still a boy. She used to find his shyness around her cute. What had changed?

She put an arm around Brandis as she stood up. "I know where you're coming from, but you have to trust us on this. We've been through a lot more with JB." As she said this, she pushed Brandis down in his chair, and as assertive as he may have been, his brown eyes turned into puppy dog eyes around Jaime. "But at the same time," she faced Bill, "we have to be skeptical."

"Guys, what do we do if we don't trust him?" Rose asked. Don't go back?"

"No," Jaime said. "He's been watching us. We develop a team to watch him."

"So you think we should become spies now?" Wes stood up and folded his arms.

"I know it's uncomfortable, Wes," Jaime said, looking around at everyone present. "Listen, you guys. I'm tired of guessing what's real and what's not. We received the tapes for a reason. People have been kidnapped and even fucking murdered. We need to stop worrying about how others may feel or how it will make us look. We grow a pair and figure this shit out. Now."

Jaime breathed heavily, and everyone else simply stared back at her. She looked directly at Bill and raised her eyebrows. She saw the defeat in his eyes, but he said, "Then let's call for a vote then. We do what the majority want, oh-right? So, raise your hand if you think we need a team to spy on JB when we return?" Only three hands didn't go up in the air: those belonging to Carol, Wes, and Bill.

"That settles it," Jaime said, but she didn't gloat. "We need to know, guys."

"I trust him," Bill said. "I know it's crazy, and I have my fears, I do. I can't explain it." He lowered his head.

"How should we organize this?" Wes asked.

"How about we have pairs? We want to be as discreet as possible. We'll have a pair for the morning, afternoon, evening, and night. What do you guys think?" Daniel asked humbly.

Wes nodded and looked at Rose for confirmation. "I like that idea. So let's pair up."

"Carol is obviously skeptical," Daniel spoke up again. "Would you work with me?"

"That's a good plan," Wes complimented. "Carol, you said you're graduating early, right? If everything works out when you get home, then you can come back after the New Year?"

"Yeah. I'll do it," she said. "I don't like the distrust here, but I do like the idea of seeing whatever you guys think you're seeing with my own eyes."

"Okay, me and Rose will team up. Jaime you and . . ."

"I'll work with her." Brandis jumped up. "I'm also graduating early, remember? I'll be able to come back."

"What about you, Bill?" Wes asked.

"I'll sit this particular adventure out, man."

Leroy and Annie looked at one another and nodded. "We'll work together too," Annie said, gesturing at Leroy.

"Let's report daily on what we find when we return," Wes said. "Now, let's try and have some fun tonight. It is our last night together."

He was greeted by a mix of empathetic and apathetic smiles. Like Bill, like them all probably, Jaime wanted to trust JB. But like she'd said, she was simply tired of guessing games. *If you can't trust the creator, you can't trust the creation.* One way or another, though, she was sure their days at Rabbit in Red were limited.

*****

"I'm gonna miss these nights," Wes whispered in Rose's ear when they finally had some alone time together. They were in Rose's room, and Jaime was out somewhere with Brandis. Everything was crazy, and only getting crazier. How many simple, peaceful nights with Rose remained at Rabbit in Red? Maybe it was time to get out, if Rose would leave with him.

"It really sucks. It's gonna be over a month till we even return." She pouted.

"I don't know how a guy like me got so lucky to get a girl like you."

She smiled back and kissed him. "You're turning into quite the leader, babe. I'm proud of you. To see you speak like you did in front of everyone, and even though your best friend doesn't agree, that's real leadership."

"I hope Bill is right. I do. But we have to learn more. I don't know how else to do that without exploring. Spying, I guess, if we have to call it that." He paused for a moment. "*You're* my best friend, though."

She blushed and cuddled closer to him. "I want Rabbit in Red to be everything I always imagined it could be," Rose said. "We have to find out the cause of these problems and extinguish them. Even—and I hope it's not—if the cause is JB."

"And if it is him?"

"I would think there would be plenty of people who could fill his shoes," Rose said. "Maybe not his wallet though. Let's not worry about it until we have to."

"I don't want to lose you. I'm . . . I'm worried if we lose Rabbit in Red, then I may lose you," Wes said softly. *I'd follow you onto the Titanic,* he thought.

"Never. You'll never lose me." She kissed him hard then, a passionate juxtaposition to her quiet personality. It was a long kiss, and all of their thoughts disappeared.

"I love you, Rose." His arms shook, and he felt more terrified in this moment than he had in any other moment at Rabbit in Red.

Rose had become his everything.

"I love you even more, Wes," she said back and kissed him hard once again.

He pulled away, and he saw the confusion on her face. Wes never pulled away first. He blinked hard, hoping she'd read his mind.

She dimmed the lights.

Wes reached for her hand, and he pulled her closer. He felt goosebumps and a chill, in every place on his body except for one.

He kissed her again, and then his mouth found her neck. He lifted up her shirt, and Rose moaned. Then she reached for Wes's shirt. He hesitated at first, but if there was one person in this world he trusted to see every inch of his body, it was this beautiful girl sharing a bed with him now.

They pulled the covers over their heads. Wes grinned from ear to ear.

It was by far the best night of his life.

*****

Not everyone was happy on the last night at this cold lodge in Minnesota. Bill walked the halls alone lost in his thoughts, and then he ran into perhaps the only person who could cheer him up.

"Tara!" he said. "I've been wondering where you were."

"Well, I was trying to spend time with Jaime, but she's . . . she's busy." Tara looked away quickly, but Bill knew what she was trying to say.

"Yeah, I can imagine."

"Why didn't you say something to her, Bill?" Tara demanded. "You two are meant to be together!"

"I tried. Honest." Bill put his hands in his pockets.

"I don't like this Brandis. He's cocky but wimpy at the same time. How can that be?"

He put an arm around Tara. "I don't know. I feel strong but weak at the same time. How can that be?"

"Because you're scared."

"I'm not scared!" he defended, his voice raising in pitch.

"You are, but it's okay. You'll always be my brother." Tara slipped her arm around his waist.

"I wish I had been lucky like Jaime to grow up with a sister like you."

"Your parents never had any other kids?" she asked. They walked and talked, moving through the hallways of the lodge.

"Nope, just me."

"You must have been too much for them." Tara giggled.

Changing the subject, he asked, "Are you looking forward to going home?"

"I don't know where we're going. Mom is still in a hotel gushing over some security dude in LA."

"I forgot about that. So maybe you'll be close to Rabbit in Red after all?"

"I guess." She took back her arm and shrugged.

"Is that okay with you? How are you doing these days?" They kept walking through the empty halls of the lodge.

"I want to be a part of the team. I know I'm still too young. You know JB's got me doing online classes for high school? That's what I work on in the trailer while you guys are freezing your butts off." She laughed. "The way I'm going though, I feel like I could finish tomorrow."

"You're not held back by all the idiots in the classroom."

"Exactly. I can work about five times faster on my own. Mom and JB don't want me in the public though. That's why I have to do it. But I do want to be a part of the team. It's like . . . some asshole tried to hurt me to hurt you guys. It makes me want to give him two middle fingers and say, 'Guess what asshole? Now I'm a part of the team too so screw yourself.' That's what I want," she said with an incredibly straight face.

Bill burst out laughing. "I've never heard you swear before." He laughed until his stomach hurt. It felt great. "Well, I'll do whatever I can to help with that, okay?"

"I know. Now, back to you and Jaime. What are you gonna do about Brandis?"

"What can I do?" Bill gestured with his palms up.

Tara just shook her head. "I know you're a lot smarter than that. Geez. Maybe you're an asshole, too?"

She made Bill laugh again, and he pushed at her jokingly. All the laughter did feel wonderful, but Tara may have been right. He probably was an asshole.

"Let's see who's up for a game," Tara suggested. "I have an idea."

*****

Bill wouldn't have been nearly as successful, but because it was Tara who went banging on everyone's door to get them to play, everyone was more than willing and excited to do so.

Well, almost everyone. She told Bill she couldn't find Wes or Rose, and he had advised her that they probably didn't want to be found.

"The game is called Jack Rabbit," she informed them all. "I thought you'd all like the name. One person is "it." That person runs off and hides, anywhere inside the lodge. The rest of us count to sixty, slowly, and then go looking for him or her. Once the person is spotted, you scream 'Jack Rabbit!' and run back to a designated base. Whoever is tagged first becomes the next Jack Rabbit, unless no one is tagged. So who wants to be the Jack Rabbit first?"

"I will," Daniel said. "Sounds fun."

"Okay. Go hide," Tara told him. They counted to sixty, and then Tara said, "Jaime come with me!" She grabbed her sister and ran off. "Everyone else join a group!"

Bill didn't join a group. Instead, he walked up and down the halls, which had a very retro cabin-in-the-woods appearance, by himself. Maroon carpeting met wooden walls with random pictures of nature. The dim lights created a haunting kind of atmosphere that enhanced the suspense of the game.

He walked around for a couple of minutes, not finding Daniel. Tara spotted Bill, and she ran toward him holding onto Jaime.

"Bill, you go with Jaime that way! I think that's where he's hiding." Then Tara took off in the opposite direction with no further explanation.

She turned to Bill after shaking her head at her sister. "Hi," she greeted simply.

"Hi," Bill said, shrugging his shoulders and looking at the ground. "Um, so this way?" He pointed in the direction Tara suggested.

"Sure," she said. It was an awkward silence as they walked. Bill thought to himself that out of everyone here, except for Tara and Jaime of course, it was Bill and Jaime who had known each other the longest. Considering the silence, it was all quite ironic.

"How are you doing?" she asked after a minute.

"I'm okay," Bill lied.

"I know I should have talked to you more about Brandis," she offered.

"I did think we were best friends. Don't best friends share everything?"

"We are, and yeah . . . I just . . . is it weird for you?" she asked.

Bill stopped walking, and Jaime had to turn around. "You know, I think Tara did this on purpose so we could talk."

"She's smart. She takes after me." Jaime smiled.

*Why does she have to be so damn beautiful?* Bill thought. *This isn't fair.*

"It is weird," Bill mumbled. "Do you like him? I mean really like him?"

Her eyes met his. "I do," she said. "I want you to give him a chance, too."

Bill frowned and started to roll his eyes. "What about me?"

"What about you?"

"I dunno . . . do you . . ." He struggled to find the words, and then someone yelled "Jack Rabbit!" from behind them.

"Let them run," Jaime said. "Come here." She pulled him into a corner.

Bill didn't know what to say, so he reacted impulsively. He leaned in quickly and kissed Jaime hard on the lips. He was off-balanced, and the kiss was awkward and sloppy. It didn't feel the way it should have felt.

"Bill, stop," she said and pulled away. "Not like this."

"Then like how? I don't know what to do."

Brandis ran down the hall with Carol, Jimmy, and Ricky. He put on the brakes hard when he saw Bill and Jaime together.

"Hey! What's going on?" Brandis asked in a stern tone.

"Nothing," Jaime said. "We were just talking."

Bill's mood snapped, and he faced Brandis. "Give us a minute."

"Why don't you get your hands off my girlfriend?" Brandis snapped. Bill looked down and saw he still had his arms around Jaime from the awkward kiss.

Jaime pulled away, and Bill let go. "Don't be an asshole," he told Brandis. "We were just talking."

That's when Brandis punched Bill in the face. He was shorter than Bill but more muscular, and Bill bounced off the wall at the force of the punch.

"Sorry, but maybe you two don't need to be hanging out anymore," Brandis said. "C'mon, Jaime." He reached out for her hand.

She looked back at Bill, who had his palm against his face. She hesitated and looked from Bill to Brandis. Brandis grabbed her hand and pulled, and she turned and walked away with him.

*Well, that sure as hell didn't go as planned,* he thought. Bill stood there, completely alone. *After everything I had faced last year, why couldn't I just punch that asshole back?*

*And what about Jaime?* That wasn't his best friend. His best friend wouldn't leave him on the ground like this. His best friend wouldn't have left him for such an asshole.

Bill just stared at nothing and wished nothing was all he felt.

*I'm ready to go home,* he thought.

## Chapter Twenty-Three

Bill stretched his long legs out on his bed back home in Illinois. A cold, gray December morning pierced through the window. He felt too big for this bed. It was the bed of his teenage years, his high school days that seemed so far away, even if it was only months ago. He had several unopened Horror Block boxes his mom tossed next to the stacks of all the opened ones he had collected through the years. Perhaps they were just silly toys or collectibles, but he never wanted to give them up. He turned on his tablet and out of habit almost called Jaime. His finger brushed over the FaceTime button, but then he closed the app and sat up in bed.

All of his posters still lined the walls, although they had gained a layer of dust. He walked downstairs to an empty kitchen and checked the cupboards, a habit he had developed since arriving home. He didn't find anything, though. His mom seemed to be doing well. She still worked as an administrative assistant at an elementary school, but she had started substitute teaching and even told Bill that she might apply for a job as a full-time teacher again.

He was proud of his mother. He didn't know anything about addictions other than what he had read, but he sensed kicking any habit was far harder than he could imagine. It would be like if someone told him to stop watching horror films. He didn't know if he could do it.

His mom had purchased Captain Crunch just for him. As he poured himself a bowl of cereal, she entered the room wearing a light blue bath robe. Her hair was disheveled but she looked rested.

"Good morning, Billy," she greeted. "How are you?"

"Okay," he said, slurping on a spoon full of milk and cereal.

"No nightmares?"

"I did, but it's okay. I'm used to them."

He paused as he recalled his dream. There had been a part of his nightmare that had bothered him about the night his father was murdered for a long time. He didn't even realize it had bothered him so much until recently. Watching as his mom put on a pot of coffee, he waited until she had a little caffeine before asking the question that had been on his mind. There was one thing about that night, one thing on which his dreams kept focusing, that he couldn't understand.

When the intruder entered his parents' bedroom all those years ago, he had something that had stood out to Bill. Remembering the dreadful memory, he closed his eyes and listened to the intruder—Jason Lamb, that was the name the reporter said when JB showed him the news footage of the arrest last year—make demands from his father and mother.

*"On your knees," a voice demanded. Bill did not recognize the voice.*

*Then he heard his father.*

*"Leave her alone! What do you want?"*

*"Quiet," the intruder barked. "You, on the floor, now. Where is your son?"*

*"He . . . he is—" his mom started to answer, the words interrupted by a sob.*

*"He's spending the night at a friend's house," his father interjected.*

*"You better be telling me the truth," the man snapped. Bill thought he sounded relieved. "Now, on your knees. Hands behind your back."*

Bill watched his mother sip on a cup of coffee. He finished his bowl of cereal, and then he mustered up the courage to bring her back to that terrible night and ask the question that was on his mind.

"Mom," Bill started, "there's something I've been meaning to ask you. It's about *that* night, though."

She choked ever so lightly on her coffee, spilling just a dab on her chin. "Go on."

"How did the intruder—uh, Jason Lamb—how did he know that I was here? Do you remember? He asked you where I was. He said 'your son.' He clearly knew you had one boy. He didn't ask about anything else. How did he know?"

"Oh, for heaven's sake, how would I know?" Sally shook her head.

"Doesn't it seem weird to you? Was he watching the house? Or did he know us somehow?"

"I guess you could ask him," she stated matter-of-factly.

The thought turned Bill's stomach upside down. It surprised him that he had never thought of that himself. There was no major trial. The evidence that had been accumulated against Lamb was overwhelming, thanks largely to the efforts of JB, Bill assumed. Seeing no chance of redemption, Lamb pleaded guilty. The newspapers did say if he went to trial that there would be zero chance for parole. Illinois had abolished the death penalty, so there was no chance for Bill to see Jason go *Green Mile* style, which he found disappointing. The papers said that by pleading guilty, he would have opportunity for parole hearings in the future. Bill hoped Jason Lamb would be dead by then.

He looked at his mother inquisitively. "Are you serious?"

She sipped her cup of coffee again before answering. "I've thought about it myself. I've talked about it at my AA meetings. I don't know. Sometimes I'd like to look the devil directly in the eyes and ask why. But then I realize I'd probably end up right next to him after I broke the glass and strangled him to death." Her face told Bill that this was no joke. No joke at all.

*Sometimes there is no why, boy*, Bill heard in his head.

"I just think it's odd that he knew about me. That's all." Bill wondered what else Jason Lamb knew about the family, and he wondered if there was a why after all.

*****

Jaime and Tara watched a movie together in the living room while waiting for their aunt and cousin to come over. They chose *The Mist*, and Tara screamed at the end. Jaime had been waiting to see her reaction on what she thought was one of the most twisted endings of any story.

"That's crazy! He . . . just as they . . . oh my God!" Tara put a hand over her mouth, trying to digest what she had seen.

"I know, right?" Jaime smiled. "I love a twisted ending."

The front door opened without so much as a knock.

"Happy New Year's Eve!" Aunt Megan cheered. Aunt Megan and Jennifer were carrying a couple of large plates of food. To celebrate the arrival of a new year, they had planned a full night of eating and drinking (for the moms anyway).

"What are you watching?" Jennifer asked Tara.

"*The Mist*!"

"Never heard of that."

"What? I'll start it over right now!" Tara giggled, and Jaime knew that laugh. Tara wanted to be the one to torture someone now.

"You girls are not watching horror films all night!" Janet yelled from the kitchen. "Do you know Tara and Jaime have probably watched three or four horror movies a day since they've been home?"

"You have two crazy kids." Aunt Megan shook her head, and Jaime walked into the kitchen with them. But she smiled at Jaime's mom, and then she jumped in and hugged her tight. "I'm so glad you're back. I was worried you'd stay in California and never come back."

Janet returned the smile and hugged her back. "Well, the weather's nicer. And I've told you about the security guard that JB hired for us? He has the tightest little ass, I just want to—"

"Mom!" Jaime rolled her eyes. "Please!"

"Well," Janet continued, lowering her voice, "he had family to visit, so we thought we'd come home for a couple weeks. JB is relentless though with security. There's a rotation of hired guards here. They work in short shifts so they can spend part of the holidays with their families, but there's always someone here."

"What's he like?" Aunt Megan asked.

"Besides that ass, he has these arms I just picture taking me and—"

"No, you dirty minded whore," Aunt Megan joked as she poured them each a glass of wine. "I want to hear about your man crush, but tell me about JB. I've been following the news, but he never does any interviews."

Jaime stared at the glass of wine. Maybe she'd have a glass or two. It was New Year's, after all.

"He's very thoughtful," Janet said. "He took great care of Tara. Covered all hospital costs, got her counseling, let those Rabbit in Red kids help out. They love her." Janet took a sip of wine. "I was *very* skeptical, mind you, about being around anything else related to horror, but the friends she's made there really have helped."

"Hmm, okay, he sounds boring," Megan joked.

"JB?" Janet asked. Megan nodded, and Janet said, "You know, I've never actually seen him. Just his security or assistants. He's always so busy."

"Yep. He sounds boring. Tell me more about that security guard's ass." Janet snorted but wasted no time refilling a glass of wine and giggling. Jaime had heard enough. She returned to the living room to her sister and cousin.

"I can't listen to them," Jennifer said and stuck out her tongue. "Turn up the TV or something."

"Good idea," Jaime agreed. She switched the TV to one of the New Year's Eve shows and cranked the volume.

"So tell me everything," Jennifer said, crossing her legs on the couch and facing Jaime and Tara. "Do you have pictures?"

"Yeah," Jaime said and took out her phone. They flipped through several, Jaime commenting briefly on each one.

"This is your boyfriend?" Jennifer asked at a picture of Bill and Jaime taking a selfie. This was taken back last summer, before things had become awkward.

"It should be!" Tara jumped in. "That's Bill. He's the coolest."

"It's a long story." Jaime gave her sister a dirty look and swiped forward to a picture of Brandis. "That's my boyfriend."

"Ooh, he's hotter than Bill. That's okay then." Jennifer laughed.

"He is not!" Tara argued.

"Have you seen those arms? I'd let him touch me!" Jennifer grinned.

"You're gross," Tara said. "Bill is sweet. Jaime is just going through a stupid phase."

"You can be a real brat sometimes, you know?" Jaime rolled her eyes. Jennifer flipped through several other pictures.

"Who's that?" Jennifer asked.

"That's Rose and Wes, I told you that. They're a sweet couple and my best friends."

"No, behind them," Jennifer said. "Here." She pointed in the background.

"Oh, that's JB. I never noticed that before. He's not really the picture type. Must have just caught him in the background when I took this of Rose and Wes."

"He looks like Frankenstein," Jennifer said.

"You mean Frankenstein's monster," Tara corrected. "But don't say that. It's cruel. He's been very good to me, even if *she* thinks he's gone crazy."

"What do you mean?" Jennifer asked.

"We shouldn't talk about it," Jaime said. Jaime and the others had done their best not to talk about it around Tara, but she had obviously overheard some things.

"There was a murder at Rabbit in Red," Tara said bluntly.

"What?" Jennifer's mouth dropped open. "Are you kidding me? What happened?"

"One of JB's assistants, a woman by the name of Donnie Chase, was found murdered," Jaime told her, rolling her eyes at Tara.

"And why haven't I heard about this?"

"JB has a lot of connections," Jaime explained. "He's kept it out of the media, which makes some of us believe it's just another twisted game within a game, a mystery for us to figure out."

"You don't sound like you believe that," Jennifer noticed.

Jaime looked at Tara, thinking about what to say in front of her. "We're all just being extra cautious. Maybe it is a game. Or maybe JB is responsible."

"You've got to be kidding me," Tara sighed. "He would never hurt a fly." Jaime bit her tongue and looked at her sister. Tara didn't know about all of the videos, and it was best to keep it that way.

"So let me get this straight," Jennifer said. "You believe there's a chance the guy who is running this whole show is actually a killer? And you're going back? Are you *crazy*?"

"A lot of people seem to think that these days," Jaime confessed. "It's one of those things . . . where you have to be there. There's been a lot of complication, but at its core, Rabbit in Red is a very special place."

"I can't believe you." Jennifer's face flushed with anger. "Tara gets abducted, hurt, then there's a murder, and both of you want to go back? How are we even related? That's just plain dumb."

Jaime nodded. "I get it," Jaime said, trying to stay calm. "I know how crazy it sounds from the outside. But you're not there. You have to trust me. We're safer there than anywhere else, really."

"Even with the host being a killer?"

"Well, we don't know that," Jaime said. "And if he is, we'll make sure he gets the justice he deserves. If we're not there to investigate, then he could get away with it. We have to be there to know for sure what's going on."

"Then call me stupid because ignorance sounds like bliss." Jennifer sighed. "Let me see that picture again." She examined the picture Jaime had taken of Rose and Wes, with JB lurking in the background.

"I recognize him, now that I think about it. I never forget a face." She paused for a moment and closed her eyes. "Yeah. He came to your graduation ceremony, didn't he?"

Jaime had almost forgotten about that. She saw JB from the crowd, a proud teacher waving from the way back. He was there to support her, wasn't he? And now she thought he could be a murderer. It was all very confusing.

"You gotta be very careful, Jaime. He's obviously taken a special interest in you and Tara. If he's crazy like you think he is, then you have to realize that you're in danger."

Jaime hadn't thought of it like that before. JB had given her extra attention this year, from the graduation ceremony to being there in every way possible when Tara was hurt. Was she in trouble?

Could she be the next victim? Was it possible JB was responsible for what had happened to Tara? He had found her so easily, all with a new app that detected rapid changes in temperature to quickly catch fires. Now that she thought about it—JB's app, finding Tara rather quickly—it was all rather convenient, wasn't it?

"I know this may make things even weirder," Jennifer said hesitantly, "but I've seen this guy before that, too. I mean before your graduation ceremony. You don't forget a guy who looks like that."

"Where?" Tara asked. She had been mostly quiet listening to Jennifer and Jaime talk. Jaime knew Tara liked JB. He had found her when she was hurt. He had saved her. At least that was what they all had thought. He was there day in and day out for her while the first years spent time on their studies. Jaime could read her sister's face, and she knew all of this talk was making Tara afraid. If the others were right that JB was mad, then he could come after her or Jaime or both, right? Jaime tried to shake away the thoughts.

"He was at Dad's funeral. I swear he was." Jennifer couldn't take her eyes off the picture. "Not the service but at the cemetery. I looked behind as they lowered Dad's coffin into the ground. He was standing next to the tree, almost as thick as the tree itself. He saw me look at him, and he turned around quietly. It was just one of those odd moments that I never forgot. But I'm telling you, he was at my Dad's funeral."

Jaime narrowed her eyes. "That was before Rabbit in Red. Before everything. Why would JB have been at your dad's funeral?"

"I don't know," Jennifer said, "but it sounds like you've got another mystery to figure out."

All three girls looked out into the kitchen. Their moms had already finished a bottle of wine and were opening another. Their continuous laughter was a refreshing sound. Jaime was resolute in not wanting her mom to know any more than she absolutely needed to about JB and Rabbit in Red. She didn't need another fight about going back and staying there. She looked at Jennifer and smiled gently. They both shared an understanding. Let their mothers enjoy the night. It had been one hell of a year.

"Maybe we should throw that movie on you were telling me about," Jennifer said.

"Okay."

The movie would be good. She had seen it a dozen times, and she could zone out with her thoughts. She took out her phone and was only thinking of one person. It wasn't Brandis.

She desperately wanted to text Bill. He would understand how she felt. She could talk to him about what Jennifer had said, but she just stared at his number in her phone, and suddenly sharp tears pierced at her eyelids.

Glancing back to the kitchen, she saw her mom and Aunt Megan laughing and drinking. She looked at her phone and wondered if there was a way she could Skype with her father. She just needed someone who would listen and understand. Not that she had any reason to think her dad would, but in those few seconds before graduation last summer, he had told her and Tara both that he loved them, missed them, and that one day he'd get home to see them again. If her father thought she'd ever understand his absence, then he could try to help her understand this.

She sighed. Her thoughts were bouncing around. She wouldn't try to get ahold of her father. She needed Bill, but she had ruined that, too, hadn't she? Jaime didn't know what to do or what to think, and maybe—she hoped—all of this was a bunch of nothing, but right now it felt incredibly overwhelming. She wiped little tears from the corner of her eyes and forced a deep breath. She wouldn't lose it in front of Tara or Jennifer or do anything to distract their moms from having a good time.

She remembered JB maintained a collection of blogs online at his frightfest4d.com website. Maybe it would help to read through those again and see if anything new had been posted. She and Bill had read through them all last year as they prepared for the riddle contest and Halloween weekend. She missed those days.

When she clicked on frightfest4d.com, she saw the Rabbit in Red logo. The rabbit did its little dance, but then a second later, it burst into flames.

The entire website was nothing but fire. No other links to click, nothing to explore whatsoever.

Everything was on fire.

# Part III:
# Burn the Rabbit

"There's no counting what kind of undesirables you might run into in these halls."
- Liz from *American Horror Story: Hotel*


"What fresh hell is this?"
 - Chanel from *Scream Queens*


"There was a crooked man, and he walked a crooked mile. The crooked man stepped forth and rang the crooked bell. And thus his crooked soul spiraled into a crooked hell. Murdered his crooked family and laughed a crooked laugh."
- The Crooked Man from *The Conjuring 2*

# Chapter Twenty-Four

In the middle of January, everyone was invited back to Rabbit in Red. An invitation was sent via e-mail with a simple message attached.

*Transportation will be arranged for you over the weekend. Click confirm to let us know you will be returning. On Tuesday, January 24, we begin our second semester program with a special tribute. The semester will feature advanced course studies, the final round of games for new recruits, and a special challenge for our first years. Enhanced security at Rabbit in Red will ensure safety.*

Time had a way of distorting memory, of making things seem better or worse than they were, JB thought. He was certainly well aware of that. He worried for his creation and for his participants. It wasn't supposed to happen like this. He had such great visions for a college of horror. With virtually unlimited resources and supplies, what couldn't they accomplish together in this industry?

He sat in the safe room back at the studios, which he had turned into his office. He sat there not to hide, but to watch. He replayed surveillance video from the summer and fall, trying to pick up on anything he had missed, and he watched to see if anything would happen at Rabbit in Red with everyone gone.

The halls were depressingly quiet and inactive. This was his nightmare. To have this world of resources in front of him with no enthusiastic participants was miserable. He knew he needed to give everyone time. They needed to distance themselves from the murder and the sabotage. Perhaps then, he could reignite their youthful energy and the desire to create and push the boundaries of terror. He reflected on the things he had done when he was their age. Not having the resources he had today but having the desire to understand horror from all perspectives, he had felt he had to resort to other means. It was his experiences, however, that led to the concept of Rabbit in Red, a place where fears could be faced head on in the safety of enhanced virtual reality.

But it wasn't really safe, was it? No, not at all, and the thing JB had completely overlooked was the fact that he had become the prime suspect in nearly every mind of those he cared about.

He watched them all return with a hopeful smile on his face. The setting was the same. He hadn't had the energy or time to change it. They walked past Freddy's basement, through *Hellraiser*, into the *Candyman* commons, and up to their *Alien* rooms to put their belongings away. He wanted to hear laughter and see hugs. Did they not understand how close they had all become? Didn't they understand that sometimes it does take terrible things to bring people even closer together? When that happened, a bond was forged that would never be broken.

But he didn't see laughter, hugs, excitement, or appreciation. He saw curiosity, but it was lined with fear and apprehension. He nodded to himself in the empty safe room. He had made deliberate efforts to remove their fears in the past, and he could do it again. He stood up, stretched his arms, rolled his neck, and listened to the joints pop after sitting for too long. It was time to say hello. A new semester of opportunity began today. He would do whatever it takes to eliminate their fears.

Whatever it takes.

*****

Rose released Wes's hand and smiled encouragingly at him.

He stood up. "We start today," Wes said to Daniel, Carol, Leroy, Annie, and Brandis. Jaime and Bill watched from the side, although they weren't speaking to one another.

"Hi, Bill," Rose greeted. "I know before you didn't want to spy, but we hope you'll join us."

Wes smiled at him, too. "You could join us, man." Rose could tell that Bill didn't want to talk or argue at all. But she also felt that he didn't want to be left out. He simply nodded. "Awesome. We'll take the first shift this afternoon. We'll rotate in and out. The idea is to see and hear whatever JB does. We may not be able to always find him easily, so I think we can spend time dropping in on the assistants and professors, too."

Bill nodded again and felt Brandis staring at him. Rose hoped there wouldn't be another fight. Rose had always thought that what people did in the movies was different than what they did in real life. Wasn't that part of Rabbit in Red's test? We can re-enact scenes all we want, but that's not real life, she thought. And what did Bill do after Brandis slugged him? Nothing. In a movie, wouldn't he have stood up and punched him back? After all, Rose thought, this was their leader who had faced people he thought were trying to *kill* him. *But a guy punches him in the face and he doesn't do anything about it?* It was a paradox Rose didn't understand.

"Carol and I can take the next shift," Daniel said. They had agreed to rotate every hour or two, or whatever felt natural so as to look like it was only a couple of friends walking around the studio in between classes and projects.

"Then how about us?" Leroy asked, looking from Wes to Annie.

"And we'll take the later hours," Brandis said of himself and Jaime. Rose caught the grin Brandis gave Bill when he said "later hours."

*This really sucks,* she thought.

"Sounds like a plan, guys. Good luck," Wes said, and he, Rose, and Bill exited the bedrooms to begin their shift.

"Where to?" Bill asked.

"Under the commons," Wes said, "where Donnie was killed."

"Oh-right," Bill said hesitantly. "I guess we're not wasting any time."

"Wes and I talked a lot over winter break," Rose told him. "We want everything to be back to normal and quick, you know?" Bill nodded as they searched the floor of the commons for the elevator that took them down a level.

"But last time only Jaime was able to activate it," Bill said.

"I figure it's worth a try." Wes felt around the area where he saw Jaime get the elevator to work. He had no luck. Neither did Bill or Rose.

"There has to be another way down," Rose said in frustration. She looked around and sighed. She wanted to get this search over with. More than anything, she absolutely hated the love triangle between Brandis, Jaime, and Bill. *What is this? Twilight? The Hunger Games? Ugh!*

"Sure!" Wes shouted in a realization. "We just have to slide down to the safe room, then go up the slide that's attached to this level!"

*The longer we wait . . .* Rose didn't want to finish the thought. She nodded and led the way back to their bedrooms. They had to climb back up, do their best to avoid everyone, which was hard. Everyone was chilling in bed or hanging out right in the open.

"Be very quiet," Rose said, as they crept to the back corner of the sleeping area. She gently pushed open the door to the slide. It wasn't that they cared a lot that the other students knew what they were doing. They worried though that others would want to help, and too many helpers—like too many cooks in a kitchen—could get messy and ruin their plans. With a look over her shoulder, Rose nodded and jumped on the slide. Wes and Bill followed suit, and they hung on at the top of the slide for a moment.

"Very slowly, now," Wes whispered. "JB could be down there, and we don't want to plop out all dramatically if he is."

They braced their arms at the sides of the slide to slow down their momentum, and just as Wes had suggested, they glided downstairs to the safe room. Slowing to a complete stop at the bottom of the slide before exiting, they could already hear JB's voice.

Rose put her finger up to her lips and made eye contact with Bill and Wes to make sure they understood. They nodded, and each stretched out as far as possible to listen to JB.

"I know that you don't understand," they heard JB say. "Listen to me, please," he started but must have been cut off. For the next minute, they only heard "uh-huh" and "mmhm." JB must be talking to someone on the phone.

"I do care!" The pitch in his voice dramatically sharpened. "Something happened. Something I've been trying to make up for." Bill, Wes, and Rose looked at one another questioningly, wishing they could hear the other voice.

"I've done more than you know," he snapped. "Damn!" They heard him shuffle around below them, thinking that the phone conversation must have ended. Rose dared to peek out from the bottom of the slide to see what JB was doing. She saw him walk toward one of the walls aligned with monitors, a wall between the two main slides that led from the guys' rooms and the girls'. He touched the monitor several times, and then the wall opened like a door. He pushed it all the way open, went inside, and shut it from behind.

*Let's get out of here before we're caught,* Rose thought. She glanced back at the others, and they all nodded, as if reading her mind. Who was JB talking to? This was beginning to feel like an episode of *Lost.* They didn't get any answers, but instead had even more questions to discuss.

They waited several minutes to make sure JB was gone, and then they returned to their rooms. Impatiently, they waited until dinner, when they could all sit together somewhat discreetly to discuss the conversation they had heard.

"It sounds like he knows he messed up," Annie said. "Last fall, with everything that happened. And now he's trying to make up for it? With us?"

"Who was he talking to?" Jaime asked.

Rose shook her head and shrugged. Throughout the day, they saw everyone: the professors, Victor Cunningham, Shirley Rice, and Curt Waggner were here. All of the assistants were here, except for Donnie of course. They saw Chester Malcolm, Michael Quinn, and Thomas Vance. They even saw Bonnie and Marcus.

"There were dozens of other stunt actors at the final game we played," Bill added. "It could be any of them or any number of people he works with in this industry."

"He's got more connections than we could possibly imagine, I'd bet," Wes agreed.

"It sounded very personal though," Rose whispered. "This wasn't a colleague, I don't think. This was someone he cares a lot about."

"We need to learn more," Daniel stated, "about his personal life then. Does he have a girlfriend? A wife? A mother? A brother? Maybe there's some kind of personal connection that we're missing. Someone who would also have an interest in Rabbit in Red."

"Yeah," Jaime said. "Good thinking." *She's complimenting Daniel*, Rose thought. *That never leads to anything good.*

"We could just ask him," Rose suggested.

The guys all laughed, and then Brandis asked, "Oh, you're serious?"

"Why not?" Rose said. "All this spying around is one thing. But maybe we just need a good ten minute conversation."

"Okay." Jaime smiled. "I'm with Rose. After dinner. We see if he's got a few minutes to chat."

"We shouldn't all bombard him at once though," Wes said. "Maybe just one or two of us?"

Rose added quickly, "I agree. Jaime and Bill, you two should do it. You've each spent time with him alone before. It would be less weird if it were just you two."

"Easy for you to say," Bill said. "But yeah, out of all of us, that's a good idea." Rose saw Bill smile at Jaime, and she returned it, even if was just polite. *That's something.*

"Good, that's settled," Rose said, putting her hands on her black purse that rested on her lap. "There's JB now."

The master host walked across the stage to address the students. "Good evening, and welcome back, my friends. It's been a long winter, has it not? There are mysteries unsolved and I'm sure you would like more answers to everything in our past. I would, too. Please, let me assure you that we are making great progress, and you will have your answers the moment I do. Until then, I want us to start fresh. To begin anew. We have two upcoming events I wish to preview. First, we must finish the games for our new recruits. They were a part of our journey at our most difficult times. I consider them family, as I do all of you. But to be fair, they haven't finished."

JB's familiar sadistic smile returned on his face, a grin from ear to ear. Rose wished she could take comfort in that smile.

"So we will have a special weekend. After that, I've prepared a special challenge for our first years. You've all been working on games, challenges, and a variety of studies. You get to have your fun, too. I was actually saving your challenges for the end of the semester, but in light of everything, you'll get your round of games the same weekend as our new recruits. We'll give them a chance to sit back and see what our first years are made of!"

No one cheered, but there were uneasy stirs throughout the commons. The last time they had any kind of game or challenge, one person went to the hospital and another wound up murdered. Rose thought that JB must have expected their hesitation and prepared for it.

"Let's break the ice tonight with some fun, then, shall we? I've added some additional programs to our game chambers, just for your amusement. Tonight we begin a new tradition. Something I could see kicking off the start of every new semester. Tonight is the first bi-annual Rabbit in Red Monster Battle!"

Several students looked at one another curiously. They listened closely as JB continued.

"Think of it like Mortal Kombat. I've tweaked the Rabbit's Eye and the game chambers for the ultimate virtual reality battle. You get to choose your favorite horror villain and you will battle one another. The winner gets a special prize. We were going to give it away to a parent last summer, but . . . well, complications ensued, didn't they? Tonight, there will be no complications. Just pure fun. Tournament style, winner moves on to the next fight, so choose wisely."

It turned out to be a night they all needed. Wes chose Pennywise the Clown, and Bill picked Michael Myers. Rose selected Cujo the dog. Jaime selected the Stay Puft Marshmallow Man and couldn't stop laughing. Brandis picked Dracula, in honor of the late, great Christopher Lee, he later told them. Others chose Chucky, Jack from *the Shining*, Leatherface, the Alien Queen, Predator, and other horror greats.

It was a night of laughter. Cujo took a bite out of Stay Puft. Stay Puft blasted the dog with marshmallow goo. Dracula tried sucking the blood out of the Alien Queen. Pennywise and Predator squared off in an epic battle. Chucky tried to kill Myers, but Michael's knife was bigger and quicker. Jack got his head sliced off by Leatherface's chainsaw. The students cheered and screamed—it was perhaps the best game they had ever played.

JB had created the perfect night. At the end of the tournament, he announced, "I will leave the game chambers open for you to play any time you wish. I will also leave the program available for you to create any other characters you wish to have. Tonight, our winner is . . . Daniel! How could you not win as Cthulhu, I suppose? A creature that is part dragon, part octopus, and part man is tough to beat." JB laughed. "Your reward, young man, is . . . here!" JB handed Daniel an object. "This mirror may have *magical* properties, so hold on to it closely and use it wisely."

Daniel looked at JB strangely, but accepted the gift. It was a handheld mirror, no bigger than his palm. and of course it didn't look magical. Daniel shrugged and slipped it in his pocket.

"I have a bonus prize, too," JB announced. "The parent who did the best at Hellfire was going to get a prize for their student. I hate to not give away a prize, so I do have one more. Wes? Would you come forward?"

Wes gasped and looked at Rose with the biggest, goofiest smile, and it made her laugh. He looked like he had just won the lottery, and he stood up and ran to JB who handed him a gift.

"This is for you. May it help provide what you've been looking for."

It was a VHS tape.

## Chapter Twenty-Five

"Good luck," Jaime told Brandis as she leaned in to kiss him. He put on the Rabbit's Eye, strapping the heart rate monitor to his bare chest. He wore only a pair of red athletic shorts and tennis shoes. Jaime wrapped her arms around his shirtless chest and felt muscles that she had never felt on Bill. The Rabbit's Eye crisscrossed on his chest, making him look part *Lord of the Flies* and part futuristic predator slasher. Jaime stepped back from the hug but kept a hand on his well-defined chest, and she heard Bill cough awkwardly from behind. Jaime was sure Brandis' goals included pissing off Bill, and that goal was successful.

The first month of the second semester at Rabbit in Red flew by without any excess trouble. JB kept them busy once again with projects and studies, and he counted down the days until the weekend of the final game for new recruits, the game they were unable to finish last year when Diane Willow was burned in the simulation.

Most of the recruits returned, even Diane. She looked more determined than most. She had straightened her previously curly dark hair, and her eyes were focused on the mission ahead. No longer an innocent girl simply trying to have fun, Jaime thought she looked like she had something to prove, a Katniss Everdeen standing in an arena of physically stronger contestants.

Carol Fisher, formerly JB's biggest cheerleader, stretched her legs and swung her arms in anticipation. She wore a tight pink tank top and her blonde hair reached down to the upper part of her back. She tied it in a ponytail, and she looked equally determined to prove something. Jaime had seen Carol out walking with Daniel on several different nights, supposedly looking for any additional clues and insights about their master host.

Jaime had sensed a change in Carol. Previously, Carol had been JB's biggest supporter. She no longer championed their master host in any way. During discussions, she sat quietly and nodded her head when others criticized JB. What had happened? Had she seen something the others hadn't? Carol's mind appeared to be consumed by dark clouds overpowering a previously sunny day.

Of course, there was the issue with the video tape, too. It would appear that JB had wanted them to see it, and more than that, it meant that he had known what they already had seen, right? But the VCR they watched the other tapes on was gone. They couldn't find a single VCR in the entire studio. They had asked JB and the assistants to get them a VCR, but every time they asked, they were told any number of excuses. "The ones we had have broken. We're getting a new one." Or "it's on its way." And, Jaime's favorite: "I'm worried no one makes them anymore, but if we can find a new one, you'll be the first to know." It was pure torture, and she assumed JB had to have been doing it on purpose. Was this another test?

They stayed up late at night speculating dozens of possibilities. They kept the VHS tape close and never let it out of sight, taking care of it as much as they took care of Falcor and Lester. They would find a way to watch the tape, and until they did, they kept all eyes on JB.

As the month passed, suddenly it was time for another game, the final part for the recruits, many months delayed. The first years walked them all to the Hellfire rooms. Ricky Thomas rubbed his fake looking goatee that never seemed to grow. Jimmy put on his favorite tie, and Jaime thought he was trying to look like James Bond getting ready to save the world. Julie strapped on shoes that looked like a cross between hiking boots and high heels. Was she planning on crushing someone? The other recruits, the ones she didn't know as well, Amelia, Samuel, Morgan, and Cameron, were all there too, making a total of ten recruits playing the final game. The only one who never returned was Kent Callahan. Kent and his cornrowed hair made no appearance. He had repeatedly told them they were all crazy, and perhaps they all were, Jaime thought, smiling to herself.

"For the final part of your contest," JB announced over a loud speaker, "you all will enter Hellfire at once. All rooms are open, but the ones you previously explored have been redesigned to add a little extra to fun to your challenge." He released the classic JB chuckle. "The goal is simple. Today you no longer are working in teams to solve a puzzle. The first one out the other side will be one of our student leaders next year. If the rest of you want to return, you must at least finish. Are you ready?"

The first years wished them all good luck one more time. Jaime stepped in close to Brandis so only he could hear. "Kick ass," she told him, and kissed him on the cheek. She turned around to catch the look of disgust on Bill's face. Then they all ran back to the commons to watch on the big screen.

The entryway outside of Hellfire went dark. The rabbit appeared before them in full 4D glory. It sat on its axe as if the axe were its child. Then the rabbit snarled, stood up, spun, and vanished. They heard it cackle from within Hellfire. It was time to enter.

All ten ran into the first room where the rabbit awaited them. "Rescue the father," it instructed. The dark room slowly came to life and they saw they were somewhere in a desert. Up on a hill before them, a man was tied up. They saw what they thought to be monsters surrounding him. Disfigured creatures, sometimes with one eye or three eyes, hissed at them. Their faces were crooked, they had one limb longer than the other, and their spines were like hoses, bending this way and that, as if their bodies were supported by gelatinous material and not bones. The monsters saw them and charged. With a surprised yelp, the recruits ran into different directions in the room. Behind them they saw a trailer.

Jaime recognized the reference. These weren't monsters, then. These were mutants. This was a challenge inspired by *The Hills Have Eyes*. She could tell from Brandis' expression that he caught the reference, too. Perhaps inside the trailer, he could find a weapon to fight the mutants. He sprinted toward it, and the other recruits took notice. They followed.

Inside the trailer were a few items he could use. Whether they were in the movie or just added by JB for the simulation, Jaime didn't know. There was one gun, and she watched Brandis dive for it. Behind him, Carol grabbed a baseball bat, Ricky found a cross bow, Diane snagged a knife, and Jimmy grabbed a huge frying pan from the kitchen. He smiled and shrugged when he saw everyone else's weapons. "It will have to make do."

The mutants had already approached the trailer. Some hopped on top while others rocked it back and forth. Seconds later before the recruits could even exit, the trailer had been knocked over. They all fell on their sides, as the floor of Hellfire shook and erupted like an earthquake had taken place.

Diane kicked open the door and crawled out. Brandis jumped through a window, and the mutants hopped out in front of them. Diane slashed at one's throat and raced toward the father that was tied up in the distance. Jaime cheered for all of them, but then a feeling surprised her: part of her wanted Brandis to lose. It would be easier to deal with Bill, who was already disgusted that she and Brandis were together. If he became a champion too and joined them as leaders, that would drive Bill over the edge. So she rooted for them all. Jaime wanted to yell and remind them that the goal wasn't to destroy the mutants but to save the father. In the story, the mutants set the father on fire. The recruits would have to save him before that happened.

Gunshots fired from behind. Brandis shot at a half-dozen mutants, Ricky launched an arrow, and Jimmy clubbed one repeatedly in the head with his frying pan. But Diane was the fastest. She reached the father in the distance and untied him. A hand pulled at her from behind, and she slashed out at it with her knife. Jaime laughed a little as she watched. That was no mutant. That was Brandis. He yelled as if he had actually been stabbed, holding on to his chest where she cut at him.

Diane jumped back. "Are you okay?"

"It hurts like hell." He groaned.

"Must be programmed the same way the fire simulations were designed to make us feel pain, except now we can hurt one another."

Brandis nodded. "Maybe you shouldn't tell the others that. It is every man for himself right now." Jaime studied Brandis through the screen. You can learn a lot about someone based on how they compete, she knew.

"And every woman." Diane smiled. "Yeah, okay." She looked up at the father she had just untied. He had vanished, and a door appeared to a new room. Without looking back at Brandis, she ran forward, but someone approached from right behind.

As she watched them, Jaime wondered if they could handle real pain. They had designed the Rabbit's Eye to simulate any sensation. If one were stabbed in this virtually enhanced reality, they'd feel it. She smiled at the thought. Which of them was tough enough?

As they entered a new room, a new object appeared. Each time one of the recruits entered the room, a new object formed, one for each of them. The other recruits had made it into the second room, and looking closer, they observed that the new objects were long, rectangular boxes of bright light.

"They look like tanning beds," Carol said.

The rabbit paused after its tenth hop and announced, "To get out, you must get in. Solve the riddles before it gets too hot!"

They looked briefly at one another, and Jaime knew they must be worried what they would actually feel, but then they ran toward the tanning beds. They climbed in and shut the lids. The lights burst on, shining a bright, intense heat. On the big screen from where Jaime and the first years watched, a temperature suddenly displayed, and it was increasing rapidly. It started at room temperature, a nice 68 degrees. Then suddenly it jumped to 75, to 80, to 85, and it kept climbing. The cameras that JB used to show what was happening shifted to first person points of view. The top of each tanning bed also turned into a screen for the recruits, and on the screen, a riddle appeared alongside the temperature display.

*In a steel room built for revenge, they die burning in chains. Where don't you want to go in this 1979 film that would have made you go insane?*

A touch screen keyboard appeared inside the tanning bed, and the temperature increased again.

Jaime knew the answer and wanted to shout it. She watched Diane closely. After all, it was Diane who had been set on fire for real. She must be trying to show JB that she really could overcome her fears. Jaime admired Diane more and more, and Jaime whispered the title of the film, "*Don't Go In the House.*" Diane came up with the answer on her own and typed *the house* as her answer. The rabbit smiled on screen, and the temperature in Diane's bed decreased. Jaime cheered.

Not everyone else was as fortunate. They typed a number of places to guess the answer, and each time they guessed incorrectly, the rabbit snarled and the temperature increased in their tanning bed.

The next riddle appeared for Diane while the others struggled to answer the first.

*You certainly don't want to die in a tanning bed, but it could be worse. When every degree matters, what sauna temperature would put you in a hearse?*

*These were not easy challenges*, Jaime thought. No questions about Michael or Freddy or Jason that even non-horror fans might know. But Diane must have been a binge-watcher just like Jaime, and she knew the answer. It was the title of a 2011 horror flick, and its tagline was *Every Degree Matters*. The name of the film was *247 Degrees Fahrenheit.*

Screams came from the other tanning beds. Jaime could only imagine just how hot it must be in there for the recruits.

'Only one more riddle,' the rabbit said. 'Read a story or burn me on the grill. If it's in word or in a look you can't get rid of what still?'

*I just saw this*, Jaime thought. *They tried to burn it on a grill. Word . . . look . . . it came from a story. Yes, that's it!* Jaime cheered as Diane typed in *The Babadook.*

"Correct!" The temperature cooled again, and Diane's tanning bed opened. She was the first out. They all heard screams, and Jaime wondered how hot JB would make it. The temperature on the screens was now at 115 degrees.

"Help!" someone cried. Diane glanced ahead at a new door that had opened, but then ran to the tanning bed.

"Are you okay?" Diane asked.

"I'm trying every number I can think of, but I don't know the answer to the second riddle." It was Jimmy's voice. "It's so hot. Please, help."

Jaime watched her closely. Would Diane help another or just try to win it all for herself? Diane answered Jaime's thoughts without any hesitation, it seemed. She shouted out the answer to Jimmy.

"Thank you!" he yelled.

"I wouldn't do that if I were you." It was Ricky. He came from behind and shoved Diane out of the way.

"Hey! You don't have to be an ass!"

He grunted at her and ran into the next room. Carol, Jimmy, and Brandis exited their tanning beds.

"What was that about?" Carol asked.

"Ricky," Diane sighed. "Maybe he has to run to the bathroom. Talk about bad timing."

Another voice called out from one of the beds, "Someone help! It's too hot!"

"Sorry," Brandis frowned and ran through the door into the next room as well.

*Well, that says a lot, doesn't it?* Jaime shook her head. Bill would have helped them. Diane did help them. *I would have helped them,* she thought.

Carol, Jimmy, and Diane exchanged looks. "A real leader helps others," Diane yelled. "Do what you want, but I'm helping them get out of there first."

Jaime couldn't help but stand up and actually cheer. "Go Diane!" she shouted, and she saw Bill smile out of the corner of her eye. She looked over at him and returned a small smile. *What have I been thinking?* She tried to dismiss relationship thoughts from her mind. *Deal with that later, Jaime. Focus.*

"I'll help, too," Jimmy said and Carol nodded in agreement. They ran to the tanning beds of the students who hadn't solved the riddles and gave them the answers. Then they all marched into the next room. They saw Brandis and Ricky fighting flying creatures, and at a closer look they recognized these creatures as vampires. Fire spit out from all directions. All of their weapons had vanished the moment they entered the new room, and they looked around for new ones.

"It's *From Dusk Till Dawn*," Jimmy yelled. "Look!"

They turned to where Jimmy was pointing. There were rifles crossed with baseball bats, a makeshift cross and firearm all in one. Giant jackhammer drills, crossbows, whips, and water guns that would have been filled with holy water were scattered around the room.

Enormous vampire bats flew down upon them, clawing and biting at their faces. Jaime saw their faces twist, and the recruits grimaced and moaned. Each swipe of a nail or sting of a tooth appeared to shoot pain throughout their bodies. Carol screamed, grabbed the crossbow, and shot at the bats. Jimmy picked up the water gun, sprayed it while spinning in a giant circle, and yelped at the top of his lungs. Diane grabbed the whip and snapped it at her attackers. They had missed the rabbit's clue and didn't know how to escape this room.

Ricky held a rifle crossed with a baseball bat. He turned to Brandis and shot him in the chest. Brandis flew backwards, screaming, and hit the floor hard.

"What are you doing?" Carol yelled at Ricky.

"Winning." He grinned and fired at her. Carol covered her chest with her hands, and that look on her face . . . Jaime jumped up again. Carol looked genuinely hurt, and Diane sprinted at Ricky, but she wasn't fast enough. He fired at her, and she shrieked as the shot hit her head. The Rabbit's Eye must have pumped a pulsating pain on her temples, and she slammed face first on the floor.

Ricky fired at them all, and then he spotted the source of one of the fires in the room. This was 4D all right—a mix of real and virtual fires. Ricky pointed his rifle at a fire emitting from some kind of propane tank, and he shot right at it. The tank exploded, and the room burst into flames.

He ran into the next room, leaving all of them to burn.

Jaime stood up and turned to the other first years watching. "Shit! Ricky's gun. What if that's not a prop?."

The first years all stood up and watched in horror.

The fires appeared far too real.

The rabbit was burning.

## Chapter Twenty-Six

Bill's mind raced: *We have to help them.* He looked from Wes to Jaime, and they had stood up, too. His heart raced, and he felt terribly hot. Something wasn't right, and Bill had a feeling that it was time to fight.

"It's only part of a simulation though, right?" Annie asked uneasily.

Jaime shook her head. "The Rabbit's Eye will make them feel pain of course, but that's too much fire." The emergency alarm system blared as she finished her sentence.

"Oh, no. Not again!" Rose clenched her firsts in angry frustration. She joined Bill, Wes, and Jaime as the four leaders standing in front of the group of first years in the common. Bill's height towered over them and his short blond hair glistened lightly with a fearful sweat. Wes stood next to him with wide, white eyes. Although shorter and rounder, his dark face tightened, and Bill knew Wes was ready to fight. Rose's knuckles matched the white in Wes's eyes. Jaime's chest moved rapidly, her longer, dark hair enveloping the front and back of her shoulders like a wave.

They were ready to confront whatever nightmare had been unleashed.

The others sat with an implicit understanding. The electronic music of the alarm vibrated throughout the studio and their bodies.

"Go to safety, now," Bill told the other first years. He turned to Wes, Rose, and Jaime. Bill couldn't explain the connection he felt with these three, no matter what drama had been going on. It was a powerful sensation that transcended logical thought. The four of them had been through all sorts of tragedies. This was no longer a game. This wasn't like last year, and Bill didn't think they would have a nice ending that revealed stunt actors and a leader telling them there really wasn't any risk. There was a great risk, but they would not idly stand by while others were getting hurt.

"Let me help you guys, too." It was Daniel. The other first years had run to the safe room as Bill instructed. All except Daniel.

Bill nodded. "I have a feeling we could use you. Thanks."

Then Bill took the lead, and the others followed. They ran to the back of the studio, to the entrance of Hellfire. Pausing for a moment outside of the storage compartment that housed the Rabbit's Eye devices, Rose asked, "Will we need these?"

Bill shook his head. "No, I don't think so." There would be no more simulations tonight.

They sprinted through the first couple of rooms to where they saw the propane tank explode. Ricky had left the other nine recruits in the *From Dusk Till Dawn* simulation, and sure enough, when they kicked open the door to that part of the newly re-created Hellfire, they felt an immense heat. They needed no Rabbit's Eye to feel it. The fires were real.

Bill had a sudden, twisted realization. The recruits would think the pain they were feeling, although horrible, was still an illusion they had to tolerate. They may not even realize if they were getting legitimately hurt.

"Take them off!" Bill shouted, pointing at his head. "Get rid of the Rabbit's Eye!"

"Jesus!" Brandis wailed after taking it off and seeing his surroundings for what they really were. "This is real? And damn! That alarm!"

"You didn't hear it?" Jaime asked. Brandis shook his head, and she gave Bill a troubled look. Then she turned back to Brandis. "Are you okay? Ricky shot you, but was it real?"

Brandis looked over his body, and there were no visible wounds, just some scratches. "I'm okay," he said.

"We gotta get you guys out of here," Wes told them.

"C'mon," Rose said, reaching out her hand for anyone who needed a push. Carol took it, and they turned to go out the way they came in.

The door slammed shut. Rose pushed on it with no luck. "Let me try," Wes yelled, charging at the door. He hit it with all of his body weight, but it wouldn't budge. Brandis approached and kicked it repeatedly. He had no luck either.

"Looks like the only way out is to move forward," Bill said. The sweltering heat of the room was becoming too much, but as the smoke from the fire spread, they all started having trouble breathing.

Bill did a quick head count. "We have to keep track of everyone. Get a partner, and keep track of your partner, okay?" They nodded while coughing, and Bill realized that Daniel had come with them to help. He nodded at Daniel who nodded back. Regardless of their past, Bill was happy he was here. Strength in numbers.

"Let's get out of here! C'mon." Jaime coughed and moved forward to the door they all saw Ricky slam shut. She tried to open it, but it was also locked. "Dammit!"

Brandis kicked at it again, but the door wouldn't budge. "Shit!"

"Guys," Bill mumbled between a cough. "What did you have to do to get out of here? What did the rabbit say to do?"

Carol, Jimmy, and Diane looked sharply at Brandis. "Ask him," Diane said. "He left us without helping the others in the tanning bed room. We didn't get there in time to hear it." She glared at Brandis with a look brighter than the flames that surrounded them.

"I was just trying to win," Brandis defended and then looked at Bill. "You're not gonna like it."

"Don't waste time. What did it say?"

"It said, 'only by explosion will the next door open. Beware the vamps, but find your fiery omen.' I can only assume that it referred to the tank Ricky shot." Brandis hacked into his hand.

"There's something I need to tell you guys about Ricky. I didn't know if it was important or not," Daniel said. "But maybe it is."

"What?" Jaime asked. "Quick! We don't have time to guess!"

"I think . . ." Daniel squinted. "I don't know what's going on with Ricky, but I think he's a girl."

"Huh?" Bill asked. "What are you talking about?"

"I saw him, the night we all were stuck together. His face isn't real or something. I think he's . . . maybe trans or whatever," Daniel said.

"I don't know, man. He seems pretty tough for a girl," Brandis said. Jaime gave him a dirty look.

"Let's worry about that later. Right now we've got to find a way out of here," Jaime said.

"There must be another tank, right?" Rose asked. "Put on the Rabbit's Eye and look around. But stay close." The recruits put on their 4D equipment and scanned the room. *Yeah, we're gonna need the Rabbit's Eye,* Bill thought. He couldn't explain how he knew that, but the combination of virtual reality and real shit was just perfect, wasn't it?

"There!" Diane pointed. "But who has a gun?"

"Ricky had the gun," Carol said, "but we can try my crossbow." The first years watched, and if the room hadn't been on fire, Bill would have been quite amused. Unlike the video feed that revealed all the 4D virtual effects, Bill watched Carol grab an imaginary crossbow that only she could see. "I'll set the arrow on fire first." She ran to the nearest fire, lit the arrow, and then took a step back. Aiming at the propane tank, she let the arrow fly.

"What the hell?" Daniel asked as another explosion erupted through the floor of this room. The tanks and the weapons may have been virtual, but somehow the explosions and fires were real.

"No time to discuss," Jaime snapped. "You did it, Carol. Look! The door is open. Quickly now!" She ran to the door and held it open as everyone marched through to what they hoped was safety. Once everyone was through the door, Jaime closed it, shutting off the fire of the previous room. They all coughed hard and long, trying to get the smoke out of their lungs.

But what they saw next took their breath away all over again.

*****

"We didn't design this one either," Jaime said. "What's going on here?"

"This is incredible," Wes admired, momentarily oblivious to the fact that they may be in danger. "How far does it stretch? This is more than one room. It looks like the size of the entire studio!"

What they saw before them was an unbelievable labyrinth, a dark maze of walls stretching in every direction. A pyramid like shape floated ominously above the maze, as if connecting everything together.

Rose gasped, "Jason's balls!"

"And Freddy's claws," Wes finished. Bill would have laughed at this inside joke from last Halloween if not for the real horror around them.

"It's *Hellraiser*," Bill said. "But not the hell from the entry hall or hell as we would think of it."

"Right," Daniel said. "In the story's mythology, hell is a labyrinth. It can take on any shape. That overhead, that's the Leviathan, the creator of the Cenobites."

"What?" Brandis asked. "I don't remember any of that. All I remember is Pinhead."

"He's like the leader of the Cenobites, the demons from hell." Daniel gave him a condescending look. "This part of the mythology wasn't explained until the second film."

"What are we supposed to do?" Carol asked. "How are we even seeing this without the Rabbit's Eye?"

"I guess we have to find our way out," Jaime said. Then she looked at Bill who shrugged in response to Carol's second question. "I would guess JB found a way to use the Rabbit's Eye technology without the virtual reality headset. Who knows?"

They moved forward hesitantly. A great wind blew forcefully in their faces and as they looked around, they realized they weren't exactly within the walls. They were walking on top of them, as if standing on a ledge. Below them were enormous pits, seemingly infinitely deep, and of all shapes and sizes. They needed no Rabbit's Eye to see them either. It appeared all to be real, and that was even more horrifying.

"It looks like it goes on forever," Wes said.

"It has to be some kind of illusion, right?' Jimmy asked. "Mirrors and lights and all that?"

"Unless we've just entered some alternate universe, then I'd say that has to be the case," Bill replied in an uncertain tone. He looked over the side and lightning shot up from below.

"Lightning should fall from the sky, not shoot up from the ground," Jaime gulped as Bill jumped.

The rabbit appeared before them. "To move forward, Leviathan requires a sacrifice. None of you will move forward if all of you play nice."

On the ledge in front of them, where the rabbit stood, a part of the labyrinth rose upward. It was shaped like a puzzle piece, a bit larger than an old outdoor telephone booth. A door opened, revealing some kind of elevator that would only fit one.

"Shit, you guys know what this means?" Jaime asked.

"One of us has to get inside that thing," Bill said.

"But where will it take us?" Diane asked, her eyes wider than ever.

"In the movie, I'm pretty sure whoever gets in is killed and sacrificed to the monster that created this hell." Daniel sighed.

"I don't trust it," Rose said. "No, not after everything that's happened here. Is this a trick?"

"I'll go," Bill told them and walked forward.

"No!" Wes pushed Bill back. "It's supposed to be me."

"Why would you say that?" Rose asked. Wes pulled an object out of his pocket that he had been holding onto for quite some time, since last summer, Bill had remembered. It was the puzzle box he was awarded last summer during the family week, the first of three prizes JB gave out to students whose parents performed the best during the family week games.

"It's time for me to use it," Wes said grimly. "I don't know how or what will happen, but it has to be me who goes in that thing."

"Let me squeeze in with you," Rose pleaded.

"Babe, I'll barely fit. It has to be me."

She looked at him with such worry in her eyes. Bill knew that look and all of the worries she must have felt. Would he have let Jaime go? Not without a fight, but it would be a fight she would probably have won, he knew.

Rose jumped forward and hugged Wes tightly. "Please be careful. How will we know if you're okay?"

"I'll come back for you. You move forward. I'll be right below." He stepped inside the puzzle shaped elevator, holding his own little Pandora's Box in his hands.

Rose kissed him hard as he stepped into the small elevator and pulled away slowly.

"Good luck, man," Bill said when Rose had stepped back. "You get back to us, oh-right?" Wes nodded as they elevator doors closed. It sank slowly downward, and the rest of the students stared in panic. When it was out of sight, they heard a scream. Wes yelled from below as if in great pain.

Rose slid to where the elevator appeared down to her hands and knees. She pounded the ground with her fist. "Wes! Wes! Are you okay?" His screams echoed around the room, and then there was nothing but silence. "Wes! Say something!" Bill thought he could see Rose's heart beating through her chest, but they heard nothing from Wes. There was complete silence from below.

She snapped her head back and shrieked, "We have to help him!"

"Then we move forward," Bill said. "We get out of here, and we find him." Tears pricked at Rose's eyelids, but she nodded. Bill wanted to comfort her, to tell her it would all be okay. It had to be, right? They couldn't lose Wes. *What would any of them do if one of them . . . disappeared or even died?* Bill couldn't even fully think about that. They had to keep moving.

Then the labyrinth rumbled, like an earthquake. The room began to shake, and they stumbled for their balance up on the ledge of the wall.

"Quick!" Jaime called. "Let's get out of here!"

They ran forward, Bill in the lead, Rose and Jaime right behind, and everyone else bringing up the rear. In the dark, with the walls and floor shaking, it was difficult to judge distance. Bill slammed into a wall in front of him. Looking at it, he realized the depth of the room may have been an illusion after all, like 3D art on paper.

The others ran into him when he stopped suddenly, and the shaking in the room intensified. Bill gasped as people begin to fall. Diane, Jimmy, Carol, Brandis, and the other recruits bringing up the rear were forced off the ledge. Bill grabbed onto Rose and Jaime and pressed them against the wall and then he took a step back. He thrust out his hand, catching Daniel right as he was about to fall. Someone had hold of Daniel's leg. They heard Brandis call out, "I can't hold on!" Nearly a dozen screams echoed from below, and Brandis's hand slowly slipped from Daniel's leg.

"Ahhhhh!"

Bill, Daniel, Rose, and Jaime held on to one another as the room continued to shake. The screaming eventually trailed off into nothing, and they listened in dread for any sounds of thuds or bodies slamming on the floor.

"Are you guys okay?" Rose shouted after the screaming stopped and silence took its place.

There was no response, but the earthquake like rumbling of the room ceased, and the wall in front of Bill shifted, revealing a new path.

"They will be okay," Bill said. "Wes, too. They have to be." But he wasn't certain. Nothing was certain anymore. He thought about Tara's kidnapping and burning. He thought about the first incident with Diane. He thought about Donnie Chase and the other professor who was supposed to be here, both of whom were murdered. And now all of this? Something even worse was happening.

"It will be okay," Jaime whispered, repeating Bill's sentiment. Bill wanted to believe it, but he had a terrible feeling in his stomach. She looked at him in the eyes then, sharing in his doubt, he knew. Daniel put his arms around them all, and they moved to the next room.

It resembled the basement of a haunted mansion, but a few things stood out more than the rest. The entrance was shaped like the trunk of car, and in the middle of the room, there was a furnace that rivaled the size of the boiler from *A Nightmare on Elm Street*. But worst of all were piles of bones: skulls, legs, arms, even full skeletons all throughout this room.

And they didn't look like props.

## Chapter Twenty-Seven

They crawled through the trunk shaped door, hands and knees pressing on skeleton bones. Some bones crushed under their weight, as if brittle and old. Jaime shuddered at the thought that they could be real, but they pushed on through. Standing on the other side, Bill, Jaime, Rose, and Daniel examined their surroundings.

Jaime didn't like the look of this one bit.

The room appeared to be that of a large basement with a gigantic furnace. The floor was muddy, and their shoes were covered in a sticky slush.

"You recognize this?" Daniel asked.

"Yeah," Jaime said. "It was my favorite comedy when I was a kid."

"A comedy?" Rose asked incredulously.

"*The 'Burbs*," Jaime said. "An old Tom Hanks comedy about neighbors who are suspected murderers and cannibals. I'm not finding it too funny at the moment."

"In the movie, the neighbors search for human remains in this basement," Bill said, "but they didn't look in one place."

"Let me guess," Daniel said. "The furnace."

"Yep," Jaime said and Bill nodded. They stared into an enormous furnace. It looked large enough to heat the entire Rabbit in Red studios.

*If it were real, that is. It's not real, is it?* Jaime couldn't tell.

"But they also hit a gas line or something and blow up the whole house when they're looking," Bill added. "So be careful."

As they inched closer to the furnace, the rabbit appeared before them. Music played, and in any other circumstance, Jaime would have laughed at the song. As the rabbit hopped up to them, the song that played through loud speakers was *I'm burning, I'm burning, I'm burning for you.*

Jaime looked at Bill and rolled her eyes. She wished it was only cheesy fun, but she worried the music was an ominous sign that things would only get worse.

The music faded and the rabbit spoke. "Your house guests require a sacrifice," it said. "Enter the fire. One of you must pay the price."

"This can't be good," Rose shook her head. "If Wes was right about the last room, then it's my turn."

Jaime cocked her head. "Why?"

"I won the second prize, and it must be about this room," she said.

"The femur!" Bill exclaimed. "But you don't have it with you, do you?"

"No, it's in my room," she sighed. "Kinda big to carry around." The femur, Jaime knew, was a bone that the characters in *The 'Burbs* found. It was the evidence they needed to know that the weird neighbors were, in fact, killing and burying actual humans, and not just animals or something.

"There's no shortage on bones," Daniel said, kicking a few on the ground. "Let's find one. If somehow those are to help you, then whoever is jumping in that thing better have something to take with them."

They pushed around all sorts of bones, digging and hoping to find a possible replacement.

"Here," Jaime groaned, picking up a femur. "God, I hope this isn't real."

"Let me see." Rose held out her hand, and Jaime handed her the femur. "Ugh, it feels real," she moaned. "I guess there's no time to waste. Let's open up the furnace."

"Let me go," Daniel told her. "I . . . I owe you. I owe you all. From last year." Jaime studied him closely. Was he being sincere?

Something had changed about Daniel. That much was for certain. Jaime wanted to trust him, but he was difficult to read.

"But you won something too, didn't you?" Rose asked.

Daniel reached into his pocket and pulled out the pocket mirror JB awarded him just before giving a VHS tape to Wes. "Yeah, this."

"Everything is designed for a purpose," Rose spoke. "I don't want to jump in that thing, but if leads me to Wes, then it's a risk I'm willing to take." Her red hair was wet with sweat, but her eyes were powerful and possessed a dark confidence. Bill and Jaime exchanged looks and nodded.

"I don't want you to go alone," Bill sighed. "But I also think you're right. We're being set up for something. What I don't know."

"Who doesn't like a good surprise?" Rose tried to smile and walked closer to the furnace. She opened it, and a wave of heat poured out.

"Oh, Rose, no," Jaime whimpered. "Maybe that last room was hell, but it's hotter than hell in that thing."

"What's the purpose of all of this?" Bill yelled out and kicked at a pile of bones.

Rose smiled gently at him. "Does it have to have a purpose? Or maybe the purpose is just to scare the shit out of us?" She looked into the furnace and grimaced at the heat. "Either one of you would do this for the other," she said looking back at Bill and Jaime. "Remember that."

Without any further hesitation, Rose jumped in. Jaime watched and saw that the furnace contained a slide, much like the ones that led from the bedrooms to the safe room. They heard a short-lived, high-pitched squeal, and then Rose was gone.

"And then there were three," Daniel groaned uncomfortably. "They're picking us off one at a time."

"You're not finished here yet," the rabbit announced as it reappeared in the room. The lights in this basement room shut off, and then dark boom echoed all around. "You have one object left and one more game to play. Think of where you gather, and think of his name—several times you must say."

"I think we all know what that is about," Daniel said as the three huddled very close to one another. He pulled out his pocket mirror and stared into it. Even though it was dark and they couldn't actually see a reflection in the mirror, Jaime felt the tension in the room increase.

This was a game you'd play as a child to scare your friends at a sleepover, she thought. This was not a game you'd play at Rabbit in Red. She shivered, thinking of what could happen next.

"*Candyman*," Jaime moaned. "He comes to life when you look in a mirror and say his name three times."

"But then—" Bill started

"Then he kills you," Daniel finished.

"Guys, I have a bad feeling about this," Bill muttered.

"Be ready for anything, okay?" Jaime pleaded. "And stay close."

Daniel looked into the pocket mirror. "Candyman," he said once. A strobe light pulsed throughout the room matching the vibrations of the electronic beat. "Candyman," he said a second time. The music blasted again from several speakers. The strobe light and the sounds pulsed faster. He swallowed hard and said it a third time. "Candyman."

The sounds and the strobe lights stopped completely. They stood there, frozen, waiting for something to happen. They could hear each other's breath and feel one another's chests heaving in and out to take in enough air.

Then the room went entirely white, as if the bright strobe light turned on with no pulsing. A shrieking sound followed next, a piercing scream that made them all wince. Then someone grabbed Daniel from behind. Bill and Jaime turned, and Daniel struggled to throw off his attacker.

But the attacker was strong. The man pulled at Daniel, stepping backward quickly. Daniel thrust his body weight back, and the attacker laughed. The strobe light flashed again, and Jaime caught a glimpse of the attacker. He wore a hooded sweatshirt, the hood draped over his head. She instantly thought of the man who approached Daniel in the final challenge last Halloween. The man had pretended to be Daniel's father.

But that "actor" turned out to be JB.

Was it actually JB attacking Daniel now?

Daniel pushed back at the man, and the two hit the wall behind them, which turned out not to be a wall at all but another door. It swung open with Daniel's force, and then the attacker slammed it shut.

Just before the door closed completely, the strobe light flashed at the attacker's face.

Jaime recognized the man immediately and gasped.

Bill and Jaime ran to the door, pushing, kicking, pounding, and screaming. But it wouldn't budge.

Jaime looked at Bill in panic, thinking a thousand thoughts. How is this possible? And why? Why would he do this?

Jaime pounded on the door harder and shouted at the attacker who pulled Daniel through to the other side. "Ricky! Ricky! Open this door! Now!"

"This isn't the way out," Ricky called back.

The furnace rumbled from behind them, and they heard Ricky's cackle from behind the wall. "Uh oh, it's almost time!" he yelled.

"Time for what?" Bill asked.

"Time to burn!" Ricky shouted.

The furnace's growl intensified and flames spit out from inside. "Rose!" Jaime yelled, running toward the flames. "Do you think she's okay?"

"She got down before the fire started spitting at us," Bill reasoned, joining Jaime. "But we better get out of here."

"How?"

Bill shrugged and ran back to the way they came in, through the shape of a vehicle's trunk. The outside had been shut and he couldn't open it. Jaime tried to open the furnace, but it had been locked, too. Bill grabbed bones from the floor and chucked them at the walls around them. He threw high and low and in every direction he could. Jaime snatched some as well and launched them up high at the ceiling.

Who was this Ricky, really? What was his motivation to do this? Was he working with someone else?

"Look! Over there!" She pointed at the sound of broken glass that the bones must have broken. "That must be the way out."

They crawled on top of some shelves in the corner of the room where they heard the sounds of broken glass had come from. Sure enough, there was a small window. Bill ran back down, grabbed another bone, and broke out the remaining fragments of the window. The fire from the furnace spit harder and faster.

"You first," he told Jaime, and she took his hand. He hoisted her up through the broken window. She wiggled through, turned around, and stretched out her arms for him. He jumped up with all of his might, grateful for his height, and squirmed through the window.

Seconds later, *The 'Burbs* room exploded in fire, and flames followed them through the window.

They looked up and found themselves in a giant room, the size of a gymnasium but even taller. In the middle of the room stood a haunting object, and they were even more surprised by who was trapped inside.

It was a human shaped cage, the size of a giant. Everything was made of wood. A long ladder stretched up in between the legs of this monstrosity to the chest of the cage. Arms stretched below and a head above. It was a wooden, human cage like that from *The Wicker Man.*

And trapped inside was JB.

# Chapter Twenty-Eight

"JB!" Jaime yelled. She couldn't believe what she was seeing.

"Jaime? Bill? Is that you?" he shouted from up above, imprisoned inside the wicker cage.

They ran to the ladder that led up to where JB was trapped. "Yes! We'll get you out of there!"

"Stop!" JB commanded. "No! You must go. It isn't safe!"

"What's going on here?" Bill asked.

"Karma. Revenge." It was a dark, harsh voice from behind them. Ricky approached holding a flamethrower. "He's right, kids. It's not safe."

"Why are you doing this?" Jaime asked.

Ricky paused and a sinister smile stretched from ear to ear. He dangled the flame thrower in one hand and then bent over. With his other hand, he reached over the top of his head to the back of his neck. He pulled at his skin, dug in with his fingernails, and Bill and Jaime groaned as they saw the top of his head wrinkle. Ricky pulled harder and removed his entire face. His entire face! It wasn't real. It wasn't a mask exactly, but in parts. Jaime gasped and what she was seeing. Ricky tossed globs of elaborate makeup, latex, and who knew what else on the floor.

Then he looked at her and smiled, and Jaime felt a chill all throughout her body. In his eyes, she saw more than hate. She saw desire, and it terrified her.

"Chester?" Jaime asked, completely shocked and taken aback.

"Close," the man said. He wasn't a woman at all like Daniel had thought. He actually looked like Chester Malcolm in the face with the long sideburns that now appeared before them. He had a receding hairline and dark hair. This man's face looked younger than Chester's though, and then it finally clicked. Jaime knew who he was.

"Fools. All of you." He laughed. "Picture what you can do if you re-mold your eyebrows, dye your hair, change the shape of your eyes, use implants around your cheek and jaw and body." He shook his head and laughed some more. "I even fooled my old employer and my very own brother, although given I never once looked them in the eye while I was here. That's how stupid your so-called geniuses really are. I was right in front of their faces the entire time, and they never noticed." He giggled and wiped away more makeup and dye and whatever else it was he used to disguise himself. That's clearly why he needed all those bathroom trips. How did they not see it? "Let me introduce myself," the man said, and he stepped closer to Jaime. "My name is Sid. Sid Malcolm. I'm Chester's brother."

Jaime and Bill exchanged terrified looks.

"You heard from me last year," Sid continued, "ever so briefly. It was me who e-mailed you after the riddle contest. I warned you this place was dangerous, didn't I?" He snarled. "I never cared about your safety. I wanted to ruin his plans for everything he had done to me even before that weekend!" He looked up at JB and then back at Jaime. "But you didn't listen to me then, and what did I get in return? I was locked in a cage like an animal for a weekend. You walked right over me last year many times. I was gagged and chained to a wall, and that trapdoor underneath the funhouse was my weekend residence. My brother, Chester, put me in there. And that's not all they did. You don't know half of what happened at this place before you all entered its doors!"

"Sid!" JB scolded from above. "We can resolve this peacefully. Let them go."

"You!" Jaime snapped. "So it was you who hurt Tara?" She felt her arms and legs shake, and her heart pounded. *I'll kill him.* It was such a simple thought, really, but Jaime meant it. *I'm going to kill you.*

"I didn't want to burn her," Sid said defensively, "but I needed to get your attention." He laughed at Jaime's anger. "You're even prettier when you're mad, you know that?"

"Back away, kids!" JB called down again.

"You shut up!" Sid yelled at JB. "You'll get yours."

Jaime lunged forward, her knuckles clenched in a tight fist, and swung at Sid's face. He grabbed her hand, twisted it, and she fell to the floor, screaming in pain.

"Let go of her!" Bill ran forward, but using his other hand, Sid aimed the flame thrower right at Bill.

"I'll burn you first, boy," Sid snarled. "Back up!" Bill froze in his steps.

"Where are the others?" Bill asked.

Sid laughed. "Don't you see yet? Each of you gets a choice. JB had designed the rooms for a final challenge for first years. I've been here all along of course, watching and spying as you watched and spied. I knew the prizes—the puzzle box, the femur, the mirror—would come into play somehow. I modified little things whenever I could to make this all work out the way I needed it to. And didn't you like the earthquake setting? You see, JB hired me as one of his mechanical engineers to design Rabbit in Red. I dare say I may have more talent than even your own mentor. And I have quite a lot of experience in makeup and costume, too, as you probably guessed by now."

"The others are okay then?" Bill questioned.

Sid laughed. "The ones who fell were caught by safety nets. They're fine. For now. I've taken special care of Rose, Wes, and Daniel. I needed them alive."

Sid grinned and licked his lips. Jaime felt disgusted. The way he looked at her—that wasn't okay. She wanted to hurt him in so many ways.

"In fact, you can see for yourself." Sid let go of Jaime, reached into his pocket, and pressed some kind of remote. A wall behind him in this gymnasium style room rumbled and opened. There, in smaller versions of the wicker prisons, were Rose, Wes, and Daniel, each trapped in their own personal cage.

"You monster!" JB yelled from above.

"Me?" Sid called back, trying to look shocked. "They've seen all of your videos, JB. I made sure to give them the home movie version of your sick past."

Bill stood up for their master host. "Yeah, we saw them. You tried to manipulate us. We didn't even see what was on the final tape."

"I had to destroy all the VCRs when JB gave Wes that tape," Sid said and giggled. "First, destroy the VCRs and then I planned on destroying the tape, too. If he wanted you to see it, then I wanted to make sure it never happened. Now, the tape will be destroyed right along with all of you." He grinned again. "And you never even realized I had someone else helping me from the inside, did you?" He looked at Bill and Jaime, then turned back to where Rose, Wes, and Daniel were trapped. "Would you like to tell them how you helped me or should I? What do you say, Daniel?"

Daniel's jaw dropped. "No! It's not true. I did no such thing."

*I knew I shouldn't have trusted him,* Jaime thought. She glared at Daniel, but his face was wide and horrified. Could he be telling the truth?

Sid's head rolled back, and he laughed until he coughed. "Oh, boy. Good luck trying to defend yourself."

Jaime's eyes flared with more anger. She had trusted Daniel. They had all given him a second chance, but he apparently had fooled them again.

"Not that I particularly care what they think about you, but allow me to bring out my first witness. Carol, darling? Would you come join us?" Sid asked.

From behind the smaller size wicker cages, Carol Fisher walked forward. She was clearly frazzled, her blond hair an absolute mess.

"Carol, dear, why don't you tell us all what Daniel told you?" She looked at the floor, head bent in uncertainty. "Now, Carol! Trust me when I say we don't have all night."

"Daniel . . . he . . . he told me JB was the villain. He told me I needed to convince Bill and anyone else who wasn't sure about JB. I was supposed to help convince you guys that JB killed Donnie and sabotaged Hellfire to intentionally hurt Diane."

"But why?" Jaime asked. She looked at JB hesitantly and softly added, "We were already thinking that."

"Daniel wanted Rabbit in Red shut down. He wanted JB arrested. He thought if he could convince me, because I was so . . . such an enthusiastic follower, that it would eliminate any doubt anyone else had." Carol had tears in her eyes.

Sid laughed again. "You see? Thanks, Daniel, for your help."

"He lies! You guys, please! I can explain!" Daniel cried from inside his cage, but Jaime didn't feel a bit sorry for him. He had fooled them twice, and she wasn't going to listen to him anymore.

"Now, as I said, we don't have all night," Sid snarled. "We have a final game to play, a game of choices. Bill, you're up first. Someone must die tonight. You get to choose between your good friend Wes or your good friend Daniel. Who will it be?"

Jaime's heart jumped in her throat. Why was Sid doing this?

"Choose now, or both burn." Sid lifted the flame thrower and pulled the trigger. "You pick one right this second, or I'll kill them both. *Now!*"

As it projected fire, Bill shouted. "Stop! Daniel! I choose Daniel." Bill had great pain on his face. He looked up at Daniel, and Jaime could see a pronounced look of apology. Even if Daniel had tried to manipulate them somehow, surely no one would actually want him to die.

Daniel screamed from inside. "No! I wasn't working with him! It's true that I wanted to ruin JB. He . . . he embarrassed me and tricked me last year, but all I wanted was for him to go away, for all of you to see him the way I saw him. I never wanted anyone to get hurt." He had tears in his eyes. "When you found those tapes and when I saw how much Carol was infatuated with JB, I thought I could use all of that to make sure you distrusted JB. That's all. I promise! I was with you guys. I really wanted to help you. It's him I didn't want to help," Daniel cried and pointed at JB. "And . . . and I'm sorry for that, too." He lowered his head and sobbed.

"Those will make for very nice last words," Sid cackled, and just like that, he lit Daniel's wicker cage on fire. Daniel jumped back against the cage, howled, and swung at the flames. "We'll let him play with that for a moment, but we don't have much time. Dear Wes. Sweet Wes. You get to choose next. Your darling Rose or your master host? Who burns next?"

"No! I won't play this game! You can't do this to us!"

Jaime couldn't believe what Sid was doing. She looked at Wes and saw the misery on his face. His eyes were red and puffy, and she thought to herself again, *as soon I get the chance, I will kill this man.*

"Yes, but I want to hear you say it. I want the words you're about to say to haunt you for the final few minutes of your life. I want you to know that you were responsible for a death." Sid almost giggled in delight. "Now, Wes! Or both burn!"

"JB!" Wes cried and hung his head in shame. "I'm so sorry!"

JB yelled from above. "Wes, you have nothing to be sorry for. My friends, I only wanted to give you the kind of experiences I wish I had. I know you saw those tapes and saw some of the choices I made when I was younger. I never hurt anyone without their permission. I know that may not mean much to you, but I promise you, that's the truth."

"Is that all?" Sid asked and rolled his eyes. Daniel screamed as the flames grew larger, swallowing his cage.

"I hope someday you'll see what was on the rest of that tape. There's so much more to the story. I love you. As if you all were my own children. I'm sorry that I cannot help you."

"How beautiful," Sid said and then he lit JB's wicker man cage on fire.

"The final choice is yours, Jaime. And I urge you to make it quick. Bill or Rose? Who burns?"

"What? No, how could you?"

"Quick now, or I will burn both."

"I refuse!"

"Then I'll give you a third option." Sid smiled, and Jaime thought that this is what he wanted all along. "You come with me tonight. And be with me. That's your option. Be with me. So one last choice: I burn them both or you come with me. Which will it be?"

"You disgusting psycho!" Jaime snapped. *You want me? You got me. I'll kill you the first chance I get.* "Take me." She snarled.

"Jaime, no!" Bill shouted and stood up. Sid shot the flame thrower at him, but it missed as Bill rolled.

She looked at Bill and Rose. She wished there was something more she could do. She didn't trust Sid at all. Would he really let them go? She looked at Bill as Sid forced her out of the room.

We never got to be together, she thought. *I love you, Bill. Our world is completely fucked up, but I will always love you.* Tears of fierce anger shot down her cheeks as she saw JB's and Daniel's cages burn.

"This way, girl. Now!" Sid pulled Jaime up, and they walked back behind where Rose, Wes, and Daniel were trapped. The flames were waist high on Daniel's cage, and he bounced around the cage in panic.

"Death by fire," Sid told him. "It hurts like hell but it's over quite quickly actually. Rest in peace." Then he turned to JB. "You, I hope, will burn in hell." He looked at Wes, Rose, and Bill next. "Oh, I almost forgot. You should say your good-byes to Rabbit in Red as well." Sid released Jaime for a second while he pulled out another remote device.

He pressed a button.

They felt what happened before they saw it.

It was an explosion. From all around them, it was as if all air and gravity had somehow been removed. Bill fell to the floor as the room burst into flames.

Then Sid pulled Jaime out the door and left everyone else to burn.

## Chapter Twenty-Nine

The heat was more intense than anything they had ever experienced. No simulation could prepare them for the fires that engulfed the walls and swallowed the floor. Covering his mouth, Bill ran to Rose. He pulled at the wood, kicking and screaming. Using all of his might, adrenaline pumping through every vein, he punched through the wooden wicker cage, bloodying his hand. He tore it open, and Rose fell out. They glanced over behind Daniel. Carol ran to Daniel's wicker cage and slammed her fists against it. Bill tried to understand Daniel's role, and he had decided to trust him. Daniel's revenge would simply have been to get everyone here to leave JB and Rabbit in Red, not to destroy it. He manipulated Carol, JB's number one cheerleader, to be on his side. But he wasn't going to hurt anyone. These thoughts flashed through Bill's mind as the fire destroyed everything.

Bill ran to Wes, and he and Rose tore at the wooden cage. Bill punched through it again and heard a crack in his hand. He yelped at the intense pain but took no time to rest. They pulled Wes out just as flames engulfed his man-made prison cell.

Bill tried not to think about Jaime. *One at a time. Help one at a time, and then I'll get to Jaime. I promise you, J, I'm coming.*

Running to Daniel, they worried they were too late. He cried out in severe pain, fire dancing on his legs. Carol had already broken some of the cage, and with a roar, Wes charged at it, tackling the wood and crashing through it head first. He pulled Daniel out of the fire, and all four jumped on the crying man, trying to put out the flames. Daniel looked up in disbelief.

Daniel reached his hand up to Wes, tears streaming down his cheeks, and coughed, "Thank you." He coughed again, harder this time. "Thank you. Thank you." Wes nodded, the three stood up, and Wes pulled Daniel off the floor.

"You okay?"

"My legs hurt bad," Daniel said. "But I'm alive." He looked forward in the distance to the giant wicker cage. "JB!" he yelled.

Wes, Bill, and Rose sprinted to their master host, and Daniel limped behind. The fire had had spread throughout the wicker man's legs and had completely destroyed the ladder. The blaze was taller than all of them, and there was no way they could reach JB.

"Go, kids, go!" JB screamed.

"We can't leave you," Bill cried.

"You'll die with me if you don't," JB told him sternly. "There's no time. What about the others?"

It was as if Bill had just been punched in the gut. The others? Shit, how many people were in danger? All of the other first years and recruits were still somewhere within Rabbit in Red, and the fire was hungry.

"JB!" Bill bawled. There was so much to say. So many questions unanswered. So many things he needed to know and needed to express. But there was no time. "I'll never forget what you did for me and my family. Thank you."

JB smiled warmly at Bill. As if reading his mind, he said, "This isn't the end, Bill. You will find your answers and so much more. In time, you will understand it all, my boy. Now, go. There are more important people than me. Save them if you can."

Bill stood for a moment as the flames grew higher, dancing at JB's feet. The fire spread even more rapidly, and in the blink of an eye, the flames engulfed the entire body of the large wicker man cage with JB inside. They heard a haunting scream, and Bill closed his eyes.

"C'mon, Bill. We have to help who we can," Rose said and pulled him away from JB. The tears rolled down his cheeks, but his sobs were interrupted with a hacking cough. He looked up at Rose, and she was crying, too. He saw the pain in her eyes. "We have to help the others," she said again. The palpable smoke covered the room like a crippling blanket. He turned with Rose, and all four ran out of the room. As they exited in the back, they heard a great crash, no doubt the wicker man cage falling along with the walls.

"Don't think about that now," Wes advised, rubbing tears from his eyes. "We have to get everyone else."

"The first years should be in the safe room, right? They should be okay, right?" Daniel asked.

"I don't know," Wes said. "I don't want to split up, but I think some of us should go to the first years and the others look for the recruits."

"Let me," Daniel said, putting a hand on Wes's shoulder. "You saved me. More than you know."

"Check the safe room and make sure our classmates got out safely. We know where the recruits are. We were down there in that hell, Rose and me. We can get them." Wes turned to Carol. "Go with him. You don't want to go back down there."

She nodded, turned to Daniel, and they ran off as fast as they could, considering Daniel looked like he was hopping on one leg.

"Follow us, Bill," Rose said, and the three ran in a giant semi-circle around the part of Hellfire that had collapsed. When the room with the wicker cages collapsed, they pushed through the back and returned to the beginning of the Hellfire entrance. The fire was spreading. In the distance, they saw Daniel run through the funhouse, the flames chasing him.

They ran through the first set of Hellfire rooms back into the labyrinth room. Wes looked down over the ledge and then at Bill and Rose.

"Ready?" he asked.

Bill started to mouth the word "what?" but there was no time. They held each other's hands and just jumped. Free falling for longer than Bill thought should be possible—*how big is Rabbit in*

*Red?*—a scream escaped his mouth just as he felt something catch his body. It was like a swing, and he kept falling for a moment before it pushed him back up. They bounced a few times on what must have been a large circus kind of net before finding their balance. Rose and Wes were the first to roll off, and Bill followed. They ran underneath the labyrinth. Bill tried to look up, but it seemed so high.

"Where are they?" Bill huffed, running out of breath.

"This way," Wes pointed. "Hurry!" They were running up a hill now, a long slope, and Bill felt completely disoriented. *Where are we?*

And then seconds later, they ran into the recruits. Brandis, Diane, Jimmy, and the rest huddled closely together. Upon seeing Wes, Rose, and Bill, they ran forward.

"What's happening?" Jimmy asked.

"Is everyone okay? Where's Jaime?" Brandis asked.

"There's no time to explain, guys," Wes said. "We have to get out of here. Now. Follow me!" Wes took the lead and they continued running up a slope deep beneath Rabbit in Red.

"I'm so confused," Diane said as they ran. "When we fell, the rabbit appeared down here. It told us to wait, that only those who could exhibit the most patience would be rewarded. So we waited."

"It was a trick to get you out of the way. You weren't the targets. We were," Rose paused for a moment. "And JB."

"Who did this?" Brandis demanded.

"Shh!" Wes snapped again. "Let's focus on getting out of here, then we'll talk."

They followed him up this seemingly infinite slope until their heads hit a wall and ceiling.

"Dead end?" Bill asked. "Wes, where are you taking us?"

Wes pulled out the puzzle box he had taken with him down into the labyrinth. "In the elevator, when I went down the labyrinth, this opened. Inside it had a map, a map of Rabbit in Red. I tried to study the map as quickly as I could. What stood out to me was a path from the bottom of the labyrinth that led all the way back here. We're under the commons. Or rather, under the other floor that is under the commons."

"What happened when you got off the elevator?" Rose asked.

"The elevator got hotter as it went down. It gets hotter in hell, right? It got so hot, I yelled, thinking the whole damn thing was gonna catch on fire. Then when it opened, Ricky stood there and shot me with something. A tranquilizer gun, maybe?" He rubbed the right side of his chest. "I don't know. I know my chest hurts like hell. And then I remember being out for a minute and waking up in the wicker cage."

"Same with me," Rose said. "He was waiting for me when I went down the slide that was in the furnace."

"Ricky?" Brandis asked. "Ricky is behind all of this?"

"It's not really Ricky," Bill said. "I'll explain later. Why don't we get out of here first?"

"Yeah," Wes said. "Okay, there must be a way that leads up. Look for a door, a staircase, an elevator, anything."

"Here!" Diane said, a step ahead of them. She was already pushing on everything and anything while they were talking.

She found a part of the wall that slid open on the side and led to a staircase. They climbed up it quickly and discovered that it led all the way up to the commons, another way in and out that they had never known about. They pushed and pulled on the wall at the top of the staircase until it opened. Stepping out, they realized they were just feet away from Candyman's mouth, the entrance to the commons. Heaving a sigh of relief, they all stepped out.

But it was short lived. The fire was spreading rapidly, and they saw the flames grow from the halls that led to the old game chambers and old sleeping quarters.

"The closest way out is the front door," Wes said. "Let's go!"

"Wait, Wes, shouldn't we check on Daniel?" Rose asked.

"He's certainly at the safe room already. We have to trust that he got to them and they got out. C'mon, Rose."

"No, wait, we should check our bedrooms," Rose insisted. "Lester and Falcor are up there! We can't just leave the bunny and the pup. And what if anyone's hiding up there, scared? We need to double check!"

Bill saw the determination in her eyes and knew arguing any more would be a waste of time. Wes must have seen it also.

"Okay," Wes said, "but Brandis, I want you to take the other recruits and wait outside. Bill, you, me, and Rose will check quickly and then get the hell out of here, okay?"

Bill nodded, and Brandis agreed. They went in their separate directions. Bill, Wes, and Rose climbed the ladder—*probably for the last time*, Bill thought—up to the *Alien* themed bedrooms. Falcor was barking continuously. "Come here, boy!" Bill called, and the puppy ran into his arms.

"I'm getting Lester," Rose said. "Check to make sure no one else is up here."

They sprinted to the back of the bedrooms, hollering for anyone, but there were no replies.

"We're good," Wes said. "Let's get out of here."

They felt the floor sink. The fire had snuck up the back of the bedrooms.

"Shit, let's go!" The fire consumed the beds, the mattresses burning all too easily. Part of the bedroom quarters crumbled and blocked off the slides that led to the safe room. The ladder back down to the commons was the only option. Bill passed Falcor to Wes and jump down several steps at a time. Wes passed the dog back to Bill, and the pup licked Bill's face repeatedly.

"Now you," Wes said to Rose.

"No, you go, that way I can pass Lester to you."

"Fine," Wes said, trying to get out of here as quickly as possible. He tried to jump down like Bill, but hit his chin hard on one of the steps. Rubbing his face, he took the last couple of steps more carefully and then looked up when he reached the floor. He held out his hands for Lester.

"Here you go, bunny. We'd never let you burn." Rose passed little Lester to Wes.

He took Lester. "C'mon, Rose."

That was when the ceiling above her collapsed. Plaster fell through the hole where the ladder stood, knocking Wes down.

"Rose!" he cried and stood back up, but the walls were crumbling. In just a matter of seconds, the hole had been filled with everything but Rose. She was trapped up above. He tried to push the debris away from the ladder, but it burned his hand.

"Ahh!" he squealed at the touch. "Rose! Rose! Can you hear me?"

There was no reply except for the continued collapsing of Rabbit in Red and the hiss of the fire.

"Wes, we have to go!" Bill called as the fire swallowed the commons. Flames were coming for them from all directions.

"No, Bill, no!" Wes cried "I can't leave her! I won't! Rose!" The only reply was another chunk of ceiling that fell and nearly crashed on Wes's head.

Bill wanted to scream and cry. None of this was fair. He knew he wouldn't have left Jaime, and he didn't want to leave Rose either. But he knew . . . he knew they'd die if they stayed. All of them would die. But to live meant leaving behind someone they loved.

"Oh, God, Wes, I know! I'm so sorry! But we're gonna die here if we don't leave!"

"What about Rose?"

Seeing the tears in Wes's eyes, Bill cried with his friend. "I don't know!"

He didn't know. He didn't know about Rose or what they could do, but he did know that staying here any longer would be their death sentence. He pulled Wes, who fought back, unwilling to move.

"Wes! She could have run the other way. There's always a chance!"

"The exit to the safe room was on fire, too," Wes moaned.

"There's always a chance. She's a fighter. C'mon!" Bill pulled at him again, and this time Wes's body moved but not his eyes. He couldn't look away until the fire completely swallowed the surrounding walls.

Bill pulled him through the commons, through the now crumbling mouth of Candyman, through the *Hellraiser* hall that was also on fire, and they pushed through the front door of Rabbit in Red. Running out the door, they tripped and fell to the ground. Wes slammed his fists on the cement.

Daniel ran up to Bill and Wes. He was standing outside with the other first years and the recruits.

"What happened?" he asked.

"Rose! Rose is inside!" Wes cried. He looked up and saw Rabbit in Red swallowed by flames. Everything burned.

Falcor jumped out of Bill's arms and licked Wes's tears. Wes still had hold of Lester, and the dog kissed the bunny, too. Everyone surrounded Wes and stared at the enormous studio in front of them as it collapsed. Bill saw Wes shrink. He fell on the concrete.

Bill sat down with his friend, unable to move, unable, really, to even breathe. They heard sirens in the distance, first responders responding way too late. When they arrived, the police and firefighters made them back away, but none could take their eyes off of Rabbit in Red on fire.

Minutes passed, maybe even hours, it was hard to tell. Police asked them questions. Paramedics checked them for injuries and tried to get them to go to the hospital. Bill couldn't remember what they had even said, but they had refused to move for the time being. Their passions were being destroyed in front of their eyes, and worse than that, they were worried about so many people they may have lost.

Sid had taken Jaime to God knows where to do God knows what.

JB had been consumed by fire in the wicker cage and surely was dead.

Rose had been trapped by the destructive flames and disintegrating walls, stuck and left to die.

And they all sat outside, helpless, unable to do anything.

All they could do was hold one another.

Finally someone said something. It was Brandis, and the word that came out of his mouth woke Bill from his shock.

"Jaime?"

Bill turned when he heard Brandis call her name, and he shot straight up and ran to her.

She walked toward them like a zombie, and blood trickled down her arm to her hand and dripped on the concrete. It looked relatively fresh, and it was also smeared on her face. Looking closer, Bill saw she was covered in blood. It was in her hair and splattered on her clothes.

"Blood?" Bill asked. "Jaime, what happened?"

"It's not my blood," she answered coldly. "None of it is my blood." She didn't make eye contact with any of them. She was also hypnotized by the fire and what was left of Rabbit in Red.

Bill reached out for her hand, and she took it willingly. Blood dripped slowly from her arm onto his, but he didn't mind.

Jaime pulled her eyes from the blazing studio and looked at everyone who was outside.

"Where's JB? Where's Rose?" Jaime asked calmly.

"Inside," Bill said. "Somewhere in all of that." Flames hissed, as if taunting them. He turned slowly toward Jaime again. "What happened, J?"

She looked at him with an expression he had never seen and never wanted to see again in his life. It was an empty, cold expression, one capable of doing anything.

"I did what I had to do. We're safe now. Finally."

They walked over to Wes, who still sat on the ground. His cries had softened, replaced by fatigue and shock. Bill held Jaime's hand with his right one and put his left hand on Wes's shoulder. Brandis stared at them but said nothing.

"Do you think there's a chance she survived?" Wes asked. "That she's somewhere in all of that, alive and waiting?"

Bill looked at the ashes and destruction. It was as wide as a city block and the smoke darkened the already black night. He didn't think anyone could survive that, but he wouldn't say that to Wes.

"It will be okay," he said. "Somehow, it will all be okay."

Blood continued to run from Jaime's hand onto Bill's and it dripped onto Wes, too. A trickle of blood fell on the rabbit. Bill thought about wiping it off the rabbit's head, but he didn't.

Bill looked at Jaime then to Wes then to the studios that were crumbling to ashes in front of them. He watched as everything they had created and fought to be a part of fell apart, and he worried that the night would be long.

Deep in his gut, he had a terrible feeling. He wouldn't say it out loud, not tonight, but he knew it to be true.

This dark night was just the beginning of their nightmares.

To Be Continued . . .

# Acknowledgments

Dear friends,

I'm finishing up the first draft of the third and final book in the *Rabbit in Red* trilogy, *Bury the Rabbit*, at the same time as we're putting the final touches on this book, *Burn the Rabbit*. I plan on having the final book ready for you by fall of 2017.

I hope you enjoyed this story, and I know you have lots of questions. I've been keeping a huge list, and—as JB said—"You will find your answers and so much more."

This book was a huge adventure, and I want to thank everyone who helped me.

Thank you to my first and most trustworthy readers: Brian McWilliams, Brandy Kennington, and Rachel Heckman. One of my favorite days was a walk on January 1 of 2016 with Brian and Brandy through the gorgeous Springdale Cemetery. They had just finished reading an early draft of this book, and I listened to them discuss the characters and what they think happened and so much more. It was such a joy, and I appreciate you all for such great feedback that helped make this story as good as it could be.

Thank you next to my wonderful editor, Kathy Teel. Kathy doesn't hold back on me when she thinks I'm getting lazy with my writing or when something doesn't make sense in the story. I treasure your criticism, and thank you for continuing to be a part of my *Rabbit in Red* journey.

Thank you next to my *Burn the Rabbit* PR Team. This is a group of friends, students, writers, and others who wanted to be a part of my official PR crew to help spread the word about this story. Thank you to Christian Harr, Sammy Spear, Brianna Schierer, Amanda Sluga, La Verne Roz Armijo, Aaron Hamilton, Kayla Fast, Eric Heyob, Alexis Benson, Stephanie Jones, Ruben Ramirez, Amanda Fox, Salina Porter, Justyce Blankenship, Rachel Heckman, Asanta Cunningham, Brittany Wagley, Zach Paine, Nashawn Webb, Micheale Potter, and Tal Porter.

Thank you to my fellow authors at Four Phoenixes Publishing for the support, too—Jennifer Gadd, Charles O'Keefe, and TP Keane.

Thank you to Apartment Two for the pictures, videos, and other media that helped promote this book.

Thank you, so much, to my friend Bryan Fitzgerald at Fitz of Horror. Fitz is doing the audio books of this series, and he's been a tremendous supporter whose influence has helped *Rabbit in Red* succeed.

Thanks also to Camron Johnson, the incredible artist who developed the *Rabbit in Red* art concept you see on the cover. I love that image.

Thank you to my final proofreader, Jennifer Gadd of Four Phoenixes Publishing. She's a fantastic writer. Give her book *Cat Moon* a read.

I also want to thank so many businesses who have supported me— Zeek's Comics and Games, I Know You Like a Book, Lit. on Fire Used Books, Barnes & Noble, and more.

To my mom, to whom I dedicated book one. She's still fighting this terrible cancer, but it's getting harder and harder. I hope you'll keep her in your thoughts. She's always been my #1 supporter.

My list could go on and on—all of my friends who encourage my dreams and don't get tired listening to me talk about my books and ideas. To Illinois Central College—my colleagues of course have been amazing, but the college as a whole has celebrated me, and I can't think of a better place to work.

To all of my Rabbiteers—fans, friends, supporters—follow the rabbit until the end with me. It's going to be a wild ride. Things get crazier. Let's do it one more time!

If you enjoyed the book, leave a review and tell a friend.

Follow me on Facebook at www.facebook.com/chianakas and join me on the web at www.joechianakas.com. You can sign up for my newsletter on my website and be the first to know more about the final book in our trilogy.

Until next time when we Bury the Rabbit, I wish you all the best.

Joe Chianakas

8/4/2016

Thank you to the creative team at **Apartment Two**, who produces media content for *Rabbit in Red*. For great photography and video, like Apartment Two on Facebook at

**www.facebook.com/Apartment2co** and follow on Instagram at **@apartment2co.**

*"Be creative. Be yourself. And inspire others to do the same."*

The Apartment Two Team: Nashawn Webb, Imanuel Acera, Nicole Carson, Remi Sweeney, Drake Sweeney, Hieu Phan, Skylar Robards, Mallory Ingles, Wes Watson, and Thomas Blood.

**Listen to "Enter the Rabbit", the hit, original song inspired by *Rabbit in Red* at terriblyhappy.bandcamp.com.**

**Thanks to Terribly Happy for the incredible song! Be sure to get their first full album, "Modern Life," available now.**

**Terribly Happy**

> Kyle Hamon - guitar/vocals
> James Wylie - bass/vocals
> Logan Kiesewetter – drums

**terriblyhappy.bandcamp.com**

**Fitz of Horror is at <u>www.facebook.com/horrorfitz</u>!**

A huge thanks to Fitz not only for the support but for the AWESOME work producing the audio book for *Rabbit in Red*. Get the audio book online today!